THE EMPHYRIO ENIGMA

What was the true ending of the fragmentary folk legend of the great hero Emphyrio?

What was the message that the ancient puppet-master from the planet Damar tried to convey during the revels of the Great Fair?

How had a proud race of humans been transformed into a servile breed that lived at the will and died at the pleasure of the corrupt and debauched Lords?

Piece by piece the young rebel Ghyl Tarvoke put together the pieces of this strange puzzle—until he faced in ultimate mortal combat the one other creature who knew the monstrous, mind-shattering truth. . . .

EMPHYRIO

JACK VANCE

DAW BOOKS, INC.
DONALD A. WOLLHEIM, PUBLISHER
1633 Broadway
New York, N.Y.   10019

FIRST DAW PRINTING, DECEMBER 1979

1 2 3 4 5 6 7 8 9

DAW TRADEMARK REGISTERED
U.S. PAT. OFF. MARCA
REGISTRADA. HECHO EN U.S.A.

PRINTED IN U.S.A.

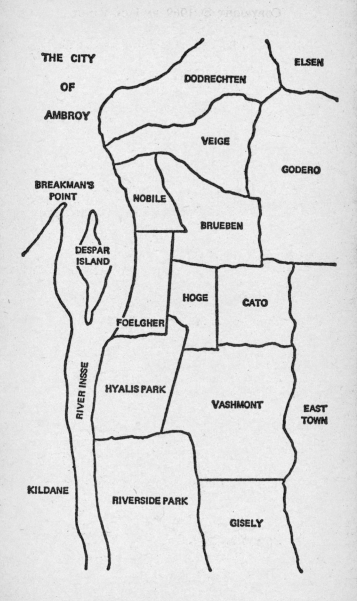

THE CITY OF AMBROY

ELSEN

DODRECHTEN

VEIGE

GODERO

BREAKMAN'S POINT

NOBILE

BRUEBEN

DESPAR ISLAND

HOGE

CATO

FOELGHER

RIVER INSSE

HYALIS PARK

VASHMONT

EAST TOWN

KILDANE

RIVERSIDE PARK

GISELY

CHAPTER 1

In the chamber at the top of the tower were six individuals: three who chose to call themselves "lords" or sometimes "remedials"; a wretched underling who was their prisoner; and two Garrion. The chamber was dramatic and queer: of irregular dimension, hung with panels of heavy maroon velvet. At one end an embrasure admitted a bar of light: this of a smoky amber quality, as if the pane were clogged with dust—which it was not; in fact, the glass was a subtle sort, producing remarkable effects. At the opposite end of the room was a low trapezoidal door of black skeel.

The unconscious prisoner was clamped into an intricately articulated frame. The top of his skull had been removed; upon the naked brain rested a striated yellow gel. Above hung a black capsule, a curiously ugly object, if only a contrivance of glass and metal. Its surface was marked by a dozen wart-like protuberances: each projected a quivering thread of radiation into the gel.

The prisoner was a fair-skinned young man, with features of no great distinction. Such hair as could be seen was tawny. The forehead and cheekbones were broad, the nose blunt, the mouth easy and generous, the jaws slanting down to a small firm chin; a face of innocent impracticality. The lords, or "remedials"—the latter term was somewhat obsolete and seldom heard—were of another sort. Two were tall and thin, with arsenical skins, thin long noses, saturnine mouths, black hair varnished close to their heads. The third was older, heavier, with vulpine features, a glaring heated gaze, a skin darkly florid, with an unwholesome magenta undertone. Lord Fray and Lord Fanton were fastidious, supercilious; Grand Lord Dugald the Boimarc seemed oppressed by worry and chronic anger. All three, members of a race notorious for its elegant revels, appeared humorless and dour, with no capability for ease or merriment.

The two Garrion at the back of the room were andromorphs: blackish purple-brown, solid and massive. Their eyes,

7

black lusterless bulbs, showed internal star-refractions; from the sides of their faces extended tufts of black hair.

The lords wore black garments of refined cut, caps of jeweled metal mesh. The Garrion wore black leathern harness, russet aprons.

Fray, standing by a console, explained the function of the mechanism. "First: a period of joinings, as each strand seeks a synapse. When the flashes cease, as now they are doing, and the indicators coincide"—Fray indicated a pair of opposed black arrows—"he becomes nothing: a crude animal, a polyp with a few muscular reflexes.

"In the computer, the neural circuits are classified by range and by complexity of cross-connection into seven stages." Lord Fray examined the yellow gel, where the scanning beams aroused no further motes of light. "The brain is now organized into seven realms. We bring him to a desired condition by relaxing control of specific realms, and, if necessary, damping, or squelching, others. Since Lord Dugald does not intend rehabilitation—"

Fanton spoke in a husky voice: "He is a pirate. He must be expelled."

"—we will relax the stages one at a time until he is able to provide the accurate statement Lord Dugald requires. Though, I confess, his motives are beyond my comprehension." And Lord Fray brushed Grand Lord Dugald with a flickering glance.

"My motives are sufficient," said Dugald, "and concern you more directly than you know. Proceed."

Fray, with a subtle gesture, touched the first of seven keys. On a yellow screen an amorphous black shape twisted and writhed. Fray made adjustments; the shape steadied, diminished to a coin-sized disk quivering to the prisoner's pulse. The young man wheezed, moaned, strained feebly against the bonds. Working with great facility, Fray superimposed a pattern of concentric circles over the dot and made a final adjustment.

The young man's eyes lost their glaze. He saw Lord Fanton and Lord Dugald: the black disk on the screen jerked. He saw the Garrion: the black disk distorted. He turned his head, looked out through the embrasure. The sun hung low in the west. By a curious optical property of the glass it appeared a pale gray disk surrounded by a pink and green aureole. The black spot on the screen hesitated, slowly contracted.

"Phase One," said Fray. "His genetic responses are restored. Notice how the Garrion disturb him?"

"No mystery," snorted old Lord Dugald. "They are alien to his genetic background."

"Why then," demanded Fanton coolly, "did the spot react similarly to the sight of us?"

"Bah," muttered Lord Dugald. "We are not his folk."

"True," said Fray, "even after so many generations. The sun however works as a reference point, the origin of mental coordinates. It is a powerful symbol."

He turned the second key. The black disk exploded into fragments. The young man whimpered, jerked, became rigid. Fray worked at the adjustments and reduced the shape once more to a small disk. He tapped the stimulator button. The young man lay quietly. His eyes roved the room, from Lord Fray to Lord Dugald, to the Garrion, to his own body. The black disk held its shape and position.

"Phase Two," said Fray. "He recognizes, but he cannot relate. He is aware but not yet conscious; he cannot distinguish between himself and the surroundings. All is the same: things and their emotional content are identical. Valueless for our purpose. To Phase Three."

He turned the third key; the tight black circle expanded. Fray again made adjustments, constricted the blot to a small dense disk. The young man heaved himself up, stared down at the metal boots and wristlets, looked at Fanton and Dugald. Fray spoke to him in a cold clear voice, "Who are you?"

The young man frowned; he moistened his lips. He spoke and the sound seemed to come from far away: "Emphyrio."

Fray gave a short curt nod; Dugald looked at him in surprise. "What is all this?"

"A rogue linkage, a deep-lying identification: no more. One must expect surprises."

"But is he not enforced to accuracy?"

"Accuracy from his experience and from his point of view." Fray's voice became dry. "We cannot expect cosmic universals—if such exist." He turned back to the young man. "What, then, is your birth name?"

"Ghyl Tarvoke."

Fray gave a brusque nod. "Who am I?"

"You are a lord."

"Do you know where you are?"

"In an eyrie, above Ambroy."

Fray spoke to Dugald: "He now can compare his perceptions to his memory; he can make qualitative identifications. He is not yet conscious. If he were to be rehabilitated, now would be the starting point, with each of his associations readily accessible. To Phase Four."

Fray turned the fourth key, made his adjustments. Ghyl Tarvoke winced and strained at his boots and wristlets. "He is now capable of quantitative appraisals. He can perceive relationships, make comparisons. He is, in a sense, lucid. But he is not yet conscious. If he were to be rehabilitated, there would be further adjustment at this level. To Phase Five."

Phase Five was concluded. In consternation Ghyl Tarvoke stared from Fray to Dugald, to Fanton, to the Garrion. "His time-scale has been restored," said Fray. "He has, in effect, his memory. With considerable effort we could extract a statement, objective and devoid of emotional color: skeletal truth, so to speak. In certain situations this is desirable, but now we would learn nothing. He can make no decisions, and this is a barrier to lucid language, which is a continuous decision-making process: a choice between synonyms, degrees of emphasis, systems of syntax. To Phase Six."

He turned the sixth key. The black disk spattered violently apart, into a set of droplets. Fray stood back in surprise. Ghyl Tarvoke made savage animal sounds, gnashed his teeth, strained at his bonds. Fray hurriedly made adjustments, constrained the squirming elements, compressed them to a jerking disk. Ghyl Tarvoke sat panting, gazing at the lords with detestation.

"Well then, Ghyl Tarvoke," spoke Fray, "and what do you think of yourself now?"

The young man, glaring from lord to lord, made no reply.

Dugald took a fastidious half-step to the side. "Will he speak?"

"He will speak," said Fray. "Notice: he is conscious; he is in full control of himself."

"I wonder what he knows," mused Dugald. He looked sharply from Fanton to Fray. "Remember, I ask all questions!"

Fanton gave him an acrid glance. "One might almost think that you and he share a secret."

"Think as you like," snapped Dugald. "Remember only who holds authority!"

"How can there be forgetting?" asked Fanton, and turned away.

Dugald spoke to his back. "If you wish my position, take it! But take responsibility as well!"

Fanton swung back. "I want nothing of yours. Remember only who was injured by this sullen creature."

"You, me, Fray, any of us: it is all the same. Did you not hear him use the name 'Emphyrio'?"

Fanton shrugged. Fray said lightly, "Well then, back to Ghyl Tarvoke! He is not yet a total person. He lacks the use of his free connections, the flexible web. He is incapable of spontaneity. He cannot dissemble, because he cannot create. He cannot hope, he cannot plan, therefore he has no will. So then: we will hear the truth." He settled himself on a cushioned bench, started a recording machine. Dugald came forward, planted himself flatfooted in front of the prisoner. "Ghyl Tarvoke: we wish to learn the background to your crimes."

Fray interceded with gentle malice: "I suggest that you ask questions of a more categorical nature."

"No, no!" retorted Dugald. "You fail to understand my requirements."

"You have not set them forth," said Fray, still waspishly polite.

Ghyl Tarvoke had been straining uneasily at his harness. He said fretfully, "Take loose these clasps; I will be more at ease."

"Your comfort is of small consequence," barked Dugald. "You are to be expelled into Bauredel. So speak!"

Ghyl Tarvoke pulled at his bonds again, then relaxed and stared at the wall beyond the lords. "I don't know what you want to hear."

"Exactly," murmured Fray. "Precisely."

"The circumstances contributing to your abominable crimes!"

"I remember a lifetime of events. I will tell you everything."

Dugald said, "I prefer that you speak somewhat more to the point."

Ghyl's forehead creased. "Complete the processing, so that I can think."

Dugald looked indignantly at Fray, while Fanton laughed. "Is this not a manifestation of will?"

Fray pulled at his long chin. "I suspect that the remark derives from ratiocination rather than emotion." He spoke to Ghyl. "Is this not true?"

"True."

Fray smiled faintly. "After Phase Seven you will be capable of inaccuracy."

"I have no wish to dissemble: quite otherwise. You shall hear the truth."

Fray went to the control board, turned the seventh key. The black disk disintegrated into a fog of droplets. Ghyl Tarvoke gave a moan of agony. Fray worked the controls; the drops coalesced; the disk at last was as before.

Ghyl sat quietly. He said at last, "So now you will kill me."

"Certainly. Do you deserve better?"

"Yes."

Fanton burst out, "But why have you performed such evil, on folk who have done you no harm? Why? Why? Why?"

" 'Why?' " Ghyl cried out. "To achieve! To make capital of my life, to stamp my imprint upon the cosmos! Is it right that I should be born, live and die with no more effect than a blade of grass on Dunkum's Heights?"

Fanton gave a bitter laugh. "Are you better than I? I live and die with equal inconsequence. Who will remember either of us?"

"You are you and I am I," said Ghyl Tarvoke. "I am dissatisfied."

"With good reason," said Lord Dugald with a dour grin. "In three hours you are to be expelled. So speak now, or never be heard again!"

CHAPTER 2

Ghyl Tarvoke's first insight into the nature of destiny came upon his seventh birthday, during a visit to a traveling pageant. His father, usually vague and remote, somehow had remembered the occasion; together they set off on foot across the city. Ghyl would have preferred to ride Overtrend, but Amiante, for reasons obscure to Ghyl, demurred, and they ambled north across the old Vashmont Development, past the skeletons of a dozen ruined towers, each supporting the eyrie of a lord. In due course they arrived at the North Common in East Town where the gay tents of Framtree's Peripatezic Entercationers had been erected. A rotunda advertised: *Wonders of the Universe: a magnificent tour without danger, inconvenience or expense, depicting the spectacles of sixteen enthralling worlds, arranged in tasteful and edifying sequence.* There was a puppet show with a troupe of live Damar puppets; a diorama illustrating notable events in the history of Halma; exhibits of off-world creatures, living, dead, or in simulacrum; a comic ballet entitled *Niaiserie*; a mind-reading parlor featuring Pagoul the mysterious Earthman; gaming stalls, refreshment counters, hucksters of gew-gaws and trifles. Ghyl could hardly walk for looking this way and that, while Amiante, with patient indifference, pushed through the crowds. Most were recipients of Ambroy, but many had come in from the back regions of Fortinone; and there were a certain number of foreigners as well, from Bauredel, Sauge, Closte, distinguished by the cockades which allowed them complimentary welfare vouchers. Rarely they saw Garrion, odd animals tricked out in human clothes and always a sign that lords walked among the underfolk.

Amiante and Ghyl visited first the rotunda, to travel vicariously among the star worlds. They saw the Battle of the Birds at Sloe on Madura; the ammoniacal storms of Fajane; tantalizing glimpses of the Five Worlds. Ghyl watched the strange scenes without understanding; they were too foreign, too gigantic, at times too savage, for his assimilation. Amiante looked with a subtle, bittersweet half-smile. Never would

13

Amiante travel, never would he accumulate the vouchers for
so much as a three-day excursion to Damar, and knowing as
much, he seemed to have put all such ambitions to the side.

Leaving the rotunda they visited a hall displaying in diorama famous lovers of myth: Lord Guthmore and the Mountain Wilding; Medié and Estase; Jeruun and Jeran; Hurs
Gorgonja and Ladati the Metamorph; a dozen other couples
in picturesque costumes of antiquity. Ghyl asked many questions, which Amiante for the most part evaded or answered
glancingly: "The history of Halma is overlong, overconfused;
it is enough to say that all these handsome folk are creatures
of fable."

Upon leaving the hall they passed into the puppet* theater,
and watched as the small masked creatures jigged, scam-
pered, chattered, sang their way through "Virtuous Fidelity to
an Ideal Is the Certain Highroad to Financial Independence."
In fascination Ghyl observed Marelvie, the daughter of a
common wire-drawer, at a Foelgher Precinct street dance,
where she attracted the attention of Lord Bodbozzle the
Chaluz, a lecherous old power tycoon of twenty-six fiefs.
Lord Bodbozzle wooed her with agile capering, a comic discharge of fireworks and declamation, but Marelvie refused
to join his entourage except as legal spouse, with full ac-
knowledgement and the settlement of four choice fiefs. Lord
Bodbozzle agreed, but Marelvie first must visit his castle to
learn ladyship and financial independence. So the trusting
Marelvie was conveyed by air-weft to his castle, high on a
tower above Ambroy, where Lord Bodbozzle immediately attempted seduction. Marelvie underwent various vicissitudes,
but at the critical instant her sweetheart Rudel leapt in
through a window, having scaled the naked girders of the ancient tower. He thrashed a dozen Garrion guards, pinned
whimpering Lord Bodbozzle to the wall, while Marelvie performed a skipping dance of glee. To buy his life, Lord Bodbozzle forfeited six fiefs in the heart of Ambroy and a
space-yacht. The happy couple, financially independent and

---

* The regulations of Fortinone and indeed of all the North Continent
prohibited both the synthesis and the importation of sentient creatures, as tending to augment the recipient rolls. The Damarans, native
to the moon Damar, fabricated small creatures of a docile, eager intelligence, with furry black heads, black beaks and laterally placed eyes;
so long as the creatures performed only as puppets, or served as pets
to lord-children, the welfare agents tended to ignore their presence.

off the rolls, bounded happily away on their travels, while Lord Bodbozzle massaged his bruises. . . .

Lamps flared on, signaling intermission; Ghyl turned to his father, hoping for but not expecting an opinion. It was Amiante's tendency to turn his feeling inward. Even at the age of seven Ghyl sensed an unorthodox, almost illicit, quality to his father's judgments. Amiante was a big man, slow of motion in a fashion which suggested economy and control rather than ponderousness. His head was big and brooding, his face wide at the cheekbones and pale, with a small chin, a sensitive mouth characteristically twisted in a musing half-smile. Amiante spoke very little and in a soft voice, although Ghyl had seen him, when he was stimulated by some apparently trivial incident, erupt words, spewing them forth as if they were under physical pressure, to halt as suddenly, perhaps in mid-sentence. But now Amiante had nothing to say; Ghyl could only guess his feelings in regard to the misfortunes of Lord Bodbozzle.

Looking around the audience, Ghyl noted a pair of Garrion in a splendid livery of lavender, scarlet, and black leather. They stood to the rear of the hall, man-like but non-human, hybrids of insect, gargoyle and ape, immobile but alert, eye-bulges focused nowhere but observing all. Ghyl nudged his father. "Garrion are here! Lords watch the puppets!"

Amiante turned a brief glance over his shoulder. "Lords or lordlings."

Ghyl searched the audience. No one resembled Lord Bodbozzle; no one radiated that near-visible effulgence of authority and financial independence which Ghyl imagined must surround all lords. He started to ask his father whom he presumed to be the lord, then stopped, knowing that Amiante's only response would be a disinterested shrug. Ghyl looked along the rows, face by face. How could lord or lordling not resent the crude caricature of Lord Bodbozzle? But no one seemed perturbed. . . . Ghyl lost interest in the matter; perhaps the Garrion visited the pageant by their own inclination.

The intermission was to be ten minutes; Ghyl slipped from his seat, went to examine the stage at closer vantage. To the side hung a canvas flap; Ghyl pulled it open, looked into a side-room, where a small man in brown velvet sat sipping a cup of tea. Ghyl glanced over his shoulder; Amiante, preoccupied with his own inner visions, paid no heed. Ghyl ducked

under the canvas, stood hesitantly, prepared to leap back
should the man in brown velvet come to seize him, for somehow Ghyl had come to suspect that the puppets were stolen
children, whipped until they acted and danced with exact precision: an idea investing the performance with a horrid fascination. But the man in brown velvet, apart from a civil
nod, seemed uninterested in capturing Ghyl. Emboldened,
Ghyl came a few steps forward. "Are you the puppet-master?"

"That I am, lad: Holkerwoyd the puppet-master, enjoying
a brief respite from my labors."

The man was rather old and gnarled. He did not appear
the sort who would torment and whip children. With added
confidence Ghyl—not knowing precisely what he meant—
asked, "You're . . . *real?*"

Holkerwoyd did not seem to find the question unreason-
able. "I'm as real as necessary, lad, at least to myself. There
have been some who have found me, shall we say, evanes-
cent, even evaporative."

Ghyl understood the general essence of the response. "You
must travel to many places."

"There's truth indeed. Up and down the great North Continent, over the Bight to Salula, down the peninsula to Wan-
tanua. All this on Halma alone."

"I've never been from Ambroy."

"You're young yet."

"Yes; someday I want to be financially independent, and
travel space. Have you visited other worlds?"

"Dozens. I was born beside a star so far that you'll never
see its light, not in the sky of Halma."

"Then why are you here?"

"I often ask myself the same. The answer always comes:
because I'm not somewhere else. Which is a statement more
sensible than it sounds. And isn't it a marvel? Here am I and
here are you; think of it! When you ponder the breadth of
the galaxy, you must recognize a coincidence of great singu-
larity!"

"I don't understand."

"Simple enough! Suppose you were here and I elsewhere,
or I were here and you elsewhere, or both of us were elsewhere: three cases vastly more probable than the fourth,
which is the fact of our mutual presence within ten feet of
each other. I repeat, a miraculous concatenation! And to

think that some hold the Age of Wonders to be past and gone!"

Ghyl nodded dubiously. "That story about Lord Bodbozzle—I'm not so sure I liked it."

"Eh?" Holkerwoyd blew his cheeks. "And why not?"

"It wasn't true."

"Aha then. In what particular?"

Ghyl searched his vocabulary to express what was hardly as much as an intuition. He said, rather lamely, "A man can't fight ten Garrion. Everyone knows that."

"Well, well, well," said Holkerwoyd, talking aside. "The lad has a literal mind." Back to Ghyl: "But don't you wish it were so? Is it not our duty to provide gay tales? When you grow up and learn how much you owe the city, you'll find ample dullness."

Ghyl nodded wisely. "I expected the puppets to be smaller. And much more beautiful."

"Ah, the captious one. The dissatisfaction. Well then! When you are larger, they will seem smaller."

"They are not stolen children?"

Holkerwoyd's eyebrows puffed like the tail of a startled cat. "So this is your idea? How could I train children to gambols and artless antics, when they are such skeptics, such fastidious critics, such absolutists?"

Ghyl thought it polite to change the subject. "There is a lord in the audience."

"Not so, my friend. A little lady. She sits to the left in the second row."

Ghyl blinked. "How do you know?"

Holkerwoyd made a grand gesture. "You wish to plunder me of all my secrets? Well, lad, know this: masks and masking—and unmasking—these are the skills of my trade. Now hasten back to your father. He wears the mask of leaden patience, to sheathe his soul. Within he shakes with grief. You shall know grief too; I see that you are fey." Holkerwoyd advanced, making ferocious gestures. "Hence! Hup! Hah!"

Ghyl fled back into the hall, resumed his seat. Amiante turned him a brief quizzical glance, which Ghyl avoided. Many aspects of the world were beyond his understanding. Recalling the words of Holkerwoyd, he looked across the room. Indeed, there in the second row: a small girl with a placid woman of middle age. So this was a lady! Ghyl examined her carefully. Pretty and graceful she was beyond question, and Ghyl, in the clarity of his vision, saw also a Difference. Her breath would be tart and perfumed, like verbena or lemon. Her mind moved to unfathomable thoughts, wonderful secrets. . . . Ghyl noticed a hauteur, an ease of manner, which somehow was fascinating . . . a challenge.

The lights dimmed, the curtains parted, and now began a sad little tale which Ghyl thought might be a message to himself from Holkerwoyd, even though such a possibility seemed remote.

The setting of the story was the puppet theater itself. One of the puppets, conceiving the outside world to be a place of eternal merriment, escaped the theater and went forth to mingle with a group of children. For a period there was antic and song; then the children, tiring of play, went their various ways. The puppet sidled through the streets, observing the city: what a dull place compared to the theater, unreal and factitious though it was! But he was reluctant to return, knowing what awaited him. Hesitating, delaying, he hopped and limped back to the theater, singing a plaintive little commentary. His fellow puppets greeted him with restraint and awe; they too knew what to expect. And indeed at the next performance the traditional drama *Emphyrio* was presented, with the runaway puppet cast as Emphyrio. Now ensued a play within a play, and the tale of Emphyrio ran its course. At the end, Emphyrio, captured by the tyrants, was dragged to Golgotha. Before his execution he attempted to deliver a speech justifying his life, but the tyrants refused to let him speak, and inflicted upon him the final humiliation of futility. A grotesquely large rag was stuffed in Emphyrio's mouth; a shining ax struck off his head and such was the fate of the runaway puppet.

Ghyl noticed that the lord-girl, her companion and the Garrion guards did not stay for the finish. When the lights came on, showing white staring faces throughout the audience, they were gone.

Ghyl and Amiante walked homeward through the dusk, each occupied with his own thoughts. Ghyl spoke. "Father."

"Yes."

"In the story, the runaway puppet who played Emphyrio was executed."

"Yes."

"But the puppet who played the runaway puppet also was executed!"

"I noticed as much."

"Did he run away too?"

Amiante heaved a sigh, shook his head. "I don't know. Perhaps puppets are cheap. . . . Incidentally, that is not the true tale of Emphyrio."

"What is the true tale?"

"No one knows."

"Was Emphyrio a real man?"

Amiante considered a moment before replying. Then he said, "Human history has been long. If a man named Emphyrio never existed, there was another man, with a different name, who did."

Ghyl found the remark beyond his intellectual depth. "Where do you think Emphyrio lived? Here in Ambroy?"

"This is a problem," said Amiante with a thoughtful frown, "which some men have tried to solve, without success. There are clues, of course. If I were a different man, if I were once again young, if I had no . . ." His voice dwindled.

They walked in silence. Then Ghyl asked, "What is it to be 'fey'?"

Amiante scrutinized him curiously. "Where did you hear the word?"

"Holkerwoyd the puppet-master said I was fey."

"Ah. I see. Well then. It means that you have about you the air of, let us say, important enterprise. That you shall be remarkable and do remarkable deeds."

Ghyl was fascinated. "And I shall be financially independent and I shall travel? With you, of course?"

Amiante laid his hand on Ghyl's shoulder. "That remains to be seen."

CHAPTER 3

Amiante's shop and residence was a tall, narrow, four-story structure of old black timbers and brown tile facing on Undle Square to the north of the Brueben Precinct. On the ground floor was Amiante's workshop, where he carved wooden screens; on the next floor was the kitchen, where Amiante and Ghyl cooked and ate, as well as a side room in which Amiante kept a desultory collection of old manuscripts. On the third floor Amiante and Ghyl slept; and above was a loft full of unusable objects, too old or too remarkable to throw away.

Amiante was the most noncommittal of men: pensive, almost brooding, working in fits of energy, then for hours or days occupying himself with the detail of a sketch, or perhaps doing nothing whatever. He was an expert craftsman: his screens were always Firsts and often Acmes, but his output was not particularly large. Vouchers, therefore, were not plentiful in the Tarvoke household. Clothes, like all the merchandise of Fortinone, were handmade and dear; Ghyl wore smocks and trousers stitched together by Amiante himself, even though the guilds discourage such "fringe encroachment." Seldom were there coins to be spared for sweets, and none for organized entertainment. Every day the barge *Jaoundi* pushed majestically up the Insse to the holiday village Bazen, returning after dark. For the children of Ambroy this was the most delightful and hoped-for excursion imaginable. Once or twice Amiante mentioned the *Jaoundi* excursion, but nothing ever came of it.

Ghyl nonetheless considered himself fortunate. Amiante imposed few restraints. Other children no older than himself were already learning a trade: at guild-school, in a home workshop or that of a relative. The children of scriveners, clerks, pedants or any others who might need advanced reading and writing skills were drilled to second or even third schedule.* Devout parents sent their children to Infant Skips and Juvenile Hops at the Finukan Temple, or taught them simple patterns at home.

Amiante, whether through calculation or perhaps absent-mindedness, made no such demands upon Ghyl, who came and went as he pleased. He explored all Brueben Precinct, then, growing bolder, wandered far afield. He explored the docks and boat-building shops of Nobile Precinct; clambered over hulks of old barges on the Dodrechten mud flats, eating raw sea fruit for his lunch; crossed to Despar Island in the estuary, where there were glass factories and ironworks, and on several occasions continued across the bridge to Breakman's Point.

South of Brueben, toward the heart of old Ambroy, were the precincts most thoroughly demolished in the Empire Wars: Hoge, Cato, Hyalis Park, Vashmont. Snaking over the forlorn landscape were rows and double rows of houses built of salvaged brick; in Hoge was the Public Market, in Cato, the Temple; elsewhere were vast areas of broken black brick and mouldering concrete, ill-smelling ponds surrounded by slime of peculiar colors, occasionally the shack of a vagabond or noncup.** In Cato and Vashmont stood the gaunt skeletons of the old central towers, preempted by the lords for their eyries. One day Ghyl, recalling Rudel the puppet, decided to test the practicality of the exploit. Selecting a tower, the property of Lord Waldo the Flowan,† Ghyl started to climb

---

* In Fortinone and across the North Continent five schedules or systems of writing were in use:

1. A set of twelve hundred and thirty-one pictograms derived from ancient interplanetary conventions, taught to all children.

2. A cursive version of the pictograms, used by tradesmen and artisans, with perhaps four hundred additional special forms.

3. A syllabary, sometimes used to augment the pictograms, sometimes as a graphic system in its own right.

4. A cursive form of the syllabary, with a large number of logographs: the system used by the lords; by priests, ordained saltants, lay leapers, expostulants; by scriveners and pedants.

5. An archaic alphabet, with its many variants, used with archaic dialects or for special effects, such as tavern signs, boat names and the like.

** Noncuperatives: nonrecipients of welfare benefits, reputedly all Chaoticists, anarchists, thieves, swindlers, whoremongers.

† The lords derived their cognomens from the public utility fiefs, which constituted their primary holdings. These, in the language of the time, were Spay, Chaluz, Flowan, Overtrend, Underline, and Biomarc: communications, energy, water, transit, sewerage, trade.

the structure: up the diagonal bracing to the first horizontal girder, across to another diagonal, up to the second horizontal, and the third, and the fourth: up a hundred feet, two hundred feet, three hundred feet, and here he stopped, hugging the girder, for the distance to the ground had become frightening.

For a space Ghyl sat looking out across the old city. The view was splendid, in a still, melancholy fashion; the ruins, lit at an angle by the gray-gold sunlight, showed a fascinating wealth of detail. Ghyl gazed off across Hoge, trying to locate Undle Square. . . . From below came a hoarse harsh voice; looking down, Ghyl saw a man in brown trousers and flared black coat: one of the Vashmont welfare agents.

Ghyl descended to the ground, where he was sternly reprimanded and required to state his name and address.

Early the following morning a Brueben Precinct welfare agent, Helfred Cobol, stopped by to have a word with Amiante, and Ghyl became very apprehensive. Would he be rehabilitated? But Helfred Cobol said nothing about the Vashmont tower and only made gruff recommendations that Amiante impose stricter discipline upon Ghyl, which Amiante heard with polite disinterest.

Helfred Cobol was stocky and barrel-shaped with a pudgy pouchy head, a bump of a nose, small gray eyes. He was brisk and business-like, and reputedly conceded special treatment to no one. Still he was a man of wide experience and tended not to interpret the Code too narrowly. With most recipients Helfred Cobol used a breezy manner, but in the presence of Amiante he was cautious and watchful, as if he found Amiante unpredictable.

Helfred Cobol had hardly departed before Eng Seche, the cantankerous old precinct delegate of the Wood-carvers' Guild came by to inspect the premises, to satisfy himself that Amiante was conforming to the by-laws, using only the prescribed tools and operations, making use of no jigs, patterns, automatic processes or multiple production devices. He remained over an hour, examining Amiante's tools one by one, until finally Amiante, in a somewhat quizzical voice, inquired precisely what he sought.

"Nothing specific, Rt. Tarvoke,* nothing especial; perhaps

---

* Rt: abbreviation for Recipient, the usual formal or honorific title of address.

the impression of a clamp, or something similar. I may say that your work of late has been peculiarly even of finish."

"If you wish, I can work less skillfully," suggested Amiante.

His irony, if he intended such, was lost on the delegate. "This is counter to the by-laws. Very well then; you are aware of the strictures."

Amiante turned back to his work; the delegate departed. From the slope of Amiante's shoulders, the energy with which he plied mallet and chisel, Ghyl realized that his father was exasperated. Amiante finally threw down the tools, went to the door, looked across Undle Square. He turned back into the shop. "Do you understand what the delegate was saying?"

"He thought you were duping."

"Yes. Something of the sort. Do you know why he was concerned?"

"No." And Ghyl added loyally, "It seemed silly to me."

"Well—not altogether. In Fortinone we live or die by trade, and we guarantee hand-crafted wares. Duplicating, molding, casing—all are prohibited. We make no two objects alike, and the guild delegates enforce the rule."

"What of the lords?" asked Ghyl. "What guild do they belong to? What do they produce?"

Amiante gave a painful grimace: half-smile, half-wince. "They are folk apart. They belong to no guilds."

"How do they earn their vouchers?" demanded Ghyl.

"Very simply," said Amiante. "Long ago there was a great war. Ambroy was left in ruins. The lords came here and spent many vouchers in reconstruction: a process called investment. They restored the facilities for the water supply, laid down the Overtrend tubes, and so forth. So now we pay for use of these facilities."

"Hmmf," said Ghyl. "I thought we received water and power and things like that as part of our free welfare benefits."

"Nothing is free," remarked Amiante. "Unless a person steals, whereupon, sooner or later, in one way or another, he pays for his stealing. So there you have it. The lords take a part of all our money: 1.18 percent to be exact."

Ghyl reflected a moment. "Is that a great deal?"

"It seems adequate," said Amiante dryly. "There are three million recipients in Fortinone and about two hundred lords—six hundred counting ladies and lordlings." Amiante pulled at his lower lip. "It makes an interesting calculation

. . . three million recipients, six hundred noble-folk. One noble for each five thousand recipients. On a basis of 1.18 percent—call it one percent—it would appear that each lord receives the income of fifty recipients." Amiante seemed perplexed by the results of his computation. "Even lords must find it hard to spend so lavishly. . . . Well, then, it is not our affair. I give them their percentage and gladly. Although it is indeed somewhat puzzling. . . . Do they throw money away? Give to far charities? When I was correspondent I should have thought to ask."

"What is a 'correspondent'?"

"Nothing of importance. A position which I held a long time ago, when I was young. A time long past, I fear."

"It does not mean being a lord?"

Amiante chuckled. "Certainly not. Do I resemble a lord?"

Ghyl examined him critically. "I suppose not. How does one become a lord?"

"By birth."

"But—what of Rudel and Marelvie at the puppet play? Did they not receive utility fiefs and become lords?"

"Not really. Desperate noncups, and sometimes recipients, have kidnaped lords and forced them to yield fiefs and great sums of money. The kidnapers would be financially independent, they might call themselves lords, but they never dared mingle with the true lords. Finally the lords bought Garrion guards from the Damar puppet-makers; and now there are few kidnapings. Additionally, the lords have agreed to pay no more ransom if kidnaped. So a recipient or a noncup can never be a lord, even should he wish to be."

"When Lord Bodbozzle wanted to marry Marelvie, would she have become a lady? Would their children have been lords?"

Amiante put down his tools and carefully considered his answer. "Very often the lords take mistresses—lady friends—from among the recipients," he said, "but are careful never to breed children. They are a race apart and apparently intend to keep themselves so."

The amber panes of the outside door darkened; it burst open and Helfred Cobol entered the shop. He stood frowning portentously toward Ghyl, whose heart sank into his shoes. Helfred Cobol turned to Amiante. "I have just read my noon briefing sheet. There is a red notation in reference to your son Ghyl: an offense of trespass and careless risk. The apprehension was made by the Ward 12B, Vashmont Precinct, welfare agent. He reports that Ghyl had climbed the girders of Lord Waldo the Flowan's tower to a dangerous and illegal height, committing an offense against Lord Waldo, and against the precincts of Vashmont and Brueben by incurring risk of hospitalization."

Amiante, brushing chips from his apron, blew out his cheeks. "Yes, yes. The lad is quite active."

"Far too active! In fact, irresponsible! He prowls at will, night and day. I have seen him slinking home after dark drenched to the skin with rain! He roams the city like a thief; he learns nothing but shiftlessness! I cannot believe that this is a benign situation. Do you have no concern for the child's future?"

"No hurry there," replied Amiante in an airy tone. "The future is long."

"A man's life is short. High time he was introduced to his calling! I assume you intend him for a wood-carver?"

Amiante shrugged. "As good a trade as any."

"He should be under instruction. Why do you not send him to the guild-school?"

Amiante tested the edge of the chisel against his thumbnail. "Let him enjoy his innocence," he said in a gruff voice. "He will know drudgery enough in his lifetime."

Helfred Cobol started to speak, then stopped. He gave a grunt which might have meant anything. "Another matter: why does he not attend Voluntary Temple Exercises?"

Amiante put down his chisel, frowned rather foolishly, as if he were puzzled. "As to that, I don't know. I have never asked him."

"You teach him leaps at home?"

"Well, no. I do small leaping myself."

"Hmmf. You should enjoin him to such matters regardless of your own habits."

Amiante turned his eyes toward the ceiling, then picked up his chisel and attacked a panel of aromatic arzack, which he had just clamped to his bench. The design was already laid out: a grove of trees with long-haired maidens fleeing a satyr. The apertures and rough differences of relief were indicated by chalk marks. Using a metal straight-bar as a guide for his thumb, Amiante began to gouge into the wood.

Helfred Cobol came across the room to watch. "Very handsome . . . what is that wood? Kodilla? Boligam? One of those South Continent hardwoods?"

"Arzack, from the woods back of Perdue."

"Arzack! I had no idea it gave so large a panel! The trees are never more than three feet through."

"I pick my trees," Amiante explained patiently. "The foresters cut the trunks into seven-foot lengths. I rent a vat at the dye-works. The logs soak in chemical for two years. I remove the bark, make a single two-inch cut up the trunk: about thirty laminae. I peel off the outer two inches entirely around the trunk, to secure a slab seven feet high by six to nine feet long. This goes into a press, and when it dries I scrape it flat."

"Hm. You peel the layer off yourself?"

"Yes."

"With no complaints from the carpenters' guild?"

Amiante shrugged. "They can't or won't do the work. I have no choice. Even if I wanted any." The last was a muttered afterthought.

Helfred Cobol said tersely, "If everyone acted to his own taste we'd live like Wirwans."

"Perhaps." Amiante continued to shave wood from the arzack slab. Helfred Cobol picked up one of the curls, smelled it. "What is the odor: wood or chemical?"

"A little of both. New arzack is rather more peppery."

Helfred Cobol heaved a sigh. "I'd like a screen like that, but my stipend barely keeps me alive. I don't suppose you have any rejects you'd part with."

Amiante glanced expressionlessly sidewise. "Talk to the Boimarc lords. They take all my screens. The Rejects they burn, the Seconds they lock in a warehouse, the Acmes and Firsts they export. Or so I suppose, since I am not consulted. I would earn more vouchers if I did my own marketing."

"We must maintain our reputation," declared Helfred Cobol in a heavy voice. "In the far worlds, to say 'a piece from Ambroy' is to say 'a jewel of perfection'!"

"Admiration is gratifying," said Amiante, "but it gains remarkably few vouchers."

"What would you have? The markets flooded with brummagem?"

"Why not?" asked Amiante, continuing with his work. "Acmes and Firsts would shine by comparison."

Helfred Cobol shook his head in dissent. "Merchandising is not all that simple." He watched a moment or two longer, then laid his finger on the straight-bar. "Better not let the guild delegate see you working with a guide device. He'd bring you before the committee for duping."

Amiante looked up in mild astonishment. "No duplicating here."

"The action of the bar against your thumb allows you to carry along or duplicate a given depth of cut."

"Bah," muttered Amiante. "Pettifoggery. Utter nonsense."

"A friendly warning, no more," said Helfred Cobol. He glanced aside to Ghyl. "Your father's a good craftsman, lad, but perhaps a trifle vague and unworldly. Now my advice to you is to give over this wandering and prowling, by day and by night. Apply yourself to a trade. Wood-carving, or if you want something different, the guild council can offer a choice where shortages exist. Myself, I believe you'd do best with wood-carving. Amiante has much to teach you." Helfred Cobol turned the briefest of glances at the straight-bar. "Another matter: you're not too young for the Temple. They'll put you at easy leaps, and teach you proper doctrine. But keep on like you're going, you'll end up a vagrant or a noncup."

Helfred Cobol gave Amiante a curt nod and departed the shop.

Ghyl went to the door, watched Helfred Cobol cross Undle Square. Then he slowly closed the door—another slab of dark arzack into which Amiante had set bulbs of crude amber glass—and came slowly across the room. "Do I have to go to the Temple?"

Amiante grunted. "Helfred Cobol is not to be taken altogether seriously. He says certain things because this is his job. I daresay he sends his own children to Saltation, but I doubt if he leaps any more zealously than I do."

"Why are all welfare agents named Cobol?"

Amiante drew up a stool, poured himself a cup of bitter black tea. He sipped thoughtfully. "Long ago, when the capitol of Fortinone was at Thadeus, up the coast, the Welfare Supervisor was a man named Cobol. He appointed all his brothers and nephews to good jobs, so that shortly there were only Cobols in the Welfare Department. So it is today; and welfare agents who are not born Cobols—most of them are, of course—change their names. It is simply a matter of tradition. Ambroy is a city of many traditions. Some are useful, some not. A Mayor of Ambroy is elected every five years, but he has no function; he does nothing but draw his stipend. A tradition, but useless."

Ghyl looked at his father respectfully. "You know almost everything, don't you? No one else knows such things."

Amiante nodded rather glumly. "Such knowledge earns no vouchers, however. . . . Ah well, enough of this." He drained his cup of tea. "It seems that I must train you to carve wood, to read and write . . . come here then. Look at these gouges and chisels. First you must learn their names. This is a plow. This is a No. two elliptical gouge. This is a lazy-tang . . ."

CHAPTER 4

Amiante was not a demanding taskmaster. Ghyl's life proceeded much as before, though he climbed no more towers.

Summer came to Ambroy. There were rains and great thunderstorms, then a period of beautiful clear weather during which the half-ruined city seemed almost beautiful. Amiante aroused himself from his musing and in a great burst of energy took Ghyl on a walking trip up the Insse River, into the foothills of the Meagher Mounts. Ghyl had never before been so far from home. In contrast to the dilapidations of Ambroy, the countryside seemed remarkably fresh and open. Tramping along the riverbank under the purple banion trees, they would often pause to gaze wistfully at some especially pleasant situation—an island, shaded under banion and water-willow, with a little house, a dock, a skiff; or perhaps a houseboat moored to the bank, with children swimming in the river, their parents lounging on the deck with mugs of beer. At night they slept on beds of leaves and straw, their fire flickering and glowing to coals. Overhead burned the stars of the galaxy and Amiante pointed out those few he knew: the Mirabilis Cluster, Glysson, Heriartes, Cornus, Alode. To Ghyl these were names of sheer magic.

"Someday," he told Amiante, "when I am bigger, we'll carve lots of screens and save all our vouchers; then we'll travel: to all those stars, and the Five Jeng Worlds as well!"

"That would be very nice," said Amiante with a grin. "I'd better put more arzack down into chemical so that we'll have sufficient panels."

"Do you think we could buy a space-yacht and travel as we wished?"

Amiante shook his head. "They cost far too much. A hundred thousand vouchers, often more."

"Couldn't we save that much, if we worked very hard?"

"We'd be working and saving all our lives, and still never have enough. Space-yachts are for lords."

They passed Brazen and Grigglesby Corners and Blonnet,

then turned aside into the hills. At last, weary and footsore, they returned home, and indeed Amiante spent precious vouchers to ride Overtrend the last twenty miles through Riverside Park, Vashmont, Hoge.

For a period Amiante, as if himself convinced of the soundness of Ghyl's proposals, worked with great diligence. Ghyl helped as best he could and practiced the use of chisels and augers, but vouchers came in with discouraging slowness. Amiante's diligence waned; he resumed his old habits of working and musing, staring into space for minutes at a time; and presently Ghyl lost interest as well. There must be some other, faster system by which to earn vouchers: gambling, for instance. Kidnaping of lords was irregulationary; Ghyl knew that his father would never hear of such a proposal.

The summer proceeded: a halcyon time, perhaps the happiest of Ghyl's life. In all the city, his favorite resort was Dunkum's Heights in Veige Precinct, north of Brueben, a grassy-topped shoulder of ground beside the estuary. Dozens of fresh mornings and as many hazy afternoons Ghyl climbed Dunkum's Heights, sometimes alone, sometimes with his friend Floriel, a big-eyed waif with pale skin, fragile features, a mop of thick black hair. Floriel lived with his mother, who worked in the brewery, sectioning and cleaning big purple hollips, from which the brew derived its characteristic musty flavor. She was a large, ribald woman, not without vanity, who claimed to be second cousin to the Mayor. Hollip odor permeated Floriel's mother, her person and all her belongings, and even attached itself to Floriel; and ever afterward whenever Ghyl drank beer, or caught the tart musk of hollips at the market, he would recall Floriel and his wan ragamuffin face.

Floriel was a companion exactly suited to Ghyl's tastes: a lad mild and acquiescent, but by no means lacking in energy or imagination, and ripe for any adventure. The two boys spent many happy hours on Dunkum's Heights, basking in the tawny sunlight, chewing the soft grass, watching the flight of shrinken-birds over the mud flats.

Dunkum's Heights was a place to laze and dream; in contrast, the space-port, in Godero Precinct, east of Dunkum's Heights, was the very node of adventure and romance. The space-port was divided into three sections, with the depot at the center. To the north was the commercial field, where two or three freight ships were usually loading or discharging. To the south, lined up along an access avenue, were space-yachts belonging to the lords: objects of the most entrancing verve and glitter. To the west was the passenger terminus. Here hulked the black excursion ships, serving those recipients who, by dint of toil and frugality, had been able to buy off-world passage. The tours were various. Cheapest and most popular was a five-day visit to the moon Damar, a strange little world half the diameter of Halma where lived the Damaran puppet-makers. At Garwan, on Damar's equator, was a tourist node, with hotels, promenades, restaurants. Puppet plays of every description were presented: legends of Faerie, fables of gothic horror, historical reenactments, farces, displays macabre and erotic. The performing puppets were small human simulacra, far more carefully bred, far more expensive than the wry little creatures exported to such enterprises as Framtree's Peripatezic Entercationers. The Damarans themselves lived underground, in circumstances of great luxury. Their pelts were black; their bony little heads were tufted with coarse black bristles; their eyes shone with curious glints, like the lights of a star sapphire; in short, they were not unlike their own export puppets.

Another tourist destination, somewhat more prestigious, was the planet next out in orbit: Morgan, a world of wind-swept oceans, table-flat steppes, pinnacles of naked rock. On Morgan were a number of rather shabby resorts, offering little recreation other than sailing high-wheeled cars across the steppes. Nonetheless, thousands paid hard-won vouchers to spend two weeks at Tundra Inn or Mountain House or Cape Rage Haven.

Far more desirable were the Wonder Worlds of the Mirabilis Cluster. When folk returned from the Wonder Worlds they had fulfilled their dreams; they had traveled to the stars; they would talk of the marvels they had seen to the end of their time. The excursion however was beyond the financial reach of all but the highly compensated: guild-masters and delegates, welfare supervisors, Boimarc auditors and bursars, those noncups who had gained wealth through mercantilism, gambling, or crime.

Worlds more remote than the Wonder Worlds were known to exist: Rodion, Alcantara, Earth, Maastricht, Montiserra with its floating cities, Himat, many others, but no one fared so far save the lords in their space-yachts.

To Ghyl and Floriel nothing was impossible. Noses pressed to the fence which surrounded the space-port, they vowed that financial independence and space-travel was the only life for them. But first to gain the vouchers, and here was the stumbling block. Vouchers were hard to come by Ghyl well knew. Other worlds were reputedly rich, with vouchers distributed without stint. How to take himself and his father and Floriel to a more lavish environment? If only by some marvelous exploit, by some miracle he could come into possession of a space-yacht! What freedom, what romance and adventure!

Ghyl recalled the exactions imposed upon evil Lord Bodbozzle. Rudel and Marelvie had gained financial independence—but it had only been a puppet play. Was there no other way?

One amazing day toward the end of summer Ghyl and Floriel lay on Dunkum's Heights sucking grass stems and talking largely of the future. "What, really, do you think you'll do?" asked Ghyl.

"First of all," said Floriel, cradling his girlishly delicate face in his hands, "I'll hoard vouchers: dozens. Then I'll learn to gamble, like the noncups do. I'll learn all the best ways to win and then one day I'll gamble and earn hundreds and hundreds of vouchers. Thousands even. Then I'll turn them in for a space-yacht and fly away! away! away! Out past Mirabilis!"

Ghyl nodded reflectively. "That would be one way."

"Or," Floriel went on, "I might save a lord's daughter from danger. Then I'd marry her and be a lord myself."

Ghyl shook his head. "That's never done. They're much too proud. They just have friends among the underfolk. Mistresses, they're called."

Floriel turned to look south, across the brown and gray crumble of Brueben to the towers of Vashmont. "Why should they be proud? They are only ordinary people who happen to be lords."

"A different kind of people," said Ghyl. "Although I've heard that when they walk the streets without Garrion no one notices them as lords."

"They're proud because they are rich," declared Floriel. "I'll earn wealth too, and I'll be proud and they'll be eager to marry me, just to count my vouchers. Think of it! Blue vouchers, orange vouchers, green vouchers! Bundles and boxes of all colors!"

"You'll need them all," observed Ghyl. "Space-yachts cost a great deal: a half-million vouchers, I suppose. A million for the really good ones: the Lixons or the Hexanders with the promenade deck. Just pretend! Fancy that we're out in space, with Mirabilis behind, heading for some wonderful strange planet. We dine in the main saloon, on turbot and roast bloorcock and the best Gade wine—and then we go along the promenade to the after-dome and eat our ices in the dark, with the Mirabilis stars behind and the Giant's Scimitar above and the galaxy to the side."

Floriel heaved a deep sigh. "If I can't buy a space-yacht—I'll steal one. I don't think it's wrong," he told Ghyl earnestly, for Ghyl wore a dubious expression. "I'd steal only from the lords, who can well afford to lose. Think of the bales of vouchers they receive and never spend!"

Ghyl was not sure that this was the case, but did not care to argue.

Floriel rose to his knees. "Let's go over to the space-port! We can look at yachts and pick one out!"

"Now?"

"Of course! Why not?"

"But it's so far."

"We'll use Overtrend."

"My father doesn't like to give vouchers to the lords."

"Overtrend doesn't cost much. To Godero, no more than fifteen checks."

Ghyl shrugged. "Very well."

They went down from the bluff by the familiar train, but instead of turning south, skirted the municipal tanneries to the Veige No. 2 West Overtrend kiosk. They descended by escalator to the on ramp, boarded a capsule. Each in turn punched the 'Space-port' symbol and held his underage card to a sensor plate. The capsule accelerated, rushed east, decelerated, opened; the boys stepped forth upon the up escalator, which presently discharged them into the space-port depot: a cavernous place, echoing to every footfall. The boys slunk over to the side and took stock of the situation, conversing in low voices. For all the comings and goings, the atmosphere of suppressed excitement, the depot was a cheerless place, with walls of dust-brown tile, a great dim vault of a roof.

Ghyl and Floriel decided to watch the passengers boarding the excursion ships. They approached the embarkation wicket, tried to pass through the field gate but a guard waved them back. "Observation deck through the arch; passengers only on the field!" But he turned away to answer a question and Floriel, suddenly bold, seized Ghyl's arm, and they slipped quickly past.

Amazed and delighted at their own audacity, they hurried

to the shadow of an overhanging buttress, where they crouched to take stock of the situation. A sound from the sky startled them: a sudden high-pitched roar from a Leamas Line excursion ship, settling like a great portly duck on its suppressors. The roar became a whine as the force-field reacted with the ground, then passed beyond audibility. The ship touched ground; the hyper-audible sound returned into sensible range, then sighed away to silence, and the ship was at rest firm against the soil of Halma. The ports opened; the passengers slowly filed forth, vouchers spent, heads bowed, ambitions sated.

Floriel gave a sudden gasp of excitement. He pointed. "The ports are open! Do you know, if we went through the crowd right now we could go aboard and hide? Then when the ship was in space we'd come out! They'd never send us back! We'd see Damar at least and maybe Morgan as well."

Ghyl shook his head. "We wouldn't see anything. They'd lock us in a little room and give us bread and water. They'd charge our fathers for the passage—thousands of vouchers! My father couldn't pay. I don't know what he'd do."

"My mother wouldn't pay," said Floriel. "She'd beat me as well. But I don't care. We'd have traveled *space!*"

"They'd list us for inclination," said Ghyl.

Floriel made a gesture of scornful defiance. "What's the difference? We could toe the line in the future—until another opportunity like this came alone."

"It's no opportunity," said Ghyl. "Not really. In the first place they'd catch us in the act and pitch us out. We'd do ourselves no good whatever. Anyway, who wants to travel in an old excursion ship? I want a space-yacht. Let's see if we can get out on the south field."

The space-yachts were ranked in a line along the far end of the field, with an access avenue running in front of them. To reach this avenue meant crossing an open area where they would be in plain view of anyone who cared to look down either from the observation deck or the control tower. Ghyl and Floriel, huddling beside the wall, discussed the situation, weighing pros and cons. "Come," said Floriel. "Let's just make a run for it."

"We'd do better just walking," said Ghyl. "We wouldn't look so much like thieves. Which we're not, of course. Then, if we were caught, we could say truthfully that we meant no harm. If they saw us running, they'd be sure that we were up to mischief."

"Very well," grumbled Floriel. "Let's go then."

Feeling naked and exposed, they crossed the open area and gained the comparative shelter of the access avenue without challenge. And now, near at hand, were the fascinating space-yachts; the first, a hundred-foot Dameron CoCo 14, jutting its prow almost over their heads.

They peered cautiously down the avenue, which was the way the lords came when they wished to embark upon their yachts. All seemed placid, the marvelous yachts crouched on rolling gear and nose-blocks as if dozing.

No Garrion were in sight, nor any lords, nor any mechanics—these latter generally men from Luschein on South Continent. Floriel's daring, drawn more from an active mind and a high-strung temperament than any real courage, began to peter out. He became timid and fretful, while Ghyl, who would never have come so far on his own, was obliged to supply staying power for both.

"Do you think we should go any farther?" Floriel asked in a husky whisper.

"We've come this far," said Ghyl. "We're doing no harm. I don't think anyone would mind. Not even a lord."

"What would they do if they caught us? Send us to rehabilitation?"

Ghyl laughed nervously. "Of course not. If anyone asks, we'll say we're just looking at the yachts, which is the truth."

"Yes," said Floriel, dubiously. "I suppose so."

"Come along then," said Ghyl.

They started south along the avenue. After the Dameron was a Wodge Blue, and next beside it a slightly smaller, more lavish, Wodge Scarlet; then a huge Gallypool Irwanforth; then a Hatz Marauder, then a Sparling Starchaser in a splendid hull of gold and silver: yacht after yacht, each more wonderful than the last. Once or twice the boys walked up under the hulls, to touch the glossy skins which had known so much distance, to examine the port-of-call blazons.

Halfway along the avenue they came upon a yacht which had been lowered off its nose-block, apparently to facilitate repair, and the boys walked furtively close. "Look!" whispered Ghyl. "You can see just a bit of the main saloon. Isn't she absolutely wonderful?"

Floriel acknowledged as much. "It's a Lixon Triplange. They all have those heavy cowls around the forward ports." He walked up under the hull to examine the port-of-call bla-

zons. "This one's been everywhere. Triptolemus . . . Jeng
. . . Sanreale. Someday, when I read, I'll know them all."

"Yes, I want to read too," said Ghyl. "My father knows a
great deal about reading; he can teach me." He stared at
Floriel, who was making urgent geatures. "What's the matter?"

"Garrion!" hissed Floriel. "Hide, back of the stanchion!"

With alacrity Ghyl joined Floriel behind the prow support.
They stood scarcely breathing. Floriel whispered desperately,
"They can't do anything to us, even if they catch us. They're
just servants; they don't have a right to give us orders, or
chase us, or anything. Not unless we're doing damage."

"I suppose not," said Ghyl. "Let's hide anyway."

"Certainly."

The Garrion came past, moving with the rolling, purposeful step characteristic of the race. He wore livery of light
green and gray, with gold rosettes, a cap of green-gray
leather.

Floriel, who took pride in his knowledgeability, hazarded a
guess regarding the Garrion's patron: "Green and gray . . .
might be Verth the Chaluz. Or Herman the Chaluz. Chaluz
lords use the gold rosette, you know: it means power."

Ghyl did not know, but he nodded acquiescence. They
waited until the Garrion entered the terminal and was gone
from sight. Cautiously the boys came out from behind the
stanchion. They looked left and right, then proceeded along
the line of yachts. "Look!" breathed Floriel. "The Deme—the
gold and black one! The port is open!"

The two boys halted, stared at the fascinating gap. "That's
where the Garrion came from," said Ghyl. "He'll be back."

"Not right away. We could climb the ramp and look inside. No one would ever know."

Ghyl gave a grimace. "I've already been reprimanded for
trespass."

"This isn't trespass! Anyway, what's the harm? If anyone
asked what we were doing, we'd say we were just looking."

"There's sure to be someone aboard," said Ghyl dubiously.

Floriel thought not. "The Garrion is probably fixing something, or cleaning. He's gone to get supplies and he'll be away
ever so long! Let's take a quick look inside!"

Ghyl gauged the distance to the terminal: a good five
minutes' walk. Floriel tugged at his arm. "Come along; as if
we were lordlets! One peek inside, to see how the lords live!"

Ghyl thought of Helfred Cobol; he thought of his father. His throat felt dry. Already he and Floriel had dared more than was proper. . . . Still, the Garrion was in the terminal, and what could be the harm in looking through the entrance? Ghyl said, "If we just go to the door . . ."

Floriel now became reluctant; evidently he had been counting on Ghyl to veto so mad a proposal. "Do you really think we should?"

Ghyl made a signal for caution and went quietly toward the space-yacht. Floriel followed.

At the foot of the ramp they stopped to listen. There was no sound from within. Visible only was the inside of the air-lock and, beyond, a tantalizing glimpse of carved wood, scarlet cloth, a rack of glass and metal implements: luxury almost too splendid to be real. Fascinated, drawn by curiosity, almost against their wills, certainly against their better judgment, the boys ascended the ramp, furtive as cats in a strange house. They peered in through the port, to hear a murmur of machinery, nothing else.

Now they backed away to look toward the terminal. The Garrion had not come forth. Hearts thumping in their throats, the boys stepped into the air-lock, peered into the main saloon.

They let out their breaths slowly in delight and wonder. The saloon was perhaps thirty feet long and sixteen feet wide. The walls were paneled in gray-green sako wood and tapestry cloth; the floor was covered with a thick purple rug. At the forward end of the saloon four steps rose to a control platform. Aft, an arch opened upon an observation deck under a transparent dome.

"Isn't it marvelous?" breathed Floriel. "Do you think we'll ever have a space-yacht? One as fine as this?"

"I don't know," said Ghyl somberly. "I hope so . . . yes. Someday I will have one . . . now we had best go."

Floriel whispered, "Think! If we knew astrogation, we could take the space-yacht right now—up and away from Ambroy! We'd own it, all to ourselves!"

The idea was tantalizing but preposterous. Ghyl was now more than ready to leave, but to his dismay Floriel skipped recklessly across the saloon, up the steps to the control platform. Ghyl called to him in an anxious voice, "Don't touch anything! Don't move a single lever!"

"Come now. Do you take me for a fool?"

Ghyl looked longingly back at the entrance port. "We'd best be going!"

"Oh but you must come up here, you can't imagine how grand it is!"

"Don't touch anything!" Ghyl warned him. "You'll cause trouble!" He came a couple of steps forward. "Let's go!"

"As soon as I . . ." Floriel's voice became a startled stammer.

Following the direction of his gaze, Ghyl saw a girl standing by the aft companionway. She wore a rich suit of rose velvet, a square, soft, flat cap of the same material with a pair of scarlet ribbons hanging past her shoulders. She was dark-haired; her face was piquant, mobile, bright with vitality, but at this moment she looked from one ragamuffin to the other in outrage. Ghyl stared back in fascination. Surely this was the same small lady the puppet-master had pointed out at the puppet show? She was very pretty, he thought, with the same fascinating hint of Difference: that peculiar quality which distinguished lords from men.

Floriel, arousing from his petrifaction, began to slink down from the control deck. The girl came a few steps forward. A Garrion followed her into the saloon. Floriel froze back against a bulkhead. He stuttered, "We meant no harm, we only wanted to look . . ."

The girl studied him gravely, then turned to inspect Ghyl. Her mouth drooped in disgust. She looked back at the Garrion. "Give them a beating; throw them away."

The Garrion seized Floriel, who chattered and howled. Ghyl might have retreated and escaped, but he chose to remain, for a reason not at all clear to him: certainly his presence was no help to Floriel.

The Garrion dealt Floriel a series of disinterested blows. Floriel yelped and writhed in dramatic fashion. The girl gave a curt nod. "Enough; the other."

Sobbing and panting Floriel fled past Ghyl, and down the ramp. Ghyl stood his ground against the Garrion, trying to control his shrinking flesh as the creature loomed over him. The Garrion's hands were cool and rough; the touch sent an odd chill along Ghyl's nerves. He hardly felt the blows, which were carefully measured. His attention was fixed on the girl, who watched the beating critically. Ghyl wondered how someone so delicate and pretty could be so unfeeling. Were all the lords so cruel?

The girl saw Ghyl's gaze and perhaps sensed the import. She frowned. "Beat this one more severely; he is insolent!"

Ghyl received a few additional blows and then was shoved roughly from the ship.

Floriel stood a fearful fifty yards down the avenue. Ghyl picked himself up from the ground where he had fallen. He looked back up the ramp. There was nothing to see. He turned away and joined Floriel; wordlessly they trudged back along the avenue.

They gained the interior of the depot without attracting attention. Mindful of his father's antipathy toward the Overtrend, Ghyl insisted on walking home: a matter of four miles.

Along the way Floriel burst out in a spasm of fury. "What abominable people the lords! Did you sense the girl's glee? She treated us as if we were muck! As if we stank! And my mother is second cousin to the Mayor! I will have my own back someday! Hear me, for I am resolved!"

Ghyl heaved a mournful sigh. "She certainly could have used us more kindly. Still—she also might have used us worse. Far worse."

Floriel gazed at him in amazement, hair tousled, face distorted. "Eh? What's all this? She ordered us beaten! While she watched, smirking!"

"She could have had our names. What if she had given us to the welfare agents?"

Floriel lowered his head. The two boys trudged on into Brueben. The setting sun, entering a band of ale-colored haze, cast amber light in their faces.

CHAPTER 5

Autumn came to Ambroy, then winter: a season of chilling rains and mists, which started a black and lavender lichen growing over the ruins, to lend the old city a dismal grandeur it lacked in the dry season. Amiante completed a fine screen which was judged Acme and which also received a Guild Citation of Excellence, with which he was quietly pleased.

He also received a visit from a Guild Leaper of the Temple, a sharp-featured young man wearing a scarlet jacket, a tall black hat, brown breeches tight around heavy legs knotted with muscle after a lifetime of leaping. He came to remonstrate in regard to Ghyl's carefree life. "Why does he not participate in Soul Endowment? What of his Basic Saltations? He knows neither Rite nor Rote nor Doxology; nor Leaps nor Bounds! Finuka requires more than this!"

Amiante listened politely, but continued to work with his chisel. He spoke in a mild voice, "The lad is hardly old enough to think. If he has a mind to devotion, he'll know fast enough; then he'll more than make up for any lack."

The Leaper became excited. "A fallacy! Children are best trained young. Witness myself! When I was an infant, I crawled upon a patterned rug! The first words I spoke were the Apotheosis and the Simulations. This is best! Train the child young! As he stands now he is a spiritual vacuum, susceptible to any strange cult! Best to fill his soul with the ways of Finuka!"

"I'll explain all this to him," said Amiante. "Perhaps he may be encouraged to worship; who can say?"

"The parent bears the responsibility," intoned the Guide Leaper. "When have you done your last leaping? I suspect months have passed!"

Amiante calculated a pensive moment. He nodded. "Months at the very least."

"Well then!" exclaimed the Leaper in triumph. "Is this not an explanation in itself?"

"Very likely. Well then, I'll have a discussion with the boy later in the day."

The Guide Leaper started to expostulate further, but, observing Amiante's absorption in his work, he shook his head in defeat, performed a holy sign and departed.

Amiante glanced up expressionlessly as the Leaper passed through the door.

Time and welfare regulations pressed in upon Ghyl. On his tenth birthday he joined the Wood-carvers' Guild, his first choice; the Mariners' Guild, was closed to all save sons of existing members.

Amiante dressed for the occasion in formal guild-meeting wear: a brown coat flared wide at the hips, peaked up at the shoulders, with black piping and carved buttons; tight trousers, with rows of white buttons down the sides, a complicated billed hat of tan felt with black tassels and guild medals. Ghyl wore his first trousers (having heretofore gone only in a gray child's smock) with a maroon jacket and a smart, polished leather cap. Together they walked north to the Guild Hall.

The initiation was a lengthy affair, consisting of a dozen rituals, questions and responses, charges and assurances. Ghyl paid his first year's dues, received his first medal, which the Guild-master ceremoniously affixed to his cap.

From the Guild Hall, Ghyl and Amiante walked east across the old Mercantilikum to the Welfare Agency in East Town. Here there was further formality. Ghyl was somatyped; his Beneficial Number was tattooed upon his right shoulder. Henceforth, by agency reckoning, he was an adult, and would be counseled by Helfred Cobol in his own right. Ghyl was asked his status at the Temple, and was forced to admit to none. The Qualification Officer and the Department Scrivener looked with raised eyebrows from Ghyl to Amiante, then they shrugged. The scrivener wrote upon the questionnaire: "No present capability; status of parent in doubt."

The Qualification Officer spoke in a measured voice: "To achieve your most complete fulfillment as a participating member of society, you must be active at the Temple. I will therefore assign you to Full Operative Function. You must contribute four hours voluntary cooperation per week to the Temple, together with various assessments and beneficial gifts. Since you are somewhat—in fact, considerably—retarded, you will be enrolled in special Indoctrination Class. . . . Did you speak?"

"I was asking if the Temple was necessary," stammered Ghyl. "I just wanted to know——"

"Temple instruction is not 'fully compulsory,' " said the officer. "It is of the 'strongly recommended' category, inasmuch as any other course suggests noncuperativity. You will therefore report to the Temple Juvenile Authority at ten o'clock tomorrow."

So, willy-nilly, and with Amiante keeping his own counsel, Ghyl presented himself at the Central Temple in Cato Precinct. The clerk issued him a dull red cloak with high hitches for leaping, a book which displayed and explained the Great Design, charts of uncomplicated patterns; then assigned him to a study group.

Ghyl made but fair progress at the Temple, and was far outshone by others younger than himself, who skipped easily through the most complicated patterns: bounding, dancing, whirling, flicking a toe to touch a sign here, an emblem there, swinging contemptuously wide over the black and green "Delinquencies," coursing swiftly down the peripheries, veering past the red demon spots.

At home Amiante, in a sudden fit of energy, taught Ghyl to read and write the third-level syllabary, and sent him to the Guild instruction chambers to learn mathematics.

It was a busy year for Ghyl. The old days of idleness and wandering seemed remote indeed. On his eleventh birthday Amiante gave him a choice panel of arzack, to be carved into a screen of his own design.

Ghyl looked among his sketches and chose a pleasant composition of boys climbing fruit trees, and he adapted the composition to the natural grain of the panel.

Amiante approved the design. "Quite suitable: whimsical and gay. It is best to produce gay designs. Happiness is fugitive; dissatisfaction and boredom are real. The folk who gaze upon your screens are entitled to all the joy you can give them, even though the joy be but an abstraction."

Ghyl felt impelled to protest at the cynicism of his father. "I don't consider happiness an illusion! Why should folk content themselves with illusions when reality is so pungent? Are not acts better than dreams?"

Amiante gave his characteristic shrug. "There are many more excellent dreams than meaningful acts. Or so it might be argued."

"But acts are *real!* Each real act is worth a thousand dreams!"

Amiante smiled ruefully. "Dream? Act? Which is illusion? Fortinone is old. Billions of folk have come and gone, pale fish in an ocean of time. They rise into the sunlit shallows; they glitter a moment or two; they drift away through the murk."

Ghyl scowled off through the amber panes, which allowed a distorted view of the comings and goings in Undle Square. "I can't feel like a fish. You're not a fish. We don't live in an ocean. You are you and I am I and this is our home." He threw down his tools and marched outside to draw a breath of air. He walked north into Veige Precinct and by force of habit mounted Dunkum's Heights. Here, to his annoyance, he found two small boys and a little girl, perhaps seven or eight years old. They were sitting in the grass tossing pebbles down the slope. Their chatter seemed much too boisterous for the spot where Ghyl had spent so much time musing. He gave them a glare of outrage, to which they returned puzzled stares. Ghyl strode off to the north, down the long, descending ridge which died upon the Dodrechten mud flats. As he walked, he wondered about Floriel, whom he had not seen for some time. Floriel had joined the Metal-benders' Guild. When Ghyl had seen him last, Floriel had sported a little black leather skullcap from under which his hair curled out in a manner almost too charming for a boy. Floriel had been somewhat remote. He had finally, so Ghyl decided, been caught up in a sensible career, for all the wild talk of his childhood.

Ghyl returned home during the late afternoon, to find Amiante sorting through a portfolio of his private treasures, which he generally kept in a cabinet on the third floor.

Ghyl had never seen at close hand the contents of the portfolio. He approached and watched over Amiante's elbow as Amiante pored over the objects, which were old writings: manuscript, calligraph, ornaments and illustrations. Ghyl noted several extremely ancient fragments of parchment on which were characters indited with great regularity and uniformity. Ghyl was puzzled. He squinted down at the archaic documents. "Who could write so careful and minute a hand? Did they employ mites? No scrivener today could do so well!"

"What you see is a process called 'printing,'" Amiante told him. "It is duplication a hundred times, a thousand times over. Nowadays, of course, printing is not allowed."

"How is it accomplished?"

"There are many systems, or so I understand. Sometimes carved bits of metal are inked and pressed against paper; sometimes a jet of black light instantaneously sprays a page with writing; sometimes the characters are burnt upon paper through a pattern. I know very little about these processes, which I believe are still used on other worlds."

Ghyl studied the archaic symbols for a period, then went on to admire the rich colors of the decorations. Amiante, reading from a little pamphlet, chuckled quietly. Ghyl looked around curiously. "What does it say?"

"Nothing of consequence. It is an old bulletin describing an electric boat which was offered for sale by the Bidderbasse Factory in Luschein. The price: twelve hundred sequins."

"What is a sequin?"

"It is money. Something like welfare vouchers. I don't believe the factory is in operation any more. Perhaps the boats were of poor quality. Perhaps the Overtrend lords laid an embargo. It is difficult to know; there are no dependable chronicles, at least not in Ambroy." Amiante heaved a sad sigh. "One can never learn anything when he so desires . . . still, I suppose that we should count our blessings. Other eras have been far worse. There is no want in Fortinone, as there is in Bauredel. No wealth, of course, except for that of the lords. But no want."

Ghyl examined the printed characters. "Are these hard to read?"

"Not particularly. Would you like to learn?"

Ghyl hesitated, considering the many demands upon his time. If he were ever to travel to Damar, to Morgan, to the Wonder Worlds (already the dream of owning a space-yacht was becoming remote) he must work with great industry, and earn vouchers. But he nodded. "Yes, I would like to learn."

Amiante seemed pleased. "I am not overly well-versed, and there are many idioms which I fail to recognize—but perhaps we can puzzle them out together."

Amiante pushed all his tools to the side, spread a cloth over the screen upon which he had been working, arranged the fragments, brought stylus and paper and copied the crabbed old characters.

During the days that followed, Ghyl struggled to master the archaic system of writing—not so simple a matter as he had originally supposed. Amiante could not transliterate the symbols into either primary pictographs, secondary cursive, or even the third-level syllabary. And even after Ghyl could identify and combine the characters, he was forced to learn archaic idioms and constructions, and sometimes allusions, regarding which Amiante could provide no enlightenment.

One day Helfred Cobol came to the shop to find Ghyl copying from an old parchment, while Amiante mused and dreamed over his portfolio. Helfred Cobol stood in the doorway, arms akimbo, a sour look on his face. "Now what occurs here in the wood-carving shop of old Rt. Tarvoke and young Rt. Tarvoke? Are you turning to scrivening? Don't tell me you evoke new patterns for your screens; I know better." He came forward, inspected Ghyl's exercises. "Archaic, eh? Now what will a wood-carver need with Archaic? I can't read it, and I'm a welfare agent."

Amiante spoke with a trifle more animation than he was accustomed to show. "You must remember that one does not carve wood every hour of the day and night."

"Understood," responded Helfred Cobol. "In fact, judging from the work performed since my previous call, you have carved wood very few hours of either day or night. Much more of this and you will be existing on Base Stipend."

Amiante glanced at his nearly finished screen, as if to appraise how much work remained. "In due course, in due course."

Helfred Cobol, coming around the heavy old table, looked down at the portfolio. Amiante made a small motion as if to fold up the covers, but restrained himself. Such an act would only stimulate a man trained to curiosity and suspicion.

Helfred Cobol did not touch the portfolio, but leaned over it with hands behind his back. "Interesting old stuff." He pointed. "Printed material, I believe. How old do you reckon it?"

"I can't be sure," said Amiante. "It makes reference to Clarence Tovanesko, so it won't be more than thirteen hundred years old."

Helfred Cobol nodded. "It might even be of local fabrication. When did anti-duping regulations go into effect?"

"About fifty years after this." Amiante nodded at the bit of paper. "Just a guess of course."

"One doesn't see much printing," ruminated Helfred Cobol. "There's not even any contraband off the space-ships, as there used to be in my grandfather's day. Folk seem to me more law-abiding, which of course, makes life easier for the welfare agents. Noncups are more active this year, worse luck: vandals, thieves, anarchists that they are."

"A worthless group, by and large," agreed Amiante.

" 'By and large'?" snorted Helfred Cobol. "Altogether, I would say! They are nonproductive, a tumor in the society! The criminals suck our blood, the small-dealers disrupt the agency's bookwork."

Amiante had no more to say. Helfred Cobol turned to Ghyl. "Put aside the erudite uselessness, boy; that's my best advice. You'll never gain vouchers as a scrivener. Also, I've been told that your Temple attendance is spotty, that you're only leaping a simple Honor-to-Finuka Half-about. More practice there, young Rt. Tarvoke! And more time with chisel and gouge!"

"Yes sir," said Ghyl meekly. "I'll do my best."

Helfred Cobol gave him a friendly slap on the shoulder and left the shop. Amiante returned to the portfolio. But his mood was broken, and he twitched the papers with quick petulant jerks.

Ghyl heard him mutter a peevish curse, and, looking up, saw that in his annoyance Amiante had torn one of his treasures: a long fragile sheet of low-grade paper printed with wonderful caricatures of three now-forgotten public figures.

Amiante, after his outburst, sat like a rock, brooding over some matter which he obviously did not plan to communicate to Ghyl. Presently, without a word, Amiante rose to his feet, slung his second-best brown and blue cape around his shoulders, and set forth upon an errand. Ghyl went to the door, watched his father amble across the square and disappear into an alley which led away into Nobile Precinct and the rough dock area.

Ghyl, also restless, could concentrate no longer on the old writing. He made a half-hearted attempt to master a rather difficult Temple exercise, then set to work on his screen, and so occupied himself the remainder of the day.

The sun had fallen behind the buildings across the square before Amiante returned. He carried several parcels, which he put without comment into a cabinet, then sent Ghyl out to buy seaweed curd and a leek salad for their supper. Ghyl went slowly and reluctantly; there was a pot of leftover porridge, which Amiante, who was somewhat frugal with food expenditures, had been planning to use. Why the unnecessary expenditure? Ghyl knew better than to ask. At best Amiante might give him a vague and irrelevant response. At worst Amiante would pretend not to have heard the question.

Something peculiar was in the wind, thought Ghyl. In a

heavy mood he visited the greengrocer's, then the marine paste dealer's. Over the evening meal, Amiante, to anyone other than Ghyl, might have seemed his ordinary self. Ghyl knew differently. Amiante, not a talkative man, alternated periods of staring glumly down at his plate with attempts at contriving an easy conversation. He inquired as to Ghyl's progress at the Temple, a subject regarding which he had heretofore shown little interest. Ghyl reported that he was doing fairly well with the exercises but found difficulty with the catechism. Amiante nodded but Ghyl could see that his thoughts were elsewhere. Presently Amiante asked if Ghyl had come upon Floriel at the Temple, where he took instruction on much the same basis as Ghyl.

"A peculiar lad, that one," Amiante remarked. "Easily persuaded, or so I would say; and with a streak of perversity to make him uncertain."

"That is what I feel too," said Ghyl. "Although now he seems to be buckling down to guild work."

"Yes, why not?" mused Amiante, as if the reverse—indolence, noncuperativity—were standard conduct.

There was another silence, with Amiante frowning down at his plate as if for the first time he had become aware of what he was eating. He made an offhand reference to Helfred Cobol. "He means well enough, the agent; but he tries to reconcile too many conflicts. It makes him unhappy. He'll never do well."

Ghyl was interested in his father's opinion. "I've always thought him impatient and rude."

Amiante smiled, and looked off into his private thoughts. But he made another comment. "We are lucky with Helfred Cobol. The polite agents are harder to deal with. They offer smooth surface; they are impervious. . . . How would you like to be a welfare agent?"

Ghyl had never considered the possibility. "I'm not a Cobol. I suppose it's very cuperative, and they gain bonus vouchers, or so I hear. I'd rather be a lord."

"Naturally; who wouldn't?"

"But it's not possible in any way?"

"Not here in Fortinone. They keep themselves to themselves."

"On their home world were they lords? Or ordinary recipients like ourselves?"

Amiante shook his head. "Once, long ago, I worked for an off-world information agency and I might have asked, but during these times my thoughts were elsewhere. I don't know the lords' home world. Perhaps Alode, perhaps Earth, which I've been told is the first home of all men."

"I wonder," said Ghyl, "why the lords live here in Fortinone. Why did they not choose Salula or Luschein or the Mang Islands?"

Amiante shrugged. "The same reason, no doubt, that we live where we do. Here we were born, here we live, here we will die."

"Suppose I went to Luschein and studied to be a space-man; would the lords hire me aboard their yachts?"

Amiante pursed his mouth dubiously. "The first difficulty is learning to be a space-man. It is a popular occupation."

"Did you ever want to be a space-man?"

"Oh indeed. I had my dreams. Still—it may be best to carve wood. Who knows? We shall never starve."

"But we will never be financially independent," said Ghyl with a sniff.

"True." Amiante, rising, took his plate to the wash-table, where he scraped it very carefully and cleaned it with a minimum of water and sand.

Ghyl watched the meticulous process with detached interest. Amiante, so he knew, begrudged every check he was forced to pay over to the lords. It was a process which puzzled him. He asked, "The lords take 1.18 percent of everything we produce, don't they?"

"They do," said Amiante. "1.18 percent of the value of imports and exports alike."

"Then why do we use so little water and power, and why do we walk so much? Is not the money paid regardless?"

Amiante's face took on a mulish cast, always the case when he spoke of vouchers paid to the lords. "Meters are everywhere. Meters measure everything except the air you breathe. Even the sewage is metered. The Welfare Agency then withholds from each recipient, on a prorated basis of use, enough to pay the lords, together with enough to pay themselves and all other functionaries. Little enough is left for the recipients."

Ghyl nodded dubiously. "How did the lords first come into possession of the utilities?"

"It happened perhaps fifteen hundred years ago. There were wars—with Bauredel, with the Mang Islands, with Lankenburg. Before were the Star Wars and before this the Dreadful War, and before this: wars without number. The last war, with Emperor Riskanie and the White-eyed Men, resulted in the destruction of the city. Ambroy was devastated; the towers were destroyed; the folk lived like savages. The lords arrived in space-ships and set all in order. They generated power, started the water, built transit tubes, reopened the sewers, organized imports and exports. For this they asked and were conceded one percent. When they rebuilt the space-port they were conceded an additional eighteen hundredths percent, and so it has remained."

"And when did we learn that duping was illegal and wrong?"

Amiante pursed his delicate mouth. "The strictures were first applied about a thousand years ago, when our crafts began earning a reputation."

"And all during past history men have duped?" asked Ghyl in a voice of awe.

"As much as they saw fit." Amiante rose to his feet and went down to the workroom to carve on his screen. Ghyl took his dishes to the sink and as he washed he contemplated the bizarre old times when men worked without reference to welfare regulations. When all was tidy, he also went down to his bench and for a period worked on his own screen. Then he went to watch Amiante, who burnished surfaces already glistening, cleared burrs from grooves smooth beyond cavil. Ghyl tried to resume the conversation, but Amiante had no more to say. Ghyl presently bade him good night and climbed up to the third floor. He went to the window, looked out across Undle Square, thinking of the men who had passed along these ancient streets, marching to triumphs and defeats now forgotten. Above hung Damar, mottled blue, pink and yellow, casting a nacreous sheen on all the old buildings.

Into the street directly below shone light from the workroom. Amiante worked late—an unusual occurrence, Amiante preferring to use the light of day in order to deprive the lords. Other houses around the square, following a similar philosophy, were dark.

As Ghyl was about to turn away, the light from the workroom flickered and became obscured. Ghyl looked down in puzzlement. He did not consider his father a secretive man: merely a person vague and given to fits of brooding. Why, therefore, would Amiante pull the blinds? Would there be a connection between the uncharacteristic secrecy and the parcels Amiante had brought home that afternoon?

Ghyl went to sit on his couch. Welfare regulations put no

explicit ban upon private or secret activity, as long as there was no violation of social policy, which meant, in effect, prior clearance with a welfare official.

Ghyl sat stiffly, hands by his side clutching the coverlets. He did not want to intrude or discover something to embarrass both himself and his father. But still . . . Ghyl reluctantly rose to his feet. He walked quietly downstairs, trying simultaneously to avoid furtiveness and noise; to go down unnoticed but without the uncomfortable feeling of being a sneak.

The cooking and living quarters smelled warm of porridge, with also a sharp tang of seaweed. Ghyl went across to the square of yellow light barred by balusters, which marked the staircase. . . . The light went off. Ghyl froze in his tracks. Was Amiante preparing to come upstairs? . . . But there were no footsteps. Amiante remained in the dark workroom.

But not quite dark. There came a sudden flash of blue-white light, which persisted a second or so. Then, a moment later, came a dim flickering glow. Frightened now, Ghyl stole to the staircase, looked down through the balusters and into the workroom.

For several moments he stared in puzzlement, pulse thudding so loudly he wondered that Amiante did not hear. But Amiante was absorbed in his work. He adjusted a mechanism which apparently had been contrived for the occasion: a box of rough fiber two feet long, a foot high, and a foot wide, with a tube protruding from one end. Now Amiante went to a basin, peered down at something in the liquid: an object which glimmered pale. He shook his head, clicked his tongue in patent dissatisfaction. He extinguished the lights, all save a candle, and uncovering a second basin dipped a sheet of stiff white paper into what appeared to be a viscous syrup. He tilted the paper this way and that, drained it carefully, then set it on a rack in front of the box. He pressed a switch; from the tube came an intense beam of blue-white light. On the sheet of wet paper appeared a bright image.

The light vanished; Amiante swiftly took the sheet, laid it flat on the bench, covered it with a soft black powder, rubbed it carefully with a roller. Then lifting the paper he shook off the excess powder, dropped it into the basin. Then he turned on the lights, bent anxiously to examine the sheet. After a moment he nodded in satisfaction. He removed the first sheet, crumpled it, threw it aside. Then he returned to the table, repeated the entire process.

Ghyl watched, fascinated. Clear, all too clear. His father was violating the most basic of all welfare regulations.

He was duplicating.

Ghyl examined Amiante with terrified eyes, as if here were a stranger of unknown qualities. His conscientious father, the expert wood-carver, duping! The fact, while undeniable, was incredible! Ghyl wondered if he was awake or dreaming; the scene indeed had something of the grotesque quality of a dream.

Amiante, meanwhile, had inserted a new item into his projection box and focused the image carefully on a blank sheet of paper. Ghyl recognized one of the fragments from Amiante's collection of ancient writings.

Amiante worked now with more assurance. He made two copies; and so he continued, duplicating the old papers in his portfolio.

Presently Ghyl stole upstairs to his room, carefully restraining himself from speculation. The hour was too late. He did not want to think. But one dreadful apprehension remained: the light leaking through the shutters into the square. Suppose someone had observed the flickering, the peculiar fluctuations, and wondered as to the cause. Ghyl looked down from his window, and the light, going on, going off, then the blue flash, seemed inordinately suspicious. How could Amiante be so careless, so sublimely absentminded, as not to wonder or worry about such matters?

To Ghyl's relief, Amiante tired of his illicit occupation. Ghyl could hear him moving here and there around the workroom, stowing away his equipment.

Amiante came slowly up the stairs. Ghyl feigned slumber. Amiante went to bed. Ghyl lay awake, and it seemed to him that Amiante likewise lay awake, thinking his strange thoughts. . . . Ghyl finally drowsed off.

In the morning Amiante was his usual self. As Ghyl ate his breakfast of porridge and fish-flakes, he pondered: Amiante had duped eight, or even ten, items of his collection on the previous evening. It seemed not unlikely that he would dupe the rest. He must be made aware that the lights were visible. In as artless a voice as he could manage, Ghyl asked, "Were you fixing our lights last night?"

Amiante looked at Ghyl with eyebrows first raised in puzzlement, then drooping almost comically in embarrassment.

Amiante was perhaps the least expert dissembler alive. "Er—
why do you ask that?"

"I happened to look out the window and I saw the lights
going on and off. You had pulled the blinds but the light
leaked past into the street. I suppose you were repairing the
lamp?"

Amiante rubbed his face. "Something of the sort . . .
something of the sort indeed. Now then—do you go to the
Temple today?"

Ghyl had forgotten. "Yes. Although I don't know the exercises."

"Well—do your best. Some folk have the knack, others
don't."

Ghyl spent a miserable morning at the Temple, hopping
awkwardly through simple patterns, while children years
younger than himself, but far more devout, sprang about the
Elemental Pattern with agility and finesse, winning commen-
dation from the Guide Leaper. To make matters worse, the
Third Assistant Saltator visited the hall and saw Ghyl's hops
and sprawling jumps with astonishment; to such an extent
that presently he threw his hands into the air and strode from
the hall in disgust.

When Ghyl returned home he found that Amiante had
started a new screen. Instead of the usual arzack, he had
brought forth a panel of costly ing as high as his eyes, wider
than his outstretched arms. All afternoon he worked transfer-
ring his cartoon to the panel. It was a striking design, but
Ghyl could not help but feel a glum amusement at Amiante's
inconsistency: that he could counsel Ghyl to gaiety, and then
himself embark upon a work pervaded with melancholy. The
cartoon indicated a lattice festooned with foliage, from which
peered a hundred small, grave faces, each different, yet somehow alike in the disturbing intensity of their gazes. Across the
top were two words—Remember Me—in a loose and graceful calligraphy.

Amiante left off work on his new panel late in the afternoon. He yawned, stretched, rose to his feet, went to the
door, looked out across the square, now busy with folk returning to their homes from work about the city: stevedores,
boat-builders, mechanics; workers in wood, metal, and stone;
merchants and servicers; scriveners and clerks; food pro-
cessors, slaughterers, fishermen; stasticians and welfare workers; house-girls, nurses, doctors and dentists—these latter all
female.

As if struck by a sudden thought, Amiante examined the blinds. He stood rubbing his chin, then turned a brief glance back to Ghyl, who pretended not to notice.

Amiante went to the closet, brought forth a flask, poured two glasses of mild reed-blossom wine, put one by Ghyl's elbow, sipped the other. Ghyl, glancing up, found it hard to reconcile this man, a trifle portly, calm of face, somewhat pale, somewhat inward-turned but wholly gentle, with the intent figure which had worked at irregulation the preceding night. If only it were a dream, a nightmare! The welfare agents, helpful and long-suffering, could become relentless when regulations were flouted. One day Ghyl had seen a wife-murderer being dragged away for rehabilitation, and the idea of Amiante being treated so caused him such terror that his stomach churned over.

Amiante was discussing Ghyl's screen: ". . . trifle more relief, here in this bark detail. The general idea is vitality, young folk romping in the country; why diminish the theme by overdelicacy?"

"Yes," muttered Ghyl. "I'll carve somewhat deeper."

"I think I'd like less detail in the grass; it seems to rob the leaves . . . but this is your interpretation, and you must do as you think best."

Ghyl nodded numbly. He put down his chisel and drank the wine; he could carve no more today. Usually he was the one to initiate conversation, to talk while Amiante listened; but now the roles were reversed. Amiante was now considering their evening meal. "Last night we used seaweed; I thought it somewhat stale. What do you say to a salad of plinchets with perhaps a few nuts and a bit of cheese? Or would you prefer bread and cold meat? It shouldn't be too dear."

Ghyl said he'd as soon eat bread and meat, and Amiante sent him off to the shopkeeper. Looking over his shoulder, Ghyl saw with dismay that Amiante was inspecting the blinds, swinging them to and fro, open and shut.

That night Amiante once more worked his duplicating machine, but he carefully muffled the blinds. Light no longer flickered out upon the square, to excite the wonder of some passing night agent.

Ghyl went miserably to bed, thankful only that Amiante—since he seemed determined upon irregulation—was at least taking precautions against being caught in the act.

CHAPTER 6

In spite of Amiante's precautions, his misconduct was discovered—not by Helfred Cobol, who, knowing something of Amiante's disposition, might have contented himself with unofficial outrage and a close watch upon Amiante thereafter, but unluckily by Ells Wolleg, the guild delegate, a fussy little man with a dyspeptic, yellow owl's face. In making a routine check of Amiante's tools and work conditions, he lifted a scrap of wood, and there, where Amiante had carelessly laid them, were three faulty copies of an old chart. Wolleg bent forward, frowning, his first emotion simple irritation that Amiante should untidily mingle charts with guild-sponsored work; then, as the fact of duplication became manifest, he emitted a comical, fluting yell. Amiante, straightening tools and cleaning away scrap at the opposite end of the table, looked around with eyebrows twisted in sad dismay. Ghyl sat rigid.

Wolleg turned upon Amiante, eyes glittering from behind spectacles. "Be so good as to Spay-line the Welfare Agency, at once."

Amiante shook his head. "I have no Spay connection."

Wolleg snapped his fingers toward Ghyl. "Run, boy, as as you can. Summon here the welfare agents."

Ghyl half-rose from his bench, then settled back. "No."

Ells Wolleg wasted no time arguing. He went to the door, looked around the square, marched to a public Spay terminal.

As soon as Wolleg had departed the shop, Ghyl jumped to his feet. "Quick, let's hide the other things!"

Amiante stood torpidly, unable to act.

"Quick!" hissed Ghyl. "He'll be back at once!"

"Where can I put them?" mumbled Amiante. "They'll search everywhere."

Ghyl ran to the cabinet, pulled down Amiante's equipment. Into the box he piled rubbish and scrap. The lens tube he filled with brads and clips and stood it among other such containers. The bulbs that furnished the blue flash and the power block were more of a problem, which Ghyl solved by running with them to the back door and throwing them over the fence into a waste area.

Amiante watched for a moment with a dull, brooding gaze, then, struck by a thought, he ran upstairs. He returned seconds before Wolleg reentered the shop.

Wolleg spoke in stiff measured tones: "My concerns, strictly speaking, are only with guild by-laws and work standards. Nevertheless I am a public official and I have done my duty. I may add that I am ashamed to find duplicated stuffs, undoubtedly of irregulationary origin, in the custody of a wood-carver."

"Yes," mumbled Amiante. "It must come as a great blow."

Wolleg turned his attention to the duplicated papers, and gave a grunt of disgust. "How did these articles reach your hands?"

Amiante smiled wanly. "As you guessed, from an irregulationary source."

Ghyl exhaled a small sigh. At least Amiante did not intend to blurt forth everything in a spasm of contemptuous candor. Three welfare agents arrived: Helfred Cobol and a pair of supervisors with keen and darting eyes. Wolleg explained the circumstances, displayed the duplicated papers. Helfred Cobol looked at Amiante with a sardonic shake of the head and a curl of the lips. The two other welfare agents made a brief search of the shop but found nothing more; it was clear that their suspicions did not range as far as the theory that Amiante himself had been duplicating.

Presently the two supervisors departed with Amiante, in spite of Ghyl's protests.

Helfred Cobol drew him aside. "Mind your manners, boy. Your father must go to the office and respond to a questionnaire. If his charge is light—and I believe this to be the case—he will escape rehabilitation."

Ghyl had heard previous references to one's charge being high or low, but had assumed the phrase to be a colloquialism or a figure of speech. Now he was not so sure. There were menacing overtones to the words. He felt too depressed to put any questions to Helfred Cobol, and went to sit at his bench.

Helfred Cobol walked here and there around the room, picking up a tool, fingering a bit of wood, looking occasionally toward Ghyl, as if there were something he wished to say but found himself unable to verbalize. Finally he muttered something unintelligible and went to stand in the doorway, looking out upon the square.

Ghyl wondered what he was waiting for. Amiante's return? This hope was dashed by the arrival of a tall, gray-haired female agent, whose function apparently was to assume authority over the premises. Helfred Cobol gave her a curt nod and departed without further words.

The woman spoke to Ghyl in a terse clear voice: "I am Matron Hantillebeck. Since you are a minor, I have been assigned to maintain the household until such time as a responsible adult returns. In short, you are in my charge. You need not necessarily vary from your normal routine; you may work, or practice devotionals, whichever is customary for you at this time."

Ghyl silently bent over his screen. Matron Hantillebeck locked the door, made an inspection of the house, turning on lights everywhere, sniffing at Amiante's less than meticulous housekeeping. She came back to the workshop, leaving lights ablaze everywhere in the house, even though afternoon light still entered the windows.

Ghyl essayed a timid protest. "If you don't mind, I'll turn out the lights. My father does not care to nourish the lords any more than necessary."

The remark irritated Matron Hantillebeck. "I do mind. The house is dark and disgustingly dirty. I wish to see where I am putting my feet. I do not care to step in something nasty."

Ghyl considered a moment, then offered tentatively: "There's nothing nasty about, really. I know my father would be furious—and if I may turn off the lights, I'll run ahead of you and turn them back on whenever you care to walk."

Matron Hantillebeck jerked about and fixed Ghyl with so ferocious a glare that Ghyl moved back a step. "Let the lights stay on! What care I for the penury of your father? The next thing to a Chaoticist, or so I reckon! Does he want to throttle Fortinone? Must we eat mud on his account?"

"I don't understand," Ghyl faltered. "My father is a good man. He would hurt no one."

"Bah." The matron swung away, made herself comfortable on a couch and began to crochet silk web. Ghyl slowly went to his screen. The matron took a rope of candied seaweed from her reticule, then a flask of soursnap beer and a slab of curdcake. Ghyl went up to the living quarters and thought no more of Matron Hantillebeck. He ate a plate of broad-beans, then in defiance of the matron, extinguished the lights throughout the upper stories and went to his couch. He had no knowledge of how the matron passed the night, for in the morning when he went downstairs, she was gone.

Not long after Amiante shuffled into the shop. His scant gray-gold hair was tousled, his eyes were like puddles of mercury. He looked at Ghyl; Ghyl looked at him. Ghyl asked, "Did—did they harm you?"

Amiante shook his head. He came a few steps farther into the room, looked tentatively here and there. He went to a bench, seated himself, ran his hand across his head, further rumpling his hair.

Ghyl watched in apprehension, trying to decide whether or not his father was ill. Amiante raised a hand in reassurance. "No need for concern. I slept poorly. . . . Did they search?"

"Not well."

Amiante nodded vaguely. He rose, went to the door, stood looking out across the square, as if the scene—the heelcorn trees, the dusty annel bushes, the structures opposite—were strange to him. He turned, went to his bench, considered the half-carved faces of his new screen.

Ghyl asked, "Can I bring you something to eat? Or tea?"

"Not just now." Amiante went upstairs. He returned a minute later with his old portfolio, which he put down upon the workbench.

Ghyl asked in terror, "Are the duplicates there?"

"No. They are under the tiles." Amiante seemed not to wonder at Ghyl's knowledge of his activities.

"But . . . why?" asked Ghyl. "Why did you duplicate these things?"

Amiante slowly raised his head, looked eye to eye with Ghyl. "If I did not," he asked, "who would?"

"But . . . the regulations . . ." Ghyl's voice trailed off. Amiante made no remark. The silence was more meaningful than anything he could have said.

Amiante opened the portfolio. "I had hoped for you to discover these for yourself, when you had learned to read."

"What are they?"

"Various documents from the past—when regulations were less irksome, and perhaps less necessary." He lifted one of the papers, glanced at it, set it aside. "Some are very precious." He sorted through the documents. "Here: the charter of old Ambroy. Barely intelligible, and now all but unknown. Nonetheless, it is still in force." He put it aside, touched another. "Here: the legend of Emphyrio."

Ghyl looked down at the characters, and recognized them for old Archaic, still beyond his comprehension. Amiante read it aloud. He came to the end of the page, halted, put down the paper.

"Is that all?" asked Ghyl.

"I don't know."

"But how does it end?"

"I don't know that either."

Ghyl grimaced in dissatisfaction. "Is it true?"

Amiante shrugged. "Who knows? The Historian, perhaps."

"Who is he?"

"Someone far from here." Amiante went to the cabinet, brought down vellum, ink, a pen. He began to copy the fragment. "I must copy these all; I must disseminate them, where they will not be lost." He bent over the vellum.

Ghyl watched a few minutes, then turned as the doorway darkened. A man came slowly into the shop. Amiante looked up, Ghyl stood back. The visitor was a tall man with a big handsome head, a brush of fine gray hair. He wore a jacket of black broadcloth with a dozen vertical ruffles under each arm, a white vest, trousers of black and brown stripe: a rich, dignified costume, that of a man of position. Ghyl, who had seen him before at guild meetings recognized Rt. Blaise Fodo, the Guild-master himself.

Amiante rose slowly to his feet.

Fodo spoke in a rich earnest voice, "I heard of your difficulties, Rt. Tarvoke, and I came to extend you the good wishes of the guild, and wise counsel, should you require it."

"Thank you, Rt. Fodo," said Amiante. "I wish you had been here to counsel Ells Wolleg from turning me in. That would have been 'counsel' when I needed it."

The Guild-master frowned. "Unluckily I can't foresee every indiscretion of every member. And Delegate Wolleg of course performed his duty as he saw it. But I am surprised to see you scrivening. What do you do?"

Amiante spoke in a voice of the most precise clarity. "I copy an ancient manuscript, that it may be preserved for the times to come."

"What is the document?"

"The legend of Emphyrio."

"Well, then, admirable—but surely this is the domain of the scriveners! They do not carve wood, we neither indite nor

inscribe. What would we gain?" He waved his hand at Amiante's inexact writing with a small smile of indulgent distaste,
as if at the antics of a dirty child. "The copy is by no means
flawless."

Amiante scratched his chin. "It is legible, I hope. . . . Do
you read Archaic?"

"Certainly. What old affair are you so concerned with?"
He picked up the fragment and tilting back his head puzzled
out the sense of the text:

> On the world of Aume, or some say, Home,
> which men had taken by toil and pain, and where
> they had established farmsteads along the shore of
> the sea, came down a monstrous horde from the
> dark moon Sigil.
>
> The men had long put by their weapons and now
> spoke gently: "Monsters: the look of deprivation
> invests you like an odor. If you hunger, eat of our
> food; share our plenty until you are appeased."
>
> The monsters could not speak but their great
> horns yelled: "We do not come for food."
>
> "There is about you the madness of the moon
> Sigil. Come you for peace? Rest then; listen to our
> music, lave your feet in the waves of the sea; soon
> you will be allayed."
>
> "We do not come for respite," bayed the great
> horns.
>
> "There is about you the forlorn despair of the
> outcast, which is irremedial, for love we cannot
> provide; so you must return to the dark moon Sigil,
> and come to terms with those who sent you forth."
>
> "We do not come for love," raved the very
> horns.
>
> "What then is your purpose?"
>
> "We are here to enslave the men of Aume, or as
> some say, Home, to ease ourselves upon their labor.
> Know us for your masters, and he who looks
> askance shall be stamped beneath our terrible feet."
>
> The men were enslaved, and set to such onerous
> tasks as the monsters devised and found needful. In
> due course, Emphyrio, the son of fisher-folk, was
> moved to rebellion, and led his band into the moun-
> tains. He employed a magic tablet, and all who

heard his words knew them for truth, so that many
men set themselves against the monsters.

With fire and flame, with torment and char, the
monsters from Sigil wrought their vengeance. Still
the voice of Emphyrio rang down from the mountain, and all who heard were moved to defiance.

The monsters marched to the mountains, batter-
ing rock from rock, and Emphyrio retired to the far
places: the islands of reed, the forests and murks.

After came the monsters, affording no respite. In
the Col of Deal, behind the Maul Mountains, Emphyrio confronted the horde. He spoke, with his
voice of truth, and his magic tablet, and sent forth
flashing words: "Observe! I hold the magic tablet of
truth! You are Monster; I am Man. Each is alone;
each sees dawn and dusk; each feels pain and pain's
ease. Why should one be victor and the other victim? We will never agree; never shall you know
gain by the toil of man! Submit to the what-must-
be! If you fail to heed, then you must taste a bitter
brew and never again walk the sands of dark Sigil."

The monsters could not disbelieve the voice of
Emphyrio and halted in wonder. One sent forth his
flashing words: "Emphyrio! Come with us to Sigil
and speak in the Catademnon; for there is the force
which controls us to evil deeds."

(end of fragment)

Blaise Fodo slowly laid the paper on the desk. For a moment his eyes were unfocused, his mouth pushed forward into
a thoughtful pink oval. "Yes . . . yes, indeed." He gave his
shoulders a twitch, settled his black jacket. "Amazing, certain
of these old legends. Still we must maintain a sense of pro-
portion. You are an expert wood-carver; your screens are excellent. Your fine son, too, has a productive future before
him. So why waste valuable worktime inditing old tales? It
becomes an obsession! Especially," he added meaningfully,
"when it leads to irregulationary acts. You must be realistic,
Rt. Tarvoke!"

Amiante shrugged, put the vellum and ink to the side.
"Perhaps you are right." He took up a chisel and began to
carve at his screen.

But Rt. Blaise Fodo was not to be put aside so easily. For
another half hour he paced back and forth across the work-

room, looking down first across Ghyl's shoulders, then Amiante's. He spoke further of Amiante's trespass and chided Amiante for allowing a collector's avidity to overcome him, so that he bought illicit reproductions. He also addressed Ghyl, urging industry, devoutness and humility. "The path of life is well-trod; the wisest and best have erected guide-posts, bridges and warning signals; it is either mulishness or arrogance to seek from side to side for new or better routes. So then: look to your welfare agent, to your guild delegate, to your Guide Leaper; follow their instructions. And you will lead a life of placid content."

Guild-master Fodo at last departed. As soon as the door closed behind him, Amiante put down his chisel and returned to his copying. Ghyl had nothing to say, though his heart was full and his throat hurt with premonition. Presently he went out upon the square to buy food, and as luck would have it met Helfred Cobol on his rounds.

The welfare agent looked down at him with a quizzical stare. "What has come over Amiante, that he behaves like a Chaoticist?"

"I don't know," said Ghyl. "But he is no Chaoticist. He is a good man."

"I realize as much, which is why I am concerned. Surely he cannot profit by irregulationary acts; and you must realize this as well."

Ghyl privately thought Amiante's conduct somewhat queer but by no means hurtful or wrong. He did not, however, argue this with Helfred Cobol.

"He is too bold, alas, for his own good," the welfare agent went on. "You must help him. You are a responsible boy. Keep your father safe. Dallying with impossible legends and inflammatory tracts can only richen his rod!"

Ghyl frowned. "Is that the same as 'increasing his charge'?"

"Yes. Do you know what is meant?"

Ghyl shook his head.

"Well then, at the Welfare Agency are trays of small rods, each numbered, each representing a man. I am represented by such a rod, as well as Amiante and yourself. Most of the rods are pure inactive iron; others are magnetized. At every offense or delinquency a carefully calculated magnetic charge is applied to the rod. If there are no new offenses the magnetism presently wanes and disappears. But if offenses continue, the magnetism augments and at last pulls down a signal, and the offender must be rehabilitated."

Ghyl, awed and depressed, looked away across the square. Then he asked, "When a person is rehabilitated, what happens?"

"Ha ha!" exclaimed Helfred Cobol dourly, "you ask after our guild secrets. We do not talk of these things. It is enough to know that the offender is cured of irregulationary tendencies."

"Do noncups have rods at the agency?"

"No. They are not recipients; they are outside the system. When they commit crimes, as often they do, they find no understanding or rehabilitation—they are expelled from Ambroy."

Ghyl clutched his parcels to his chest, shivered, perhaps to a gust of cold wind which dipped down out of the sky. "I had best be home," he told Helfred Cobol in a small voice.

"Home with you then. I'll look in on your father in ten or fifteen minutes."

Ghyl nodded and returned home. Amiante had fallen asleep at his workbench, head down upon his arms. Ghyl stood back in horror. To right and left, spread out on the bench, was duplicated material: every item that Amiante had processed. It seemed as if he had been attempting to organize his papers when drowsiness had overtaken him.

Ghyl dropped the parcels of food, closed and bolted the door, ran forward. It was useless to awaken Amiante and expect alertness. Frantically he gathered all the material together, stacked it into a box, covered it over with shavings and scrap and thrust it under his desk. Only now did he try to arouse his father. "Wake up! Helfred Cobol is on his way!"

Amiante groaned, lurched back, looked at Ghyl with eyes only half-aware.

Ghyl saw two more sheets of paper he previously had missed. He seized them, and as he did so there came a knock at the door. Ghyl shoved the papers down into the shavings, made a last survey of the room. It appeared to be bare, innocent of illicit paper.

Ghyl opened the door. Helfred Cobol looked quizzically down at him. "Since when do you bar the door against the arrival of the welfare agent?"

"A mistake," stammered Ghyl. "I meant no harm."

Amiante by this time had come to his wits and was looking back and forth along the bench with a worried expression.

Helfred Cobol came forward. "A few last words with you, Rt. Tarvoke."

" 'Last words'?"

"Yes. I have worked this ward many years, and we have known each other just so long. But I am becoming too old for field duty and I am being transferred to an administrative office in Elsen. I came to say good-bye to you and Ghyl."

Amiante slowly rose to his feet. "I am sorry to see you go."

Helfred Cobol gave his sardonic grimace of a smile. "Well then, my last few words: attend to your wood-carving, try to lead your son into the ways of orthodoxy. Why do you not go leap with him at the Temple? He would profit by your example."

Amiante nodded politely.

"Well then," said Helfred Cobol, "I'll say good-bye to you both, and commend you to the best attention of Schute Cobol, who will take over in my place."

CHAPTER 7

Schute Cobol was a man with a style distinctly different from that of Helfred Cobol. He was younger, more punctilious in manner and dress, more formal in his interviews. He was a man brisk and precise, with a lean visage, a down-drooping mouth, black hair bristling up behind his head. On his preliminary rounds he explained to all that he intended to work by the strict letter of Welfare Agency regulations. He made clear to Amiante and Ghyl his disapproval of what he considered a lax way of life. "Each of you, with above-average capacity, according to your psychiatric rating, produces well under the norm for this rate. You, young Rt. Tarvoke, are far from diligent at either guild-school or Temple—"

"He takes instruction from me," said Amiante in measured voice.

"Eh? You teach what, additional to wood-carving?"

"I have taught him to read and write, such calculation as I know and hopefully a few other matters as well."

"I strongly suggest that he prepare more earnestly for his Secondary Status at the Temple. According to my records, he attends without regularity and is not proficient in any of the patterns."

Amiante shrugged. "Perhaps later in life . . ."

"What of yourself?" demanded Schute Cobol. "It appears that during the last fourteen years you have visited the Temple but twice and leapt but once."

"Surely more than that. Are the agency records accurate?"

"Of course the agency records are accurate! What a thing to ask! Do you have records in conflict, may I ask?"

"No."

"Well then, why have you leapt only once during these last fourteen years?"

Amiante ran his hands fretfully through his hair. "I am not agile. I do not know the patterns . . . time presses . . ."

Schute Cobol at last departed the shop. Ghyl looked to Amiante for some comment but Amiante merely gave his head a weary shake and bent over his screen.

Amiante's screen of the hundred faces received a 9.503, or 'Acme' rating at the Judgment,* and his total submission averaged at 8.626, well into 'First Class,' or export, category.

Ghyl's single screen received a 6.855 rating, comfortably within the 6.240 limit of the 'Second Class' or 'Domestic Use' category and so went to the holding warehouse in East Town. Ghyl was complimented upon the ease of his design but was urged to greater finesse and delicacy.

Ghyl, who had been hoping for a 'First Class' rating, was dejected. Amiante refused to comment upon the judgment. He said merely: "Start another screen. If we please them with our screens, we produce 'Firsts.' If we do not, our screens are 'Seconds' or 'Rejects.' Therefore, let us please the judges. It is not too difficult."

"Very well," said Ghyl. "My next screen will be 'Girls Kissing Boys.'"

"Hmm." Amiante considered. "You are twelve years old? Best wait a year or so. Why not produce a standard design: possibly 'Willows and Birds'?"

So the months passed. Despite Schute Cobol's explicit disapproval, Ghyl spent little time at Temple exercises, and avoided guild-school. From Amiante he learned Archaic One and such human history as Amiante himself knew: "Men originated on a single world, a planet called Earth, or so it is generally believed. Earthmen learned how to send ships through space, and so initiated human history, though I sup-

---

* The Judgment, from the standpoint of the Ambroy craftsman, was the year's most important event, establishing as it did his stipend for the following year. The judgments were conducted in accordance with an elaborate ritual and generated vast drama—to such an extent that the judges were applauded or criticized for the ceremonial richness of their performances.

Three separate teams of judges worked independently, at the great Boimarc warehouse in East Town and rated each item of work produced by the Ambroy craftsmen. The first team included the master of the Craftsmen's Guild, an expert on the particular class of item from one of the trans-stellar depots, and a Biomarc lord, presumably selected also for his expertise. On the second team was the chairman of the Inter-Guild Benevolent Association, the Craft Guidance Director of the Welfare Agency, the Arbiter of Comparative Beatitudes from the Main Temple. The third team consisted of two Boimare lords and an ordinary recipient chosen by random lot from the population, who received the title Independent Dignitary and a doubled stipend.

The first team investigated only a single category of objects, with ratings weighted double. The second and third teams inspected all articles.

pose there was previous history on Earth. The first men to come to Halma found colonies of vicious insects—creatures as big as children—living in mounds and tunnels. There were great battles until the insects were destroyed. You will find pictures of the things at the Hall of Curios—perhaps you've seen them?"

Ghyl nodded. "I always felt sorry for them."

"Yes, perhaps . . . men have not always been merciful. There have been many wars, all forgotten now. We are not a historical people; we seem to live for the events of the day— or more accurately, from one Judgment to the next."

"I would like to visit other worlds," mused Ghyl. "Wouldn't it be wonderful if we could earn enough vouchers to travel elsewhere, and make our living by carving screens?"

Amiante smiled wistfully. "Other worlds grow no such woods as ing and arzack, or even daban or sark or hacknut . . . and then the crafts of Ambroy are famous. If we worked elsewhere—"

"We could say we were Ambroy craftsmen!"

Amiante shook his head doubtfully. "I have never heard of it being done. The Welfare Agency would not approve, I am certain."

On Ghyl's fourteenth birthday he was accepted into the Temple as a full member, and enrolled in a class for religious and sociological indoctrination. The Guide Leaper explained the Elemental Pattern more carefully than had Ghyl's previous instructors: "The pattern, of course, is symbolic; nonetheless it provides an infinite range of real relevancies. By now you know the various tablets: the virtues and vices, the blasphemies and devotions which are represented. The sincere affirm their orthodoxy by leaping the traditional patterns, moving from symbol to symbol, avoiding vices, endorsing virtues. Even the aged and infirm endeavor to leap several patterns a day."

Ghyl leapt and skipped with the others and finally managed a fair degree of precision, so that he was not singled out for derision.

During the summer of his fifteenth year his class made a three-day pilgrimage to Rabia Scarp in the Meagher Mounts to inspect and study the Glyph. They rode Overtrend cars to the farm village Libon; then, accompanied by a wagon which carried bedrolls and provisions, set out on foot toward the hills.

The first night the group camped at the foot of a rocky knoll, beside a pond fringed with reeds and water-willow. There were fires and singing and talking; Ghyl had never known so merry a time. The adventure was given spice by the not-too-distant presence of Wirwans, a race of semi-intelligent beings about eight feet tall with heavy snouted heads, black opal eyes, rough hard skins mottled purple, black and brown. The Wirwans, according to the Guide Leaper, were indigenous to Halma and had existed in the Meagher Mounts at the time of the human advent. "They are not to be approached should we sight them," warned the guide, an intense man who never smiled. "They are inoffensive and secretive, but have been known to strike out if molested. We may see some among the rocks, although they live in tunnels and holes and do not range very far."

One of the boys, a brash youngster named Nion Bohart, said, "They throw their minds; they read thoughts; isn't that so?"

"Nonsense," said the guide. "That would be a miracle, and they have no knowledge of Finuka, the single source of miracles."

"I have heard that they do not talk," Nion Bohart insisted with a kind of flippant obstinacy. "They throw their thoughts across far distances, by a means no one understands."

The leader turned sharply away from the conversation. "Now then, all to your blankets. Tomorrow is an important day; we climb Rabia Scarp to see the Glyph."

Next morning, after a breakfast of tea, biscuits and dried sea-plum, the boys set forth. The country was barren: rocks and slopes covered with a harsh thorny scrub.

About noon they reached Rabia Scarp. During some ancient storm the scarp had been struck by lightning, with the result that a boss of black rock was traced with a set of complicated marks. Certain of these marks, which priests had enclosed in a gold frame, bore the semblance of Archaic characters, and read:

FINUKA DISPOSES!

Before the sacred Glyph a large platform had been built, with an Elemental Pattern inlaid in blocks of quartz, jasper, red chert, onyx. For an hour the guide and the students performed ritual exercises, then, taking their gear, moved on up to the crest of the scarp, and there pitched camp. The out-

look was glorious. Ghyl had never known such far vistas. To
the east was a deep valley, then the lowering mass of the
Meagher Mounts, the haunt of Wirwans. To north and south
the ridges thrust and bulked away, at last to become indis-
tinct, in Bauredel to the north, in the Great Alkali Flats to
the south. To the west lay the inhabited areas of Fortinone,
an expanse of muted brown, gray, black-green, all toned yellow-brown by the sunlight, as if under a transparent film of
old varnish. Far away shone a quicksilver glimmer, like a
heat vibration: the ocean. A moribund land, with more ruins
than inhabited buildings, and Ghyl wondered how it had
seemed two thousand years ago when the cities were whole.
Sitting on a flat rock, knees clasped in his arms, Ghyl thought
of Emphyrio and imposed the locale of the legend upon the
landscape. There, in the Meagher Mounts, Emphyrio had
confronted the horde from the mad moon Sigil—which might
well have been Damar. There, that great gouge to the
northeast: surely the Col of Deal! And there the field of
battle where Emphyrio had called through his magic tablet.
The monsters? Who but the Wirwans? . . . A peremptory
summons broke into Ghyl's musings; it was the group leader
announcing a need for firewood. The spell of the moment
was broken, presently to be replaced by another: the spectacle of the sunset, with the land and sky to the west drowned
in a sad effulgence, the color of antique amber.

Pots hanging over tripods gave off a savory odor of ham
and lentils; bramble wood fires crackled and spat; smoke
drifted off against the dusk. The scene twitched a deep-lying
node in Ghyl's mind, sent peculiar chills across his skin. In
just such a manner, by just such fires, had crouched his pri-
meval ancestors: on Earth, or whatever far planet men had
first asserted their identity.

Never had food tasted so good to Ghyl. After the meal,
with fires burning low and the heavens awesomely immediate,
he felt as if he were on the verge of some wonderful new
comprehension. Regarding himself? The world? The nature of
man? He could not be sure. The knowledge hung at the brink
of his mind, trembling. . . . The Guide Leaper also was in-
spired by the wonder of the night sky. He pointed and stated,
"Before us, and I wish all to observe, is magnificence beyond
human conception! Notice the brilliance of the Mirabilis
stars, and there, somewhat above, the very rim of the galaxy!
Is it not glorious? You, Nion Bohart, what do you think?
Does not the open sky enthrall you to your very marrow!"

"Yes indeed," declared Nion Bohart.

"It is grandeur of the most excellent and majestic sort. If no other indication offered, here at least is vindication for all the leaping done in praise of Finuka!"

Recently, among the bits and fragments in Amiante's portfolio, Ghyl had come upon a few lines of philosophical dialogue which had haunted him; and now, innocently, he spoke them:

" 'In a situation of infinity, every possibility, no matter how remote, must find physical expression.'

" 'Does that mean yes or no?'

" 'Both and neither.' "

The group leader, irked by the interruption and by the break in the mood he was trying to establish, asked in a cold voice, "What is all this obscurantist ambiguity? I fail to understand!"

"Simple really," drawled Nion Bohart, a year or so older than Ghyl and inclined to impertinence. "It means that anything is possible."

"Not quite," said Ghyl, "it means more than that; I think it's an important idea!"

"Bah, rubbish," snorted the leader. "But perhaps you will deign to elucidate."

Ghyl, suddenly in the focus of everyone's attention, felt awkward and tongue-tied, the more so that he did not fully comprehend the proposition he had been called upon to explain. He looked around the circle of firelight, to find all eyes upon him. He spoke in a diffident stammer: "As I see it, the cosmos is probably infinite, which means—well, infinite. So there are local situations—a tremendous number of them. Indeed, in a situation of infinity, there are an infinite set of local conditions, so that somewhere there is bound to be anything, if this anything is even remotely possible. Perhaps it is; I really don't know what the chances—"

"Come, come!" snapped the leader. "You are blithering! Declare us this dramatic enlightenment in plain words!"

"Well, it might be that in certain local regions, by the very laws of chance, a god like Finuka might exist and exert local control. Maybe even here, on the North Continent, or over the whole world. In other localities, gods might be absent. It depends, of course, upon the probability of the particular

kind of god." Ghyl hesitated, then added modestly, "I don't
know what this is, of course."

The leader drew a deep breath. "Has it occurred to you
that the individual who attempts to reckon the possibility or
probability of a god is puffing himself up as the spiritual and
intellectual superior of the god?"

"No reason why we can't have a stupid god," muttered
Nion Bohart in an undertone which the leader failed to catch.
With no more than a glare for Nion Bohart, he continued, "It
is a posture, may I say, of boundless arrogance. And also, the
local situation is not under discussion. The Glyph reads, 'Finuka disposes!' This clearly means that Finuka controls *all*!
Not just a few acres here and a few acres there. If this were
the case the Glyph would read 'Finuka disposes across the
township of Elbaum, in Brueben Precinct, likewise along the
Dodrechten mud flats' or some such set of qualifications. Is
this not obvious? The Glyph reads 'Finuka disposes!' which
means Finuka rules and judges—*everywhere!* So then—let us
hear no more logic-chopping."

Ghyl held his tongue. The leader once again turned his attention to the skies and pointed out various celestial objects.

One by one the boys dropped off to sleep. Early the next
morning they broke camp, leapt a final exercise before the
Glyph and marched back downhill to the Overtrend depot at
a nearby mining town.

During the entire return trip the leader said nothing to
Ghyl or to Nion Bohart, but upon their next visit to the
Temple both were transferred to a special section for difficult,
obstreperous or recalcitrant boys; in charge of the section was
a resolute, special indoctrinator.

The class, to Ghyl's surprise, included his old friend Floriel
Huzsuis, now a gentle unconventional lad, almost girlishly
handsome. Floriel was reckoned a problem not from obstinacy, or insolence, but rather from daydreaming vagary,
compounded by an involuntary half-smile, as if he found the
class irresistibly amusing in all its aspects. This was far from
the truth, but poor Floriel, by reason of his expression, was
continually upbraided for facetiousness and levity.

The indoctrinator, Saltator Honson Ospude, was a tall,
grim man with a clenched, passionate face. Intensely dedi-
cated to his profession, he was without lightness, flexibility or
humor and sought to compel the minds of his charges by the
force of his own fervent orthodoxy. Nonetheless he was an

erudite man, widely read, and introduced dozens of interesting topics into the classwork routine.

"Every society is constructed upon a foundation of assumptions," stated Honson Ospude on one occasion. "There is a multiplicity of such assumptions, from which each society selects: hence the multitude of galactic civilizations, all different. The society of Fortinone, of course, is one of the most enlightened, based as it is upon the most lofty aspirations of the human spirit. We are a lucky people. The axioms which shape our lives are ineffable but indisputable; equally important, they are efficacious. They guarantee us security from want, and offer each of us, as long as he be diligent, the chance to become financially independent."

At this, Nion Bohart could not restrain a caw of laughter. "Financial independence? If you kidnap a lord, perhaps."

Honson Ospude, neither outraged nor nonplussed by the interruption, met the challenge—for such it was, head on. "If you kidnap a lord, you'll gain not financial independence but rehabilitation."

"If you get caught."

"The chances are strong for rehabilitation," stated Honson Ospude. "Even if you succeeded in kidnaping a lord, you could no longer profit. The lord would not pay. Conditions are no longer barbaric. The lords have bound themselves to pay no further ransoms; hence there is no longer a financial incentive to the crime of kidnaping."

Ghyl remarked, perhaps inadvisedly, "It seems to me that if the lords had to choose either payment or death, they would ignore the compact and pay."

Honson Ospude looked from Nion Bohart to Ghyl, then around the class, all of whom were attending with great interest. "It seems that we have here a fine collection of would-be bandits. Well, my lads, a word of warning: you'll encounter grief and woe by working for chaos. Regulation is the single frail barrier between savagery and welfare; break down the barrier and you destroy not only yourselves but all else besides. Enough for the day. Think well upon what I have told you. All to the Pattern."

Over the course of time certain members of the class— among them Floriel Huzsuis, Nion Bohart, Mael Villy, Uger Harspitz, Shulk Odlebush, one or two others—drew together to form a clique, with Nion Bohart, a swaggering, restless, reckless youth, the informal leader. Nion Bohart was a year or two older than the others: a tall, broad-shouldered youth, handsome as a lord, with beautiful green eyes, a thin mouth twitching first down the right side and up the left, then down the left and up the right. In many ways Nion Bohart was an amusing companion, always ready for deviltry, although he never seemed to be apprehended in mischief. It was always the obstinate Uger Harspitz or dreamy Floriel who were discovered and punished for mischief conceived by Nion Bohart.

Ghyl held himself apart from the group, though he was fond of Floriel. Nion Bohart's mischief seemed to verge on irresponsibility, and Ghyl thought his hold upon Floriel's imagination to be both unfortunate and unhealthy.

Honson Ospude detested Nion Bohart, but tried to deal as fairly as possible with the contumacious youth. Nion Bohart, however, and others of the clique, took pains to attack his equanimity: doubting his assumptions, weighing the value of universal orthodoxy, marking as if by mistake incorrect or even blasphemous symbols during the leaping which opened and closed each class. Ghyl, anxious only to attract a minimum of notice, conducted himself with discretion, to the disgust of Floriel and Nion Bohart, who wanted him to take a more active part in their mischief. Ghyl merely laughed at them, and his association with the group became almost non-existent.

The years passed. At last, according to statute, the class was terminated. Ghyl, now eighteen years old, was sent forth as a presumably responsible recipient of Fortinone.

To celebrate his discharge from the school, Amiante consulted the victuallers and ordered in a grand feast: roast biloa-bird with wickenberry sauce, rag-fish, candied sea-calch, bowls of whelks, corpentine, hemmer garnished with that choice purple-black seaweed known as livret, a profusion of cakes, tarts and jellies, and jugs of edel wine.

To the feast Ghyl invited Floriel, who had no father and whose ribald mother had refused to take note of the occasion. The two lads gorged themselves on delicacies while Amiante picked at this and tasted that.

Somewhat to Ghyl's annoyance, Floriel, immediately after the meal, began to show signs of restlessness and to hint that best he should be on his way.

"What?" exclaimed Ghyl. "The sun's hardly down on the afternoon! Stay on for supper."

"Supper, bah; I'm so stuffed I can't move. . . . Well, to tell the truth, Nion spoke of a little get-together at a place we know and made sure that I'd be on hand. Why don't you come along as well?"

"I'd fear to go to a house where I wasn't invited."

Floriel smiled mysteriously. "Don't trouble yourself on that score. Nion gave orders to bring you along." This latter was transparently a fabrication, but Ghyl, after half a dozen mugs of wine, felt rather in a mood for further celebration. He looked across the room to where Amiante was assisting the victualler in the repacking of pots, pans and trays. "I'll see what my father has in mind."

Amiante made no objection to the outing, so Ghyl arrayed himself in new plum-colored breeches, a black coat with scarlet sculpture, a jaunty black hat with the rim aslant. In his new clothes Ghyl felt that he cut a passably fine figure, and Floriel made no bones about endorsing his opinion. "That's an absolutely smashing outfit; beside you I look a frump! . . . Oh well, we can't all be rich and handsome. Come along then; the sun is down in the west and we don't want to miss any fun."

To mark the occasion they rode Overtrend south through Hoge and into Cato. They surfaced and walked east into a district of peculiar old houses of stone and black brick which by some freak chance had stood against the last devastation.

Ghyl was puzzled. "I thought Nion lived across Hoge, toward Foelgher."

"Who said we were going to his house?"

"Where are we going then?"

Floriel made a cryptic sign. "In a moment you'll see." He led the way along a dank alley smelling of the ages, through a gate on which hung a lantern with green and purple bulbs, into a tavern which occupied the whole ground floor of one of the old houses.

From a table across the room Mael Villy raised a call. "There's Floriel, and Ghyl as well! Over here, this way!"

They crossed to where their friends had been making free with ale and wine, found seats and had mugs pressed into their hands. Nion Bohart proposed a toast: "Here's a pimple on the tongue of Honson Ospude, sore feet for all the Guide Leapers: may they try the Double Sincere Eight-Nine Swing, fall flat and slide to rest with their noses upon Animal Corruption!"

With bravos and catcalls the group drank the toast. Ghyl took occasion to inspect his surroundings. The room was very large, with carved posts supporting an elegant old ceiling of green sapodilla and yellow tile. The walls were stained dull scarlet, the floor was stone. Light came from four candelabra supporting dozens of little lamps. Sitting in an alcove an orchestra of three men, with zither, flute and tympany, played jigs and reels. Below the orchestra, on a long couch, lolled twenty young women wearing a variety of costumes, some flamboyant, others severe, but all characterized by an element of fantasy, setting them apart from the ordinary women of Ambroy. At last Ghyl fully realized where he was: in one of the quasi-legal taverns offering wine and food, music and good cheer, and also the services of a staff of hostesses. Ghyl looked curiously along the line of girls. None were particularly comely, he thought, and a few were actually grotesque, with garments of incredible complication and cosmetics all but concealing their faces.

"See any you fancy?" Nion Bohart called over to Ghyl. "They're all here tonight. Business is poor. Pick out the one you favor; she'll tingle your toes for you!"

Ghyl shook his head to indicate disinclination, and looked around the other tables.

"What do you think of the place?" Floriel asked him.

"It's splendid, certainly. But isn't it very expensive?"

"Not so much as you might think, if you drink only ale and stay away from the girls."

"Too bad old Honson Ospude isn't here, eh, Nion?" called Shulk Odlebush. "We'd pour him so full he wouldn't know up from down!"

"I'd like to see him tackle that fat woman!" remarked Uger Harspitz with a lecherous grin. "Her with the green feather neckpiece. What a tussle that would be!"

Into the room came three men and two women, the men somewhat cautious of step and gaze, the women by contrast bold, even insolent. Nion nudged Floriel, muttered into his ear, and Floriel in turn spoke to Ghyl: "Noncups: those five just taking a table."

Ghyl stared in surreptitious fascination at the five men and women, who, after quick glances into all corners, were now relaxing into their chairs.

Ghyl asked Floriel, "Are they criminals—or just ordinary nonrecipients?"

Floriel put the inquiry to Nion, who replied tersely, with a flicker of a cynical grin. Floriel reported to Ghyl: "He doesn't know for sure. He thinks they deal in 'scrap': old metal, old furniture, old artware—probably anything else they lay their hands on."

"How does Nion know all this?" asked Ghyl.

Floriel shrugged. "He knows all sorts of things. I think his brother is a noncup—or was. I'm not really sure. The folk who own this tavern are noncups too, for that matter."

"What of *them*?" Ghyl nodded to the girls on the long bench.

Floriel put a question to Nion, received a reply. "They're all recipients. They belong to the Matrons, Nurses and Service Workers' Guild."

"Oh."

"On occasion lords come in here," said Floriel. "Last time I was here with Nion there were two lords and two ladies, drinking ale and chewing pickled skauf like longshoremen."

"Not really!"

"Really and absolutely," stated Nion, who had hitched around to join the conversation. "There may be lords in tonight, who knows? Here, old fellow, fill your mug—good strong ale!"

Ghyl allowed his mug to be replenished. "Why would lords and ladies come down to a place of this sort?"

"Because here is life! Excitement! Real people! Not flat-nosed voucher-douchers!"

Ghyl gave his head a marveling shake. "I thought that when they dropped to the ground they always flew to Luschein or the Mang Islands, or someplace out of Fortinone for their fun!"

"True. But sometimes it's as easy to drop down to good old Keecher's Inn. Anything to escape the boredom of the eyries, I suppose."

" 'Boredom'?" Ghyl tested the word.

"Certainly. You don't think the life of the lords is all Gade wine and star-travel, do you? A good many of them find time hanging heavy on their hands."

Ghyl considered this novel perspective regarding the life of the lords. What with air-boats to sweep them here and there, not only to Luschein and the Mangs, but to Minya-judos, or the wild Para Islands, or the Wewar Glaciers, the idea was not wholly convincing. Still—who could say? "Do they come without Garrion?"

"As to that I don't know. You'll never see Garrion here in the tavern. Perhaps they watch from behind that lattice yonder."

"So long as it's not a Special Agent," suggested Mael Villy with a glance over his shoulder.

"Don't worry, they know you're here," said Nion Bohart. "They know everything."

Ghyl grinned. "Maybe the Garrion and welfare agents sit together behind the screen."

Nion Bohart spat upon the floor. "Not much. The agents come to play with the girls, like all the rest."

"The lords too?" asked Ghyl.

"The lords? Ha! You should see them. *And* the ladies! They vie in lechery!"

"Have you heard of Lord Mornune the Spay?" asked Uger Harspitz. "How he inveigled my cousin's fiancée? It was at a place up the Insse—some resort. Brazen? Grigglesby Corners? I forget the name—anyway my cousin was called aside on a false message and when he returned Lord Mornune was with the girl, and next morning she never appeared for breakfast. She wrote that she was well, that Mornune was taking her traveling, to the Five Worlds and beyond. Isn't that the life?"

"All one needs is 1.18 percent," said Nion Bohart grimly. "If I had it I'd inveigle the girls no less."

"You could try with your one voucher and eighteen checks," suggested Shulk Odelbush. "Inquire of that fat one with the green neckpiece."

"Bah. Not even one check . . . but hello! Here's my friend Aunger Wermarch. Hi Aunger! This way! Meet my friends!"

Aunger Wermarch was a young man dressed in the most extreme style, with pointed white shoes and a black-tasseled yellow hat. Nion Bohart introduced him to the group: "A noncup is Aunger and proud of the fact!"

"Right and correct!" declared Aunger Wermarch. "They can call me Chaoticist, thief, pariah—anything they want—as long as they don't put me on their damned welfare rolls!"

"Sit, Aunger—drink a mug of ale! There's a good fellow!"

Aunger pulled a stool up under his splendid shanks and accepted a mug of ale. "A merry life to all!"

"And sand in the eyes of all the water-watchers!" proposed Nion. Ghyl drank with the rest. When Aunger Wermarch turned away, he asked Floriel for an explanation. Floriel gave back a significant wink, and Ghyl suddenly understood the reference to "water-watchers," those welfare agents who patrolled the shoreline to apprehend smugglers of duplicated items, cheap elsewhere but handmade and expensive in Fortinone. So here was a smuggler: an antisocial leech and bloodsucker—so Ghyl had learned at guild meetings.

Ghyl gave a silent shrug. Perhaps. Smuggling violated welfare regulations, just as Amiante's duplicating had done. On the other hand Amiante had not been motivated by profit. Amiante was hardly an antisocial leech, certainly no bloodsucker. Ghyl sighed, shrugged once more. Tonight he would withhold all judgments.

Perceiving the jug to be empty, Ghyl provided replenishment, and filled mugs all around the table. Then he sat back to watch the events of the evening.

Two other young men came to speak to Aunger Wermarch, and presently drew up chairs. Ghyl was not introduced. Sitting at the far end of the table, he was somewhat removed from the node of conversation, which suited him well enough. His head was becoming light, and he decided to drink no more ale. It might be a good idea to think about leaving for home. He spoke to Floriel, who looked at him with a vacant face, mouth looped in a loose grin. Floriel was drunk, in a facile, ready fashion that suggested long habit. Floriel said something about hiring girls, but Ghyl had no enthusiasm for the project. Particularly so used and forlorn a set of drabs as these. He said as much to Floriel, who recommended that Ghyl drink a mug or two more ale. Ghyl pulled a wry face.

He was preparing to leave, when at the other end of the table he noted tension. Aunger Wermarch was speaking from the corner of his mouth to his two friends; surreptitiously they studied a group of four somberly dressed men who had just entered: Welfare Specials. This was clear even to Ghyl. Nion Bohart sat looking interestedly into his mug of ale, but Ghyl saw his hand flicker under the table.

Events moved with great swiftness. The Welfare Specials approached the table. Aunger Wermarch and his two friends sprang away, tumbled over two of the agents, ran for the door and were gone, almost before the mind could appreciate the fact. Nion Bohart and Shulk Odlebush rose to their feet in outrage. "What does this mean?"

"What does it mean, indeed?" said one of the Special Agents drily. "It means that three men have departed the premises without our permission."

"Why shouldn't they?" demanded Nion hotly. "Who are you?"

"Welfare agents, Special Department—who do you suppose?"

"Well then," said Nion virtuously, "why didn't you say so? You came in so furtively my friends considered you criminals and decided to leave."

"Come along," said the agent. "All of you. Certain questions must be answered. And if you please," he told Nion Bohart, "be so good as to pick up the parcel you threw to the floor and hand it to me."

The group was marched to a wagon and conveyed to the Hoge Detention Center.

Ghyl was released two hours later. He was questioned only cursorily; he told the precise truth and was instructed to go home. Floriel, Mael Villy and Uger Harspitz were released with warnings. Nion Bohart and Shulk Odelbush, with parcels of contraband material in their possession, were required to expiate their antisocial behavior. Their Base Stipends were diminished by ten vouchers a month; they were obliged to work two months on the Cheer and Cleanliness Walk-about Squad, removing rubbish from the streets, and they were enjoined to one day a week of intensive Temple exercises.

CHAPTER 8

Undle Square was cool and absolutely quiet when Ghyl arrived home. Damar, a thin sickle, hung low, backlighting the featureless black hulks to the east. No light showed; the air was cool and fresh; the only sound to be heard was the scrape of Ghyl's footsteps.

He let himself into the workroom. The odor of wood and finishing oil came to his nostrils: so familiar and secure and redolent of everything that he loved that tears came to his eyes.

He stopped to listen, then climbed the stairs.

Amiante was not asleep. Ghyl undressed, then went over to his father's bed and described the events of the evening. Amiante made no comment. Ghyl, peering vainly through the dark, was unable to sense his opinion of the scrape. Amiante finally said, "Well then, go to bed; you've done no harm and suffered none; you've learned a great deal: so we must count the night a success."

Somewhat cheered, Ghyl laid himself down on his couch, and fell asleep from sheer weariness.

He awoke to Amiante's hand on his shoulder. "The welfare agent is here to discuss the events of last night."

Ghyl dressed, washed his face in cold water, combed back his hair. Descending to the second floor, he found Schute Cobol and Amiante sitting at the table, drinking tea, apparently on a basis of courtesy and good fellowship, though Schute Cobol's mouth was even tighter and paler than usual and his eyes had a far-off glint. He greeted Ghyl with a curt nod and a glance of careful appraisal, as if he found himself face to face with a stranger.

The discussion began on a note of polite restraint, with Schute Cobol asking only for Ghyl's version of last night's events. Presently his questions became keener and his comments cutting; Ghyl became angry rather than abject. "I have told you the truth! To the best of my knowledge I did nothing irregulationary; why do you imply that I am chaotic?"

"I imply nothing. You are the one who draws inferences.

Certainly you have been irresponsible in your friendships. This fact, coupled with your previous lack of orthodoxy, compels me to an open mind, rather than the trust I automatically extend to the typical recipient."

"In this case, not enjoying your trust, it is pointless for me to say more. Why waste my breath?"

Schute Cobol's mouth tightened; he looked toward Amiante. "And you, Rt. Tarvoke—you must realize that you have been remiss as a father. Why have you not inculcated in your son a more abiding respect for our institutions? I believe that you have been reproached on this score before."

"Yes, I recall something of the sort," said Amiante with the ghost of a smile.

Schute Cobol became even more brittle than before. "Will you answer my question then? Remember, on you rests the ultimate responsibility for these sad events. Truth is what a father owes to his son, not evasion and ambiguity."

"Ah, truth indeed!" mused Amiante. "If only we could identify truth when we perceive it! Here would be reassurance!"

Schute Cobol snorted in disgust. "This is the source of all our difficulties. Truth is orthodoxy, what else? You need no reassurance beyond the regulations."

Amiante rose to his feet, stood with his hands behind his back, looking from the window. "Once there lived the hero Emphyrio," said Amiante. "He spoke such truth that monsters halted to hear him. Did he, I wonder, expound Welfare Agency regulations through his magic tablet?"

Schute Cobol also rose to his feet. He spoke in a voice passionless and rigidly formal. "I have carefully explained what the Welfare Agency expects in return for the benefits you derive. If you wish to continue to derive these benfits, you must obey regulations. Do you have any questions?"

"No."

"No."

Schute Cobol gave a curt bow. He went to the door and, turning, said, "Even Emphyrio, were he alive today, would be obliged to obey regulations. There can be no exceptions." He departed.

Amiante and Ghyl followed him down to the workroom. Ghyl slumped upon his bench, put his chin on his hands. "I wonder if this is true? Would Emphyrio obey welfare regulations?"

Amiante seated himself at his own bench. "Who knows?

He would find no enemy, no tyranny—only inefficiency and perhaps peculation. No question but that we work hard for very little return."

"He would hardly be a noncup," mused Ghyl. "Or would he? One who worked hard and honestly, but off the welfare rolls?"

"Possibly. He might choose to be elected Mayor of the city, and try to increase everyone's stipend."

"How could he do that?" asked Ghyl with interest.

Amiante shrugged. "The Mayor has no real power—although the Charter names him the city's chief executive. He could at least demand higher prices for our goods. He could urge that we build factories to produce things we need but now import."

"That would mean duplication."

"Duplication is not inherently wrong, as long as it does not diminish our reputation for craftsmanship."

Ghyl shook his head. "The Welfare Agency would never permit it."

"Perhaps not. Unless Emphyrio were, in fact, Mayor."

"Someday," said Ghyl, "I will learn the rest of the tale. We will know what happened."

Amiante gave his head a skeptical shake, as if his thoughts had many times coursed the same road. "Perhaps. But more likely Emphyrio is legend after all."

Ghyl sat brooding. Presently he asked, "Is there no way we could learn the truth?"

"Probably not in Fortinone. The Historian would know."

"Who is the Historian?"

Amiante, becoming uninterested in the conversation, began to strop one of his chisels. "On a far planet, so I am told, the Historian chronicles all the events of human history."

"The history of Halma and Fortinone, as well?"

"Presumably."

"How would such information reach the Historian?"

Amiante, bending over the screen, plied his chisel. "No difficulty there. He would employ correspondents."

"What a curious idea!" remarked Ghyl.

"Curious indeed."

Across Undle Square, a few steps up Gosgar Alley to a door with a blue hourglass painted on the panel, up four flights of steps to a pleasant little penthouse: here was the home of Sonjaly Rathe and her mother. Sonjaly was a small slight girl, extremely pretty, with blond hair and innocent gray eyes. Ghyl thought her enchanting. Unfortunately, Sonjaly was something of a flirt, well aware of her charms, always ready with a provocative pout, or a clever tilt of the head.

One afternoon Ghyl sat with Sonjaly at the Campari Cafe trying to make earnest conversation, to which Sonjaly would only give back pert irrelevancies, when who should appear but Floriel. Ghyl frowned and slumped back in his seat.

"Your father told me you'd probably be here," said Floriel, dropping into a chair. "What's that you're drinking? Pomardo? None for me. Waitress, a flask of edel wine, please: the Amanour White."

Ghyl performed introductions. Floriel said, "I suppose you've heard the news."

"News? A Mayor's election in a month or so. I've finished a new screen. Sonjaly thinks she'll change from the Marble-polishers to the Cakes, Tarts and Pastry-makers."

"No, no," complained Floriel. "I mean *news!* Nion Bohart is free of the Cheer Squad. He wishes to celebrate, and has called for a party tonight!"

"Oh indeed?" Ghyl frowned down into his goblet.

"Indeed. At the Twisted Willow Palace, if you know of it."

"Naturally," said Ghyl, not wishing to appear stupid in front of Sonjaly.

"It's in Foelgher Precinct, on the estuary—but then I'd better take you; you'd never find your way."

"I'm not certain of going," said Ghyl. "Sonjaly and I—"

"She can come too; why not?" Floriel turned to Sonjaly, who was practicing her most outrageous beguilements. "You'd enjoy the Twisted Willow; it's a delightful old place, with a marvelous view. The most interesting and clever folk go there, and many noncups. Even lords and ladies: on the sly, of course."

"It sounds delightful! I'd so like to go!"

"Your mother would object," Ghyl stated more gruffly than he intended. "She'd never allow you to go to such a tavern."

"She doesn't need to know," declared Sonjaly with a sauciness Ghyl found astonishing. "Also, as it happens, she works tonight, catering a guild banquet."

"Good! Fine! Excellent! No problems whatever," declared Floriel heartily. "We'll all go together."

"Oh very well," said Ghyl crossly. "I suppose we must."

Sonjaly drew up her shoulders. "Indeed! If you find my company so disturbing, I need not go."

"No, no, of course not!" protested Ghyl. "Do not misunderstand!"

"I misunderstand nothing," declared the outrageous Sonjaly. "And I'm sure Rt. Huzsuis would tell me the location of the Twisted Willow Palace, so that I might find my own way through the dark."

"Don't be ridiculous!" snapped Ghyl. "We'll all go together."

"That's better."

Ghyl brushed his plum-colored breeches, steamed and pressed the jacket, inserted new stiffeners into his boots, and polished to a glitter the articulated bronze greave. With a side glance toward Amiante—who maintained a studious disinterest—he fixed to his knees a pair of black ribbon rosettes, with streaming ends, then pomaded his golden-brown hair almost dark. With another quick glance toward Amiante, he teased the ends, where they hung over his ears, into gallant upturned curls.

Floriel was unflatteringly surprised at Ghyl's elegance. He himself wore an easy graceful suit of dark green, with a soft black velvet cap. Together they went to the house with the blue hourglass on Cosgar Alley. Sonjaly anticipated their knock and cautioned them to silence. "My mother is still home. I've told her I'm out to visit Gedée Anstrut. Go to the corner and wait."

Five minutes later she was with them, somewhat breathlessly, her face more charming than ever for its mischief. "Perhaps we can take Gedée with us; she's very jolly and she'd love a party. I don't think she's ever been to a tavern. No more than I, of course."

Ghyl grudgingly assented to Gedée's presence, although it would void all hope of a private hour or two with Sonjaly. She also would impose a strain on his wallet, unless Floriel could be persuaded to act as her escort—a dubious hope, since Gedée was tall and spare, with a keen beak of a nose and an unfortunately sparse head of coarse black hair, which she wore in symmetrical fore and aft shingles.

Still, Sonjaly had proposed, and if Ghyl disposed she would pout. Gedée Anstrut eagerly assented to the party and Floriel, as Ghyl had assumed, quickly made it clear that he did not intend to participate in Gedée's entertainment.

The four rode Overtrend to South Foelgher, only a few yards from Hyalis Park. They climbed a little hill: an outcropping of the same ridge which, farther north in Veige, became Dunkum's Heights. But here the river was close below, reflecting the tawny violet, gold, and orange dust of the sunset. The Twisted Willow Palace was close at hand—a rickety structure open to the air in warm weather, screened and shuttered when the wind blew. The specialty of the house was grilled mud eel, esperges in spice sauce, and a pale light wine from the coastal region south of Ambroy.

Nion Bohart had not yet arrived; the four found a table. A waiter approached, and it developed that Gedée was tremendously hungry, having not yet dined. Ghyl watched glumly while she devoured vast quantities of eel and esperges. Floriel mentioned that he hoped to build or buy a small sailing craft, and Sonjaly declared herself keenly interested in sailboats and travel in general, and the two became involved in a spirited conversation, while Ghyl sat to the side dispiritedly watching Gedée attack the platter of eel which he had ordered for Sonjaly, but which she now decided she didn't care for.

Nion Bohart arrived, in company with a somewhat overdressed young woman a year or two his senior. Ghyl thought to recognize her as one of the girls who had sat on the bench at Keecher's Inn. Nion introduced her as Marta, without reference to her guild. A moment later Shulk and Uger arrived, and presently Mael Villy, escorting a girl of rather coarse appearance, far from inconspicuous by reason of flaming red hair. As if to emphasize her disdain for othodoxy, she wore a tight sheath of black fish-skin which concealed few, if any, of her bodily contours. Sonjaly raised her eyebrows in disparagement; Gedée, wiping her mouth with the back of her hand, stared blankly, but seemed to care nothing one way or the other.

Pitchers of wine were brought; goblets were filled and emptied. Evening became night. Colored lanterns were lit; a lutist, purportedly from the Mang Islands, played lilting Mang Island love songs.

Nion Bohart was strangely taciturn. Ghyl suspected that his experience had chastened him, or at least had made him less flamboyant. But after a goblet or two of wine, a glance toward the door, a quick look at Sonjaly, Nion hitched his chair forward and became something like his old self: grim and cynical, yet easy and expansive and gay, all at once. To Ghyl's relief, Shulk Odelbush engaged Gedée in conversation and went so far as to pour her goblet full of wine. Ghyl moved his chair closer to Sonjaly, who was laughing at something Floriel had said; she turned Ghyl an unseeing glance, as if he were not there. Ghyl took a deep breath, opened his mouth to speak, shut it again, and sat back sulking.

Now Nion was speaking, telling of his experience at the Welfare Agency. Everyone grew quiet to listen. He told of how he had been conveyed to the office, of his questioning, of the stern injunctions against further trafficking with smugglers. He had been warned that the charge of his rod was high, that he risked rehabilitation. Gedée chewing on the last of the esperges, asked, "Something I've never understood: the noncups aren't recipients, so they aren't on the welfare rolls and they don't have deportment rods. Well then—can a noncup be rehabilitated?"

"No," said Nion Bohart. "If he is determined a criminal he is expelled, over one of the four frontiers. A simple vagrant is expelled east into Bayron. A smuggler fares worse and is expelled into the Alkali Flats. The worst criminals are expelled into the first two inches of Bauredel. The Special Investigator explained all this to me. I told him I wasn't a criminal, that I had committed no great wrong; he said I had disobeyed the regulations. I told him that maybe the regulations should be changed, but he refused to laugh."

"Isn't there a way to change regulations?" asked Sonjaly.

"I've no idea," said Nion Bohart. "I suppose the Chief Supervisor does what he thinks best."

"Strange, in a way," said Floriel. "I wonder how it ever started."

Ghyl leaned forward. "In the old days Thadeus was the capital of Fortinone. The Welfare Department was a branch of the state government. When Thadeus was destroyed there wasn't any more government, and there wasn't anyone to change Welfare Department Regulations. So there never was change."

Everyone turned now to look at Ghyl. "Eh, then," said Nion Bohart. "Where did you learn all this?"

"From my father."

"Well, if you're so knowing, how *are* regulations changed?"

"There's no state government. The Mayor headed the city government until the Welfare Department made a city government unnecessary."

"The Mayor can't do anything," grumbled Nion Bohart. "He's just the custodian of city documents: a nonentity."

"Come now!" cried Floriel in mock outrage. "I'll have you know the Mayor is my mother's second cousin. He is bound to be a gentleman!"

"At the least he can't be expelled or rehabilitated," said Ghyl. "If a man like Emphyrio were elected—the elections, incidentally, are next month—he might insist on the provisions of the Ambroy City Charter, and the Welfare Department would have to obey."

"Ha ha!" chuckled Mael Villy. "Think of it! All the stipends raised! Agents cleaning the streets and delivering parcels!"

"Who can be elected Mayor?" asked Floriel. "Anyone?"

"Naturally," jeered Nion. "Your mother's cousin manged to land the job."

"He is a very distinguished man!" protested Floriel.

Ghyl said, "Generally the Council of Guild-masters nominate one of their elders. He is always elected and then reelected and usually holds the job till he dies."

"Who was Emphyrio?" asked Gedée. "I've heard the name."

"A mythical hero," said Nion Bohart. "Part of the interstellar folklore."

"Perhaps I'm stupid," said Gedée with a determined grin, "but where is the advantage in electing a mythical hero Mayor? What is gained?"

"I didn't say we should elect Emphyrio," explained Ghyl. "I said a man *like* Emphyrio would perhaps insist upon changes."

Floriel was becoming drunk. He laughed rather foolishly. "I say, elect Emphyrio, mythical hero or not!"

"Right!" called Mael. "Elect Emphyrio. I'm all for it!"

Gedée wrinkled her nose in disapproval. "I still can't see what would be gained."

"Nothing real is gained," Nion Bohart explained. "It just becomes a bit of nonsense: tomfoolery, if you like. A thumb to the nose toward the Welfare Agency."

"It seems silly to me," sniffed Gedée. "A childish prank."

It needed only Gedée's disapproval to stimulate Ghyl's endorsement. "If nothing else, the recipients might become aware that existence is more than waiting for welfare vouchers!"

"Right!" exclaimed Nion Bohart. "Well spoken, Ghyl! I had no idea you were such a firebrand!"

"I'm not, really. . . . Still, the ordinary recipient could stand a bit of stimulation."

"I still think it's silly," snorted Gedée, and seizing her goblet, turned a great gulp of wine down her throat.

Floriel said, "It's something to do, at least. How does one go about becoming Mayor?"

"Peculiarly," said Nion Bohart, "I can answer that, even though my mother has no cousins. It is very simple. The Mayor himself is in charge of the election, since, in theory, the office is outside the province of the Welfare Agency. A candidate must pay a bond of a hundred vouchers to the Mayor, who then is required to post his name on the bulletin board in the Municipal Parade. On election day, all who wish to vote go to the parade, inspect the names on the bulletin board, and announce their choice to a scrivener who keeps a tally."

"So then, all that is needed is a hundred vouchers," said Floriel. "I'm good for ten."

"What?" giggled Sonjaly. "You'd put your mother's cousin from his job?"

"He's a dim-witted old mountebank. Not a month ago he walked past my mother and me as if he failed to see us. In fact, I'll pledge fifteen vouchers!"

"I wouldn't give a tainted check," sniffed Gedée. "It's ridiculous, and childish to boot. It might even be irregulationary."

"Put me down for ten," Ghyl immediately declared. "Or fifteen, for that matter."

"I'll give five," said Sonjaly, with a mischievous glance toward Nion Bohart.

Shulk, Mael, and Uger all volunteered ten vouchers, and the two girls who had come with Nion and Shulk laughingly promised five vouchers each.

Nion sat looking from face to face with hooded eyes and a half-smile. "As I count it, the pledges come to seventy-five vouchers. Very well, I'll go twenty-five, to make up the hundred, and what's more I'll take the money to the Mayor."

Gedée sat up straight in her chair and muttered something into Sonjaly's ear, who frowned and made an impatient sign.

Floriel filled goblets all around and proposed a toast. "To the election of Emphyrio as Mayor!"

Everyone drank. Then Ghyl said, "Another matter! Suppose, by some fantastic chance, that Emphyrio is elected? What then?"

"Bah! No such thing will happen," retorted Nion Bohart. "And what if it did? It might set people to thinking."

"People had best be thinking of how to behave themselves," declared Gedée stiffly. "I think the whole idea is beastly."

"Oh come now, Gedée," said Floriel. "Don't be so hoity-toity! What's a little jollity, after all?"

Gedée spoke to Sonjaly. "Don't you think it about time we were going home?"

"Why the rush?" demanded Floriel. "The party is just beginning!"

"Of course!" echoed Sonjaly. "Come now, Gedée, don't fret. We can't go home so early! Our friends would think we were ridiculous."

"Well, I want to go home."

"And I don't!" snapped Sonjaly. "So there!"

"I can't go by myself," said Gedée. "This is a very boisterous part of town." She rose to her feet and stood waiting.

Ghyl muttered, "Oh very well. Sonjaly, we'd better leave."

"But I don't want to leave. I'm having a good time. Why don't you take Gedée home, then come back?"

"What? By the time I get back here everyone else will be ready to leave!"

"Hardly, my boy," said Nion Bohart. "This is a celebration! We're good for the whole night! In fact, from here we'll presently move on to a place I know, where we'll meet some other friends."

Ghyl turned to Sonjaly. "Wouldn't you like to come along? We could talk along the way . . ."

"Really, Ghyl! It's such a little matter, and I'm having fun!"

"Oh very well," Ghyl said to Gedée. "Come along."

"What a coarse crowd!" declared Gedée as soon as they had left the tavern. "I thought things were to be nicer; otherwise I never would have come. I believe your friends are all noncups! They should be reported."

"They're nothing of the sort," said Ghyl. "No more than I myself."

Gedée gave a meaningful snort and said nothing more.

Back to Brueben Precinct they rode, then walked to Undle Square, across to Gosgar Alley and Gedée's home. She opened the door and looked back at Ghyl with a coy, gap-toothed grin. "Well then, we're here, and well away from that disreputable crowd. Not Sonjaly, of course, who is simply spoiled and perverse. . . . Would you care to come in? I'll brew a nice pot of tea. After all, it isn't too late."

"Thank you, no," said Ghyl. "I had better be returning to the party."

Gedée closed the door smartly in his face. Ghyl turned and marched back across Undle Square. In the workshop a dim light burned; Amiante would be carving at a screen or poring over an old document. Ghyl slowed his steps, and wondered if his father would like to come to the party. Probably not . . . but, as he crossed the square, he looked several times back over his shoulder at the lonely light behind the amber glass panes.

Back to the Overtrend, back to South Foelgher, up the ridge to the Twisted Willow Palace. To Ghyl's dismay the lights were turned down; the tavern was empty save for the janitor and the waiter.

Ghyl went to the waiter. "The party I was with, at that table yonder—did they say where they were going?"

"No, sir; not to me. They were all jolly and laughing; much wine they'd been drinking. I'm sure I don't know."

Ghyl walked slowly back down the hill. Would they have gone to Keecher's Inn in Cato? Unlikely. Ghyl gave a hollow laugh, and set out afoot across the dark, echoing streets of Foelgher: past stone warehouses and huts of ancient black brick. Fog blew in off the estuary, creating moist auras around the infrequent streetlamps. Finally, gloomy and sagging of shoulder, he tramped into Undle Square. He halted, then slowly crossed to Gosgar Alley and proceeded to the door with the blue hourglass. Sonjaly lived on the fourth floor. The windows were dark. Ghyl sat on the step and waited. Half an hour passed. Ghyl heaved a sigh, rose to his feet. She probably had come in long ago. He went home and put himself to bed.

CHAPTER 9

The next morning Ghyl roused himself to find Amiante already up and busy. He washed and dressed in his work smock and went below to his breakfast.

"Well then," asked Amiante, "how did the party go?"

"Nicely. Have you ever heard of the Twisted Willow Palace?"

Amiante nodded. "A pleasant place to visit. Do they still serve mud eel and esperges?"

"Yes." Ghyl sipped his tea. "Nion Bohart was at the party, and Floriel, and several others from the special class at the Temple."

"Ah, yes."

"You know that there is a mayoralty election next month?"

"I hadn't thought of it. I suppose it's about time."

"We spoke of raising a hundred vouchers and putting up the name Emphyrio to be voted upon."

Amiante raised his eyebrows. He sipped his tea. "The welfare agents will not be amused."

"Is it any of their affair?"

"Anything which concerns the recipients is the Welfare Agency's affair."

"But what can they do? It is certainly not irregulationary to propose a name for Mayor!"

"The name of a dead man, a legend."

"Is this irregulationary?"

"Technically and formally, I would think not, since there would seem to be no intent to deceive. If the public wished to elect a legend to the Mayor's office. . . . Of course, there may be age or residence or other qualifications. If so, then of course the name cannot even be placed on the boards."

Ghyl gave a terse nod. After all, it meant little one way or another. . . . He went down to the workroom, honed his chisels, and began carving upon his screen—with all the time an eye cocked on the door. Surely there would come a knock, Sonjaly would look in, tearful, meek, to make amends for the previous evening.

90

No knock. No wan face.

Halfway through the afternoon, with the door open to the amber sunlight, Shulk Odlebush appeared. "Hello, Ghyl Tarvoke. Hard at work then?"

"As you see." Ghyl put down his chisels, swung around on the bench. "What brings you here? Is anything wrong?"

"Nothing whatever. Last night you mentioned fifteen vouchers for a certain project. Nion asked me to drop by to collect."

"Yes, of course." But Ghyl hesitated. In the full light of day the prank seemed somehow pointless. Even malicious. Or more properly: mocking and jeering. Still, as Amiante had pointed out, if the population wished to vote for a legend, why should the opportunity not be extended to them?

Ghyl temporized. "Where did everyone go from the Twisted Willow?"

"Upriver to a private home. You should have come. Everyone had a wonderful time."

"I see."

"Floriel certainly has good taste in girls." Here Shulk cocked his head to look at Ghyl sidewise. "I can't say the same for you. Who was that fearful goat you brought?"

"I didn't bring her. I just had to take her home."

Shulk gave an uninterested shrug. "Give me the fifteen vouchers, I'm in a bit of a hurry."

Ghyl frowned and winced, but could see no help for it. He looked toward his father, half-hoping for some sort of admonition against foolishness, but Amiante seemed oblivious to all.

Ghyl went to a cabinet, counted fifteen vouchers, handed them to Shulk. "Here."

Shulk nodded. "Excellent. Tomorrow we'll go to the Municipal Parade and post up our candidate for Mayor."

"Who is going?"

"Anyone who wants. Won't it be great? Imagine the fuss!"

"I suppose so."

Shulk gave a casual wave and departed.

Ghyl went to the workbench, seated himself across from Amiante. "Do you think I am acting correctly?"

Amiante carefully put down his chisel. "You certainly are doing no wrong."

"I know—but am I being foolish? Reckless? I can't decide. After all, the mayoralty isn't an important office."

"To the contrary!" declared Amiante with a vehemence

that Ghyl found surprising. "The office is specified by the Civic Charter, and is very old indeed." Amiante paused, then gave a soft grunt of disparagement—toward whom or what Ghyl could not divine.

"What can the Mayor do?" Ghyl asked.

"He can—or at least he can try to—enforce the provisions of the Charter." Amiante frowned up at the ceiling. "I suppose it could be argued that Welfare Regulation effectually supersedes the Charter—though the Charter has never been abrogated. The mayoralty itself testifies to the fact!"

"The Charter is older than Welfare Regulation?"

"Indeed yes. Older and rather more general in scope." Amiante's voice was again dispassionate and reflective. "The mayoralty is the last functional manifestation if the Charter, which is a pity." He hesitated, pursed his lips. "In my opinion the Mayor might usefully take it upon himself to assert the principles of the Charter . . . difficult, I suppose. Yes, difficult indeed."

"Why difficult?" asked Ghyl. "The Charter is still valid?"

Amiante tapped his chin thoughtfully and stared through the open door out into Undle Square. Ghyl began to wonder if Amiante had heard his question.

Amiante at last spoke—obliquely, hyperbolically, so it seemed to Ghyl. "Freedom, privileges, options must constantly be exercised, even at the risk of inconvenience. Otherwise they fall into desuetude and become unfashionable, unorthodox—finally irregulationary. Sometimes the person who insists upon his prerogatives seems shrill and contentious—but actually he performs a service for all. Freedom naturally should never become license; but regulation should never become restriction." Amiante's voice dwindled; he picked up his chisel and examined it as if it were a strange object.

Ghyl frowned. "You think then that I should try to become Mayor and enforce the Charter?"

Amiante smiled, shrugged. "As to this, I can't give advice. You must decide for yourself . . . long ago I had the opportunity to do something similar. I was dissuaded, and I have never felt completely comfortable since. Perhaps I am not a brave man."

"Of course you're brave!" declared Ghyl. "You're the bravest man I know!"

But Amiante only smiled and shook his head and would say no more.

At noon the following day Nion, Floriel, and Shulk came to visit Ghyl. They were excited, keyed-up, alive. Nion, wearing a suit of black and brown, looked older than his years. Floriel was casually friendly. "What in the world happened to you the other night?" he asked ingenuously. "We waited and waited and waited. Finally we decided that you had gone home, or maybe"—he winked—"had stopped to cuddle a bit with Gedée."

Ghyl turned away in disgust.

Floriel shrugged. "If you want to be that way about it."

Nion said, "There was a minor difficulty. We couldn't register the name Emphyrio for election unless it was attached or affixed to a recipient in residence, of good moral standing. Naturally, just off Cheer and Health Squad, I was out. Floriel and Shulk are in trouble with their guild. Mael was expelled from Temple. Uger—well, you know Uger. He just wouldn't do. So we nominated you, under the cognomen Emphyrio." Nion came forward, slapped Ghyl jovially on the back. "My lad, you may be the next Mayor!"

"But—I don't want to be Mayor!"

"Realistically, the chances are small."

"Are there no age qualifications? After all . . ."

Nion shook his head. "You're a full recipient, you're in good standing with your guild, you're not listed by the Temple. In short, you're an acceptable candidate."

From the bench Amiante chuckled; all turned to look at him, but there was no further sound from Amiante. Ghyl frowned. He had not wished to become so intimately involved with the program. Especially since, with Nion involved, he had no real control over events. Unless, again, he exerted himself to exercise leadership, which meant contention with Nion, or, at the very least, a test of wills.

On the other hand—as Amiante had pointed out—the candidacy was neither irregulationary nor disreputable. There was no reason whatever why, if he so chose, he should not become a candidate, using the name Emphyrio as a cognomen, after clearly identifying himself as Ghyl Tarvoke."

Ghyl said, "I have no objection—if one condition is met."

"Which is?"

"That I am in control of the entire affair. You will have to take orders from me."

" 'Orders'?" Nion's mouth twisted wryly. "Really, now!"

"If you want it otherwise—use your own name."

"As you know, I can't do that."

"Well then, you will have to agree to my conditions."

Nion rolled his eyes up toward the ceiling. "Oh well, if you want to be pompous about the situation . . ."

"Call it what you like." From the corner of his eye Ghyl could see that Amiante had been listening intently. Now Amiante's mouth curved in the smallest of smiles and he bent over his screen.

"Do you agree to my conditions?"

Nion grimaced, then smiled, and at once was as before. "Yes, of course. The main thing, however, is not authority or prestige, but the whole great farcical situation."

"Very well then. I want no noncups or criminals involved, directly or indirectly. The affair must be totally regulationary."

"Noncups are not necessarily immoral," argued Nion Bohart.

"True," intoned Amiante from his bench.

"But the noncups you know are," Ghyl told Nion, after a look toward his father. "I don't care to be at the mercy of your acquaintances."

Nion drew his lips back, to show, for an instant, sharp white teeth. "You certainly want things your own way."

Ghyl threw up his hands in a gesture of heartfelt relief. "Do without me! In fact—"

"No, no," Nion Bohart cut in. "Do without you—the originator of the whole wonderful scheme? Nonsense! A travesty!"

"Then—no noncups. No statements or expositions or activity of any kind without my prior endorsement."

"But you can't be everywhere at once."

Ghyl sat for ten seconds looking at Nion Bohart. Just as he opened his mouth to disassociate himself irrevocably from the project, Nion shrugged. "Whatever you say."

Schute Cobol made a heated protest to Amiante. "The idea is absolutely ridiculous! A stripling, a mere lad, among the candidates for Mayor! And calling himself Emphyrio to boot! Do you consider this social conduct?"

Amiante asked mildly, "Is it irregulationary?"

"It is certainly bumptious and improper! You mock an august office! Many people will be disturbed and distracted!"

"If an activity is not irregulationary, then it is right and proper," said Amiante. "If an activity is right and proper, then any recipient may indulge in it to his heart's content."

Schute Cobol's face flushed brick-red with anger. "Do you

not realize that you are bringing difficulty, if not censure, down upon me? My superior will ask why I do not control such antics! Very well. Obduracy works both ways. It so happens that the orders for your yearly stipend increases are in my office for discretionary recommendation. I must make a 'Not Approved' indication on the basis of social irresponsibility. You gain nothing by affronting me!"

Amiante was unmoved. "Do as you think best."

Schute Cobol swung around to Ghyl. "What is your final word?"

Ghyl, previously the most lukewarm of candidates, could hardly control his voice from outrage. "It is not irregulationary. Why should I not become a candidate?"

Schute Cobol flung himself from the shop.

"Bah!" muttered Ghyl. "Maybe Nion and the noncups are right after all!"

Amiante made no direct response. He sat pulling at his little chin, an unimpressive foundation to his massive face. "It is time," said Amiante in a heavy voice.

Ghyl looked at him questioningly, but Amiante was talking to himself. "It is time," he intoned once more.

Ghyl went to his bench, seated himself. As he worked he turned puzzled glances toward Amiante, who sat staring out the open doorway, his mouth occasionally moving as he made soundless but emphatic utterances to himself. Presently he went to the cabinet and brought forth his portfolio. With Ghyl watching in disquietude, Amiante turned through his papers.

That night Amiante worked late in his shop. Ghyl tossed and turned on his couch, but did not go down to learn what his father was doing.

The following morning a curious sour odor permeated the shop. Ghyl asked no questions; Amiante volunteered no explanation.

During the day Ghyl attended a guild outing to Pyrite Isle, twenty miles to sea: a little knob of rock with a few wind-beaten trees, a pavilion, a few cottages, a restaurant. Ghyl had hoped that his involvement with the mayorality campaign—a relatively obscure and unpublicized affair—might escape attention, but such was not the case. All day he was patronized, taunted, inspected covertly, avoided. A few young men and a few girls inquired regarding his eccentric cognomen, his motives, his plans if elected. Ghyl was unable to supply intelligent answers. He did not care to identify his candidacy either as a prank, or a Chaoticist ploy, or an act of drunken bravado from which he was unable to disengage himself. At the day's end he felt humiliated and angry. When he arrived home, Amiante was out. In the shop was yet a trace of the sour odor he had noticed that morning.

Amiante did not return home until late, an unusual occurrence.

On the following day it was discovered that throughout the precincts Brueben, Nobile, Foelgher, Dodrechten, Cato, Hoge, Veige and out into Godero and East Town placards had been posted. In dark brown characters on a gray background a message read:

Let us promote change for the better
EMPHYRIO SHOULD BE OUR NEXT MAYOR

Ghyl saw the placards with amazement. They clearly had been printed by some manner of duplication; how else to explain the large number of placards?

One of the placards hung on a wall across Undle Square. Ghyl went close to the printing, sniffed the ink, and recognized the sour smell which had permeated the workroom.

Ghyl went to sit on a bench. He looked blankly across the square. A harrowing situation! How could his father be so irresponsible? What perverse motivation could so obsess him?

Ghyl started to rise to his feet, then sank back. He did not want to go home; he did not want to talk to his father. . . . And yet, he could not sit on the bench all day.

He pulled himself upright, walked slowly across the square.

Amiante stood at his bench blocking out the pattern for a new screen: a Winged Being plucking fruit from the Tree of Life. The panel was a dark and glossy slab of perdura which Amiante had been saving for this specific design.

Seeing his father so placid, Ghyl stopped short in the doorway to stand staring. Amiante looked up, nodded. "So then—the young political aspirant arrives home. How goes the contest?"

"There is no contest," muttered Ghyl. "I'm sorry I ever agreed to the foolishness."

"Oh? Think of the prestige—assuming of course that you are elected."

"Small chance of that. And prestige? I have more prestige as a wood-carver."

"If you were elected as Emphyrio, the situation would be

different. The prestige would derive from the extraordinary circumstances."

" 'Prestige' or ridicule? More likely that latter. I know nothing about being Mayor. It is absurd."

Amiante shrugged, returned to his design. A shadow fell across Ghyl's bench. He turned. As he had feared: Schute Cobol with two men in dark blue and brown uniforms— Special Agents.

Schute Cobol looked from Ghyl to Amiante. "I regret the necessity for this visit. However I can prove that an irregulationary process has occurred in this shop, resulting in the duplicated production of several hundred placards."

Ghyl leaned back on his bench. Schute Cobol and the two agents stepped forward. "Either one or both of you are guilty," declared Schute Cobol. "Prepare . . ."

Amiante stood looking from one to the other in a puzzled fashion. " 'Guilt'? In printing political placards? No guilt whatever."

"You printed these placards?"

"I did, certainly. It is my right to do so. There is no guilt involved.

"I choose to think differently, especially after you have been warned. This is a serious offense!

Amiante held out his hands. "How can it be an offense, when I exercise a right guaranteed by the Great Charter of Ambroy?"

"Eh then? And what is this?"

"The Great Charter: are you not familiar with it? It provides the basis for all regulation."

"I know nothing of any charter. I know the Welfare Code of Regulations, which is sufficient."

Amiante was more than courteous. "Permit me to show you the passage to which I refer." He went to his cabinet, brought forth one of his ancient pamphlets. "Notice: the Great Charter of Ambroy; surely you are acquainted with it?"

"I have heard of such a thing," Schute Cobol grudgingly admitted.

"Well then, here is the passage. 'Any citizen of virtuous quality and good reputation may aspire to public office; furthermore he and his sponsors may present to public attention notice of such candidacy, by means of advertisement, public posting of printed bulletins or placards, verbal messages and exhortation, on or off of public property. . . . ' There is more, but I believe this is sufficient."

Schute Cobol peered at the pamphlet. "What gibberish is this?"

"It is written in Formal Archaic." said Amiante.

"Whatever it is, I can't read it. If I can't read it, it can't bind me. This trash might be anything! You are trying to swindle me!"

"No indeed," said Amiante. "Here is the basic law of Ambroy, to which the Welfare Code and Guild Regulations both must yield."

"Indeed?" Schute Cobol gave a grim chuckle. "And who enforces the law?"

"The Mayor and the people of Ambroy."

Schute Cobol made a brusque motion to the agents. "To the office with him. He has performed irregulationary duplicating."

"No, no! I have not done so! Do you not see this passage? It avows my rights!"

"And have I not told you I cannot read it? There are hundreds, thousands, of such obsolete documents. Get along with you! I have no sympathy for Chaoticists!"

Ghyl leapt forward, striking at Schute Cobol. "Let my father alone! He has never done a wrong act!"

One of the agents thrust Ghyl aside, the second tripped him and sent him sprawling. Schute Cobol stood above him with flared nostrils. "Luckily for you, the blow did not strike home; otherwise . . ." He did not finish his sentence. He turned to the agents. "Come along then; to the office with him." And Amiante was hustled away.

Ghyl picked himself up, ran to the door, followed the welfare agents to their five-wheeled car.

Amiante looked from the window, his expression strained and wild, but in some curious manner, calm. "Make a representation to the Mayor! Demand that he enforce the Charter!"

"Yes, yes! But will he heed?"

"I don't know. Do what you can.

The agents thrust Ghyl aside; the car departed; Ghyl stood looking after it. Then, ignoring aghast stares of friends and neighbors, he returned to the shop.

He thrust the charter into a folder, took money from the cabinet, ran forth once more to the Undle Overtrend kiosk.

Eventually Ghyl located the Mayor, cousin to Floriel's

mother, at the Brown Star Inn. As Ghyl had expected, he had never heard of the ancient Charter and squinted at it with less than no interest at all. Ghyl explained the circumstances and implored the Mayor to intervene, but the Mayor shook his head decisively. "The case is clear-cut, or so it seems to me. Duping is prohibited, for good and sufficient reason. Your father seems a capricious sort to violate such an important regulation."

Ghyl glared into the bland face, then turned furiously away and strode through the dusk back to Undle Square.

Once more in the shop he sat brooding for hours as the sepia gloom of twilight became darkness.

At last he stumbled up to bed, to lay staring into nothing, his stomach churning at the thought of what was being done to his father.

Poor innocent Amiante! thought Ghyl. He had trusted the magic of words: a sentence on one of his ancient bits of paper.

But presently, as the night wore on, Ghyl became doubtful. Recalling Amiante's actions of the last few days, Ghyl began to wonder if, after all, Amiante had not done what he felt he had to do, in full cognizance of his risks.

Poor, foolish, brave Amiante, thought Ghyl.

Amiante was brought home a week and a half later. He had lost weight. He seemed dazed and listless. He came into the shop, and at once went to a bench and sat down as if his legs were too weak to support him. "Father!" said Ghyl huskily. "Are you well?"

Amiante gave a slow heavy nod. "Yes. As well as can be expected."

"What . . . did they do?"

Amiante drew a deep breath. "I don't know. He turned to look at his screen, tentatively picked up a chisel in fingers which seemed suddenly blunt and clumsy. "I don't even know why they took me away."

"For printing placards!"

"Ah yes. Now I recall. I read something to them; what was it?"

"This!" cried Ghyl, trying to keep the heartbreak from his voice. "The Great Charter! Do you not remember?"

Amiante picked it up without great interest; turned it this way and that; returned it to Ghyl. "I seem to be tired. I cannot read."

Ghyl took his arm. "Come along upstairs, and lie down. I'll fix supper and we'll talk together."

"I am not very hungry."

Jaunty footsteps sounded along the sidewalk. There was a rap at the door and Nion Bohart, wearing a tall green cap and a pointed bill, a green suit, black and yellow boots, stepped into the shop. At the sight of Amiante he stopped short, then came slowly forward, shaking his head dolefully. "Rehabilitation, eh? I was afraid of that." And he looked down at Amiante as if he were an object of wax. "They showed little restraint I must say."

Ghyl slowly straightened himself, turned to face Nion. "You are the cause of all this."

Nion Bohart stiffened in indignation. "Come now! Let's have no abuse! I wrote neither the regulations nor the Great Charter! I've done nothing wrong!"

"'Nothing wrong,'" echoed Amiante in a small clear voice.

Ghyl gave a small, skeptical snort. "Well then, what is it you want?"

"I came to discuss the election."

"There is nothing to discuss. I am not interested."

Amiante's mouth moved as if once again he were repeating what he had heard.

Nion Bohart threw his cap to a bench. "Now look here, Ghyl, you're distressed, justifiably. But put the blame where it belongs."

"And where is that?"

Nion Bohart shrugged. "Hard to say. He glanced through the window, made a quick movement as if to depart the room. "More visitors," he muttered.

Into his shop came four men. Only Schute Cobol was known to Ghyl.

Schute Cobol nodded curtly to Ghyl, turned a quick flash of a glance toward Nion Bohart, gave Amiante a grim inspection. "Well then, as a rehabilitate you are entitled to special counsel. This is Zurik Cobol. He will help provide you a healthy new basis of existence."

Zurik Cobol, a small round man with a round bald head, gave a small nod and stared at Amiante intently.

Nion Bohart, as Schute Cobol spoke, had been unobtrusively edging toward the door; but now a sign from a man standing behind Schute Cobol—a tall man in black, with a keen haughty face, wearing a great, black, much-beribboned hat, compelled Nion Bohart to remain.

Schute Cobol turned from Amiante toward Ghyl. "Now then, I must inform you that your charge is high. Expert opinion has defined your conduct as verging upon felonious."

"Indeed?" asked Ghyl, a harsh, acid flavor rising in his throat. "Why is this?"

"First: your candidacy is clearly a malicious prank, an attempt to demean the city. Such an attitude is irreverent and intolerable.

"Secondly, you are attempting obfuscation of the welfare rolls by naming yourself with the name of a legendary and nonexistent man.

"Thirdly, by associating yourself with this legend of rebellion against established order, you implicitly advocate chaoticism.

"Fourthly, you have consorted with noncuperatives—"

Nion Bohart swaggered forward. "And what, may I ask, is irregulationary about consorting with noncups?"

Schute Cobol spared him a glance. "Noncuperatives are beyond welfare regulations, hence irregulationary, though not actively proscribed. The candidacy of Emphyrio is undoubtedly a noncuperative conception.

"Fifthly, you are the son and associate of a man twice admonished for duplicating. We cannot prove collusion, but surely you were aware of what was transpiring. You made no report of the crime. Purposeful failure to report a crime is a felony.

"In none of these five instances is your delinquency definite enough to be brought home to you; in this regard you are a subtle young man." (At this, Nion Bohart turned Ghyl a look of searching new appraisal.) "Still, be assured that you deceive no one, that you will be subjected to careful observation. This gentleman"—he indicated the man in black—"is Chief Executive Investigator of Brueben Precinct, a very important person. His interest has been attracted, and from your point of view this is not a propitious circumstance."

"Indeed not," said the official, in a light, pleasant voice. He pointed to Nion. "This would be one of the accomplices?"

"It is Nion Bohart, a notorious ne'er-do-well," said Schute Cobol. "I have his dossier at hand. It is not appetizing."

The official made a negligent gesture. "He is warned. We need not proceed further."

The welfare agents departed, with the exception of Zurik Cobol, who took Amiante out into the sunlight of the square, seated him on a bench, and spoke earnestly to him.

Nion Bohart looked at Ghyl. "Phew! What a hornet's nest!"

Ghyl went to sit down at his workbench. "Have I done something terribly wrong? I can't decide . . ."

Nion, finding nothing more to interest him, went to the door. "Election tomorrow," he called over his shoulder. "Don't forget to vote!"

CHAPTER 10

There were five candidates for the office of Mayor. The incumbent received a plurality of the votes and was returned to his sinecure. Emphyrio was a surprisingly strong third, with approximately 10 percent of all votes cast—enough to disturb the welfare agency anew.

Schute Cobol came to the shop and demanded all of Amiantes private papers. Amiante, sitting at his work bench, working listlessly at his screen, looked up with a peculiar light in his eyes. Schute Cobol came a stride closer; Amiante, to Ghyl's astonishment, sprang erect and struck Schute Cobol with a mallet. Schute Cobol fell to the ground; Amiante would have struck again, had not Ghyl taken away the mallet. Schute Cobol, moaning and holding his head, tottered from the shop and out into the golden afternoon light.

Amiante said to Ghyl in a voice Ghyl would never have recognized, "Take the papers. They are yours. Keep them safe." He went into the square and sat upon a bench.

Ghyl hid the portfolio under the roof tiles. An hour later welfare agents came to take Amiante away.

When he returned after four days, he was bland, easy, indifferent. A month later he fell into a dull mood and slumped into a chair. Ghyl watched him anxiously.

Amiante dozed. When Ghyl brought him a bowl of gruel for his lunch, Amiante was dead.

Ghyl was alone in the old shop. It was full of Amiante's presence; his tools, his patterns, his mild voice. Ghyl could hardly see for eyes full of grief. What now? Should he continue to work as wood-carver? Go noncup and live the life of a vagabond? Perhaps he should emigrate to Luschein or Salula? He brought Amiante's portfolio down from the roof, went through the papers which Amiante had handled so lovingly. He puzzled through the ancient Charter, shook his head sadly at the idealistic vision of the city's founders. He reread the Emphyrio fragment, from which he drew courage. *Emphyrio strove and suffered for truth. I shall do likewise!*

If only I can find the strength within myself! This is what Amiante would want!

He removed the fragment and the Charter from the portfolio and hid them separately; the portfolio he put in the accustomed place.

He went back to stand in the workshop. The building was quiet, except for strange little noises he had never before noticed: creaks of the ancient timbers, a flutter of wind in the tiles. Afternoon came; a flood of mellow light poured in through the amber windows. How often had Ghyl sat in this light, with his father at his own bench across the room!

Ghyl fought the tears back from his eyes. He must use his strength, he must develop, gain knowledge. There was no single focus for the great dissatisfaction he felt. The Welfare Agency worked, by and large, for the benefit of the recipients. The guilds enforced the standards of excellence by which Ambroy survived in relative ease and security. The lords extracted their 1.18 percent from the economy, but the amount hardly seemed excessive.

What then was wrong? Where was truth? What course would Emphyrio have taken? In desperation, to ease his need for activity, Ghyl seized up chisels, and going to Amiante's bench worked on his great perdura panel: the Winged Being plucking fruit from the Tree of Life. He worked with feverish energy; chips and scrapings covered the floor. Schute cobol passed outside the shop, rapped, opened the door, peered within. He said nothing. Ghyl said nothing. The two looked into each other's eyes. Schute Cobol nodded slowly, departed.

Time passed: a year, two years. Ghyl saw none of his old friends. For recreation he took long hikes in the country, often sleeping the night under a hedge. Living by himself he became a different person: a young man of average height, with hard shoulders, taut muscles. His features were blunt but hard and compressed; there were ridges of muscle around his mouth. He wore his hair cropped short, his garments were plain and devoid of ornamentation.

One day in early summer he finished a screen and by way of relaxation walked south through Brueben and Hoge, into Cato, and by chance passed Keecher's Inn. Obeying a random impulse, he went in, ordered a mug of ale, a plate of steamed whelks. All was precisely as he remembered, though the scale seemed smaller and the decorations not quite so splendid. Girls from the bench looked him over, approached; Ghyl sent them away, and sat watching the folk come and go.

. . . A face he knew: Floriel! Ghyl called out; Floriel turned and, seeing Ghyl, evinced astonishment. "What in the world do you do here?"

"Nothing unusual." Ghyl indicated his ale, his plate. "I eat, I drink."

Floriel cautiously pulled up a chair. "I must say I'm surprised. . . . I heard that after your father's death you had—well, become quiet, distant. Even a recluse. A real voucher-grabber for work."

Ghyl laughed—the first time in how long? Years, it seemed. It was good to laugh again. Perhaps the ale was responsible. Perhaps a sudden yearning for companionship. "I've been pretty much alone. What of you? You've changed since I saw you last." And indeed Floriel had become, not a new person, but an augmented version of his previous self. He was as handsome as ever, as debonair, with added control, craft, alertness. He said, with a trace of complacence, "I've changed a bit, I suppose. At heart the same Floriel, of course."

"You're still in Metal-benders?"

Floriel gave Ghyl a glance of injured surprise. "Of course not. Haven't you heard? I've gone noncup. You're sitting with a man outside organized society. Aren't you ashamed?"

"No, I hadn't heard." Ghyl looked Floriel up and down, noting the signs of prosperity. "How do you live? You don't seem to be deprived. Where do you get your vouchers?"

"Oh, I manage, one way or another. I fell into a little cottage up the river, a lovely place. I rent this out over the weekends, and do a fair business. And, to be candid, sometimes I bring up girls for men on a bit of a tear. Nothing absolutely criminal, you understand. One way or another I make out. And you?"

"Still carving screens."

"Ah then, you'll continue in the trade?"

"I don't know . . . remember how we used to talk of travel?"

"Yes, of course. I've never forgotten."

"Nor I," Ghyl leaned forward, gazing down into his ale. "Life here is futility. We'll live and die, and realize no glimmer of truth. There's something terribly wrong here in Ambroy. Do you realize this?"

Floriel looked at him askance. "Still the same old Ghyl! You haven't changed a bit!"

"How do you mean?"

"You always were idealistic. Do you think I care a whit for truth or knowledge? No. But I'll travel, and in style too. In fact"—Floriel looked right and left—"you remember Nion Bohart, of course."

"Certainly."

"I see him often. He and I have some grand ideas. The only way to get is to take—from those who have: the lords."

"You mean: kidnaping?"

"Why not? I don't consider it wrong. They take from us; we must redress the balance and take from them."

"One difficulty: if you are caught, you'll be expelled into Bauredel. What good is wealth to a man an inch thick?"

"Ha ha! We won't be caught!"

Ghyl shrugged. "Go ahead, with my blessings. I don't mind. The lords can stand to lose a few vouchers. They extract enough from us."

"That's the way to talk!"

"Has Nion gone noncup?"

"Certainly. He's been quietly noncup for years."

"I always suspected as much."

Floriel ordered more ale. "To Emphyrio! What a marvelous put-on, that election! So many folk in a dither, welfare agents out looking here and there, simply wonderful!"

Ghyl put down his mug with a grimace. Floriel rattled on, unheeding. "I've had good times as a noncup, I tell you! I recommend it! You live by your wits, true, but there's no bowing and scraping to welfare agent and guild delegate."

"So long as you don't get caught."

Floriel nodded owlishly. "One must be discreet, of course. But it's not too hard. You'd be astounded by the opportunities! Cut the twig! Go noncup!"

Ghyl smiled. "I've thought of it, many times. But—I don't know how I'd make a living."

"There are hundreds of chances for clever men. Nion chartered a river barge, let it be known that indiscreet behavior was quite all right, and earned three thousand vouchers over one weekend! There's the way to operate!"

"I suppose so. I don't have the golden touch."

"I'll be glad to show you the ropes. Why don't you come up to my cottage for a few days? It's right on the river, not far from County Pavilion. We'll do nothing—just lounge about, eat, drink, talk. Do you have a girl friend?"

"No."

"Well, I might be able to fix you up. I'm living with a girl myself; in fact, I think you know her: Sonjaly Rathe."

Ghyl nodded with a grim smile. "I remember her."

"Well, then what do you say?"

"It sounds pleasant. I'd like to visit your cottage."

"Good! Let's say—next weekend. An opportune time, just right for the County Ball!"

"Very well. Do I need new clothes?"

"Of course not! We're very casual. The County Ball is costume, of course, so buy some sort of whack-up and a domino. Otherwise—just a swimsuit."

"How do I find the place?"

"Ride Overtrend to Grigglesby Corners. Walk back two hundred steps, go out a blank bridge to the blue cottage with the yellow sun-strike."

"I'll be there."

"Er—should I ask along an extra girl?"

Ghyl considered a moment. "No," he said at last. "I think not."

"Oh come," teased Floriel. "Surely you're not puritanical!"

"No. But I don't want to become involved in anything. I know myself. I can't stop halfway."

"Don't stop halfway! Why be a coward?"

"Oh, very well. Do as you like."

CHAPTER 11

The ride along the Insee was pleasant. The Overtrend cars slid on magnetic cushions without jar or sound; through the windows the Insse reflected back the sunlight. From time to time thickets of willow or horsewhistle intervened, or banks of sponge-tree or black-web. To the other side were pastures where biloa birds grazed.

Ghyl sat back, lost in reverie. It was time, he thought, to broaden his life, to take in more territory. Perhaps here was the reason he had so readily accepted Floriel's invitation. Schute Cobol would certainly disapprove. A fig for Schute Cobol. If only it were easier to travel, to achieve some measure of financial independence ...

The car halted at Grigglesby Corners; Ghyl alighted, received his bag from the ejector. What a pleasant spot! he thought. Enormous sad-apple trees towered above the brown buildings of the little depot and store, the yellow-green foliage streaming in the smoky sunlight, filling the air with a pleasant acrid scent.

Ghyl walked back along the riverbank on a cushion of old leaves. Along the other shore a dark-haired girl in a white frock lazily paddled a skiff; she saw him watching; she smiled and waved her hand; then the current eased her around a bend and into a dark little inlet, away from sight. It was as if never, never, had a girl in a white dress floated along the sunlit river. . . . Ghyl shook his head, grinned at his own vagaries.

He continued along the bank, and presently came to a trestle leading through the reeds to a pale blue cottage under a water-cherry tree.

Ghyl walked out along the precarious planks, to a porch overlooking the river. Here sat Floriel in white shorts, and a cool, pretty blond girl whom Ghyl saw to be Sonjaly Rathe. She nodded, smiled and simulated enthusiasm; Floriel jumped to his feet. "So you've arrived! Good to see you. Bring your bag on in; I'll show you where to chuck your gear."

Ghyl was assigned a small chamber overlooking the river, with yellow-brown ripples of light coursing across the ceiling. He changed to loose, light clothes and went out to the porch. Floriel thrust a goblet of punch into his hand, indicated a sling chair. "Now, simply relax! Laze! Something you recipients never know how to do. Always striving, cringing when the delegate points his dirty fingernail at a flaw! Not for me!"

"Not for me either," sighed Sonjaly, snuggling against Floriel, with an enigmatic glance toward Ghyl.

"Not for me either," confessed Ghyl, "if I knew how to live otherwise."

"Go noncup!"

"What if I did? All I know is carving screens. Where would I sell? Certainly not to the guild. It looks after its own."

"There are ways, there are ways!"

"No doubt. I don't care to steal."

"It all depends," stated Sonjaly, with the air of one reciting a liturgy, "from whom one steals."

"I regard the lords as fair game," said Floriel. "And perhaps a few other portly institutions as well."

"The lords, yes," said Ghyl, "or olmast yes, at any rate. I'd have to consider each case on its merits."

Floriel laughed, waved his goblet. "Ghyl, you are far too serious, far too earnest! Always you want to delve to some impossible fundamental, like an impet diving for a mud eel."

Ghyl laughed also. "If I'm too serious, you're too irresponsible."

"Bah," retorted Floriel. "Is the world responsible? Of course not! The world is random, vagrant, heedless. To be responsible is to be out of phase, to be insane!"

Ghyl pondered a moment. "This is perhaps the case, in a world left to itself. But society imposes order. Living in a society, it is not insane to be responsible."

"Total bosh!" And Floriel went on to detail the irrationality of certain guild practices, the Temple ritual, of agency regulation: none of which Ghyl could refute. "I agree, much of our society is absurd. But should we throw out the baby with the bath? The guilds, the agency, no matter how insane at times, are necessary instruments. Even the lords serve a purpose."

"We need a change!" declared Floriel. "The lords originally provided valuable capital and expertise. Undeniable. But they have earned back their capital many times over. Do you realize how much 1.18 percent of our gross product is? Have you ever calculated the sum? No? Well, it is enormous. Over the course of years, it becomes stupendous. In fact, it is incredible how so few lords are able to spend so much money. Not even space-yachts cost so much. And I've heard it said that the eyries are by no means paved with gold. Nion Bohart knows a plumber who services eyrie drains, and, according to this plumber, some of the eyries are almost austere."

Ghyl shrugged. "I don't care where or how they spend their money—though I'd prefer they bought my screens rather than, say, Lu-Hang stain-silk. But I don't think I'd care to abolish the lords. They provide us with a spectacle, with drama, with vicarious elegance."

"My dearest goal is to live like a lord," declared Floriel. "Abolish them? Never! Parasites though they may be."

Sonjaly rose to her feet. She wore only a brief skirt and a bit of a loose blouse. Walking past Ghyl she swung her slender body provocatively. Floriel winked at Ghyl. "Pour us all more punch and less strutting back and forth. We know you're beautiful!"

Sonjaly languidly poured punch. "Beautiful, yes. What good does it do me? I want to travel. Floriel won't take me even so far as the Meagher Mounts." And playfully she put her hand under Ghyl's chin. "Would you?"

"I'm as poor as Floriel," said Ghyl, "and not even a thief. My traveling must be by shank's mare, which you're very welcome to share."

Sonjaly made a wry face and went off into the house. Floriel leaned toward Ghyl and muttered hurriedly, "About that girl I wanted to invite: the one I had in mind was busy elsewhere. Sonjaly tried Gedée—"

"What?" cried Ghyl in consternation.

"But she is studying to pass a fish-packing examination."

" 'Fish-packing'?"

"You know—packing preserved fish in cans and cartons. There is an art to the process—so Gedée tells me. You curl the dear little toe fins and place the specimen just so, and with a sweeping motion pull the feelers down into the oral cavity."

"Spare me the details," said Ghyl. "Spare me, likewise, Gedée."

"It's all for the best," Floriel assured him. "You can go to the ball unencumbered, and your eye can rove as far as it likes. There's bound to be lords and ladies present."

"Really now! How do you know?"

Floriel pointed. "Look yonder, around the bend. See that bit of white? That's the County Pavilion. Off beyond is a vast park, the estate of Lord Aldo the Underline. During the summer many lords and ladies—especially the young ones—come down from the eyries, and they all dote on the County Ball! I wager there'll be fifty on hand."

"With a hundred Garrion," said Ghyl. "Will the Garrion be in costume, with dominoes and all?"

Floriel laughed. "What a sight! We shall see. Naturally you brought a costume?"

"Yes. Nothing very much. I'll be a Zambolian Warrior."

"Good enough. I'm a pierrot. Nion is coming as a Jeng serpent-man."

"Oh? Nion will be here also?"

"Of course. Nion and I are associates, so to speak. We do quite well, as you may imagine."

With a faint frown, Ghyl sipped his punch. Floriel was easy and amiable; Ghyl could relax and enjoy Floriel's nonsense. Nion, on the other hand, always aroused in Ghyl a vague and formless challenge. Ghyl drained his goblet. He would ignore Nion completely; he would remain calm in the face of all provocation.

Floriel took the pitcher, went to pour punch, but the pitcher was empty. "Inside there!" he called to Sonjaly. "Mix us punch, there's a good girl."

"Mix it yourself," came a petulant voice. "I'm lying down."

Floriel went inside with the pitcher. There were a few muffled words of altercation, then Floriel came forth with a brimming pitcher. "Now tell me about yourself. How are you making it without your father? Isn't that great old house lonesome?"

Ghyl responded that he lived modestly but adequately; that indeed the shop was sometimes lonely.

The hours passed. They ate cheese and pickles for lunch and later all plunged into the river for a swim. Nion Bohart arrived just as they were emerging from the water. "Halloo, halloo! All you wet creatures! Ghyl too I see! It's been a long time! And Sonjaly! Adorable creature—especially in that wet clinging trifle. Floriel, you really don't deserve her."

Sonjaly turned Floriel a rather spiteful glance. "I keep telling him the same thing. But he doesn't believe me."

"We'll have to do something about that. . . . Well then, Floriel, where shall I stow my bags? The usual little den? Anything's good enough for old Nion, eh? Well, all right, I don't mind."

"Come now," said Floriel. "You always demand and receive the best bed in the house."

"In that case—better beds!"

"Yes, yes, of course. . . . You've brought your costume?"

"Naturally. This shall be the most exalted County Ball of all time. We'll make it that way. . . . What is that you're drinking?"

"Montarada punch."

"I'll have some, if I may."

"Allow me," said Sonjaly. And bowing sinuously she handed Nion a goblet. Floriel turned away in disgust, obviously not amused.

Floriel's disapproval failed to influence either Sonjaly or Nion, and during the remainder of the afternoon they flirted with ever more daring, exchanging glances, casual touches which were barely disguised caresses. Floriel became increasingly disturbed. At last he made a sarcastic comment, to which Sonjaly gave a flippant rejoinder. Floriel lost his temper. "Do what you like!" he sneered. "I can't control you; I wouldn't if I could; I've seen too much control!"

Nion laughed in great good humor. "Floriel, you're an idealist, no less than Ghyl. Control is necessary and even good—as long as I do the controlling."

"How strange," muttered Floriel. "Ghyl tells me the same thing."

"What?" asked Ghyl in surprise. "I said no such thing. My point was that organization is necessary to social living!"

"True!" stated Nion. "Even the Chaoticists agree to that: paradoxical as it may seem. And you, Ghyl, you're still a staunch recipient?"

"Not really . . . I don't know what I am. I feel I must learn."

"A waste of time. There's your idealism again. Life is too short for pondering! No indecision! If you wish the sweets of life, you must reach forth to take them!"

"And also be prepared to run when the owner comes to punish you."

"That too. I have no false pride; I'll run very fast. I have no desire to set anyone a good example."

Ghyl laughed. "At least you are honest."

"I suppose so. The Welfare Agency suspects me of rascality. However, they can't prove it."

Ghyl looked across the brimming river. This sort of life, in spite of Sonjaly's waywardness and Floriel's bickering, seemed much more gay and normal than his usual routine: carving, polishing, a walk to the shop for food, eating, sleeping, more of the same. All for the sake of a monthly stipend! If Floriel could earn enough to live in ease and leisure, in a cottage on the river, why could he not do the same?

Ghyl Tarvoke, a noncup? Why not? He need not steal nor blackmail nor procure. Undoubtedly there were vouchers to be earned legitimately—or almost legitimately. Ghyl turned to Nion: "When a person goes noncup, how in the world does he stay alive?"

Nion looked at him quizzically, obviously well aware of what was going on in Ghyl's mind. "No trouble whatever. There are dozens of ways to stay afloat. If ever you make the decision, come to me. You'd very likely do well, with your air of respectability. No one would suspect you of sharp practice."

"I'll keep you in mind."

The sun declined; the sky burnt with such a sunset as Ghyl had not seen since his childhood, when he had often watched the sun sink into the ocean from Dunkum's Heights. "Time we were dressing for the ball," said Floriel. "The music starts in half an hour, and we want to be on hand for everything. First, I'll bring up the skiff, to ferry us across the river."

He walked ashore by the trestle. Ghyl went to his room, then came out to surprise Nion and Sonjaly locked in an unmistakably ardent embrace. "Excuse me," said Ghyl.

Neither heeded him and he returned to his room.

CHAPTER 12

Floriel Huzsuis, Sonjaly Rathe, Nion Bohart, Ghyl Tarvoke: wearing fantastic costumes, with normal personalities suppressed by their dominoes, the four stepped into the skiff.

Floriel sculled across the river to the pavilion, already aglow from flares of chalk-green, pink, and yellow, and thousands of tiny, sparkling white coruscations.

Floriel held the skiff while his passengers alighted, then tied the painter to a ring and clambered up to the dock. The pavilion lay before them: an expanse of polished wood, with private boxes and observation areas to either side. At the floor level a double row of exquisitely decorated booths provided wine and other refreshment for the celebrants.

An officer accosted the four, collected admission fees. They wandered out upon the floor in company with perhaps a hundred others. Lords? Ladies? Recipients from the surrounding countryside? From the city? Noncups like Floriel, Sonjaly, Nion? Ghyl could not identify one from the other and he wondered if Nion, usually so knowledgeable, would be able to do so.

At a booth all provided themselves with green crackle-glass flasks of edel wine and stood watching the spectacle. Now musicians mounted to a dias, all wearing buffoon's garments of checkered black and white. They tuned instruments: a sound thrilling and premonitory of gaiety, as sweet as music itself. Then they scraped their fiddles, droned on their concertinas, and struck up a gay tune.

The dances of the time were extremely sedate, a far cry from the caracoles of the Last Empire or the orgiastic whirling and twitching to be seen at the seaports of the South Continent. There were several types of pavannes, as many promenades, and for the young a kind of a swinging hand-in-hand skipping dance, of considerable vivacity. In all cases the couples stood side by side, holding hands or locking elbows.

This first tune was an adagio, the corresponding dance consisting of a slow step, a shuffle, a bow forward, another far back, the knee raised as high as possible and held stationary, while the music played a fluttering little figure, whereupon the whole series was repeated.

Ghyl, with neither skill nor inclination, watched as Nion moved purposefully toward Sonjaly, only to have Floriel step quickly in front of him and take the half-amused, half-petulant Sonjaly out upon the floor.

Nion went back to stand by Ghyl, his grin benign and indulgent. "Poor Floriel, when will he learn?"

Back and forth along the floor stepped the dancers, graceful-grotesque, grotesque-graceful. There were simulations of a hundred sorts: clowns, demons, heroes; folk from far stars and ancient times; creatures of fantasy, nightmare, faery. The pavilion was rich. There was glitter of metal, the soft sheen of silk; gauze in every color; black leather, black wood, black velvet. Nion touched Ghyl's arm: "There gather the lords and their ladies, by the archway. Look at them peering this way and that; a shame they must be so cautious. Why cannot they mingle more freely with ordinary folk?"

Ghyl refrained from pointing out that fear, as well as pride and haughtiness, was at work. He asked curiously, "How do you know them for lords?"

"Mannerisms. They are distinct in many ways. Look how they stand by the walls. Some say they have learned a fear of space from living so long in the upper air. Their equilibrium is also affected; should you dance with a lady, you'd know at once; she'd be supple but erratic, without feeling for the music."

"Oh? Have you danced with ladies?"

"Danced, and more, if you'll believe me. . . . Look, watch them now: preening, twittering, debating advisabilities—oh, they're a sage, fastidious people!"

The lords and ladies had come in several groups, which now fragmented. One by one, they slipped out upon the pavilion, like magical creatures daring a voyage on a perilous sea.

Ghyl scanned the upper tiers. "Where are the Garrion? Do they stand in the dark booths above?"

"Perhaps." Nion shrugged ignorance. "Look at them, those lords! Watch how they stare at the girls! Randy as buck wisnets! Give them ten minutes, they'd impregnate every female in the pavilion!"

Ghyl followed his gesture, but now all looked alike; lords and ladies were lost in the crowd.

The music stopped; Sonjaly brought Floriel across the floor.

"The lords are here," Nion told them. "One contingent at any rate, and there may be more."

Sonjaly wanted the lords pointed out, but now even Nion was hard put to differentiate lord from recipient.

The music started again: a slow pavanne. Floriel instantly took possession of Sonjaly, but she gave her head a shake. "Thank you, no; I'd like to rest."

Ghyl, watching the dancers, decided that the step was within his capabilities. Determined to prove himself as rake-helly and gallant as the others, Ghyl presented himself to a shapely girl in a costume of green scales with a green domino, and led her out upon the floor.

He acquitted himself well enough, or so he congratulated himself. The girl had little to say; she lived in the outlying suburb of Godlep, where her father was a public weigh-master.

"Weighmaster?" pondered Ghyl. "Does that go to Scriveners' Guild or Instrument-tenders'? Or Functionaries'?"

"Functionaries." She signaled to a young man in over-lapping rings of black and red stripes. "My fiancé," she told Ghyl. "He's a functionary also, with excellent prospects, though we may have to move south to Ditzim."

Sonjaly had recovered from her fatigue; she and Nion were dancing now. Nion moved with a sure precision and far more gusto than Ghyl could summon. Sonjaly clasped his arm and leaned against him with regard for Floriel's sensibilities.

The music ended; Ghyl relinquished the girl in green scales to her fiancé, drank a cup of wine to calm his nerves.

Nion and Sonjaly strolled off to the far side of the pavilion. Floriel scowled and muttered.

At the far end of the pavilion appeared another contingent of lords and ladies, the lords costumed variously: Rhadamese warriors, druids, Kalks, barbaric princes, mermen. One lady wore gray crystals; another blue flashes of light; another white plumes.

The musicians readied their instruments; once more there was music. A person in a cuirass of black enamel and brass, breeches striped ocher and black, a bronze and black morion came to bow before Sonjaly. With an arch glance toward Nion, Sonjaly swept away on the stranger's arm. A lord? wondered Ghyl. So it seemed. A prideful quality of conduct, a poise of head, identified him as such. Ghyl thought Nion appeared vexed.

So went the evening. Ghyl attempted the acquaintance of several girls with indifferent success. Sonjaly, when visible, kept to the company of the young lord in black, brown, and brass. Floriel drank more wine than was good for him and glowered here and there. Nion Bohard seemed even more vexed by Sonjaly's frivolity than did Floriel.

The atmosphere at the pavilion loosened. The dancers moved more freely, performing the measures with verve, toes splayed smartly aside, knees crooking sometimes grotesquely high, heads tilting and leaning, this way and that. Ghyl, through perversity or crochet, would not fall in with the general mood. He became disturbed and angry with himself. Was he so dour then, so tightly clenched, that he could not abandon himself to pleasure? He gritted his teeth, determined to out-gallant the gallants, through the exercise of sheer will, if by no other means. He walked around the periphery of the pavilion, to stop short near a delightfully shaped girl in a white gown, wearing a white domino. She was dark-haired and slender, and very graceful; Ghyl had noticed her previously. She had danced once or twice; she had drunk a certain amount of wine; she had seemed as gay and wild as Ghyl wanted to be. Every movement pressed her gown against her body, which evidently, below the gown, was nude. Observing Ghyl's attention, she tilted her head teasingly sidewise. Ghyl's heart expanded, rose into his throat. Step by step he came forward, suddenly shy, though scenes of this sort had occurred a hundred times in his imagination: the girl seemed dear and familiar, and the instant fraught with *déjà-vu*. The feeling became so intense that, a step or two away, Ghyl halted.

Shaking his head in perplexity, he considered the girl from the toes of her little white sandals to her white domino.

She made a sound of amused dismay. "You are so critical! Am I grotesque or startling?"

"No, no!" stammered Ghyl. "Of course not! You are absolutely enchanting!"

The corners of her mouth twitched, and she thought to beguile him even more utterly. "Surely others here are beautiful, but you stare only at me! I feel sure that you think me strange or remarkable!"

"Of course not! But I felt that we have met, that we have

known each other . . . somewhere . . . but I can't imagine the circumstances. I certainly would have remembered!"

"You are more than polite," said the girl. "And I would have remembered you, as well. Since I don't"—here she turned him her most bewitching glance—"or do I? I seem to recognize—as you say—something familiar, as if somewhere we have known each other."

Ghyl stepped forward, his heart pounding, his throat heavy with a wonderfully sweet ache. He took her hands, which she yielded readily. "Do you believe in dreams of the future?"

"Well . . . yes. Perhaps."

"And predestination and mysterious kinds of love?"

She laughed, a delightful husky sound, and gave his hands a tug. "A hundred wonderful things I believe in. But won't folk think us strange, standing here at the ball and declaring our philosophies?"

Ghyl looked this way and that in confusion. "Well, then— will you dance? Or, if you like, we could sit over yonder and drink a cup of wine together."

"I would as lief drink wine . . . I really don't care to dance."

A startling new thought came to Ghyl, or rather, a bubble of certainty floating up from his subconscious. This girl surely was no recipient; she was a lady! The Difference was manifest! In the quality of her voice, the poise of her head, the tart perfume which surrounded her!

Exalted, Ghyl procured goblets of Gade wine and led the girl to a cushioned bench in the shadows. "What is your name?"

"I am Shanne."

"I am Ghyl." He turned her a searching side-glance. "Where do you live?"

She made an extravagant gesture; she was a vivacious girl, with hundreds of gay tricks and wry expressions. "Here, there, everywhere. Wherever I am, this is where I live."

"Of course. And I, as well. But do you live in the city—or up on an eyrie?"

Shanne held out her hands in mock despair. "Would you rob me of all my secrets? And if not secrets, my dreams? So I am Shanne, a girl vagabond, with no reputation or money or hope."

Ghyl was not deceived. The Difference was evident: that indefinable apartness which distinguished lords and ladies from the underfolk. A parapsychic umbra? An almost imperceptible odor, clean and fresh, like ozone, perhaps from long intimate contact with the upper air? Whatever the case, the effect was delightful. Ghyl squirmed at an uncomfortable thought. Might not the reverse be true? Might not the common folk seem louts, dull and lumpish, exhaling a stale reek? The lords who were so keen to seduce recipient girls could not think so. They panted after honest and unaffected passion. Perhaps the same situation prevailed *vis-à-vis* ladies and undermen. . . . The idea was unwelcome, in fact vaguely repugnant. Ghyl had never been seriously in love. His infatuation with Sonjaly now seemed stupidity. At this moment Sonjaly herself, again with Nion, danced close by. How coarse was Sonjaly in contrast to Shanne!

Shanne seemed at least favorably disposed toward him, for—wonder of wonders!—she tucked her hand under his arm and leaned back with a sigh of relaxation, her shoulder touching his.

"I love the County Ball," said Shanne in a soft voice. "There is always such excitement, such wondering who you will meet."

"You've come before?" asked Ghyl, aching for all the experiences he had not shared with her.

"Yes, I came last year. But I was not happy. The person I met was—gross."

" 'Gross'? How so? What did he do?"

But Shanne only smiled cryptically and gave his arm a companionable squeeze.

"The reason I ask," said Ghyl, "is so I won't perform any of the same errors."

Shanne only laughed, with just the slightest sense of restraint, so that Ghyl was left to wonder what indelicacies and crudities the man had performed.

Shanne jumped to her feet. "Come; this is music I like: a Mang serenade. I would like to dance."

Ghyl looked dubiously out at the floor. "It seems very complicated. I know almost nothing of dancing."

"What? Aren't you trained to leap and skip at the Temple?"

The girl was a tease, thought Ghyl. Well, he didn't mind. And his instinct was correct: she was certainly a young lady. "I have done very little leaping," said Ghyl. "As little as possible. In retribution Finuka has cursed me with a heavy foot, and I would not like you to think me clumsy. But there is a skiff at the dock; would you like me to row you out on the river?"

Shanne gave him a quick glance of calculation, ran the tip of her pink tongue over her lips. "No," she said in a thoughtful voice. "That would not be . . . advantageous."

Ghyl shrugged. "I'll try to dance."

"Wonderful!" She pulled him to his feet, and for a breathless second leaned against him so that he felt all the contours of her body. Ghyl's skin tingled; his knees felt warm and weak. Looking down into Shanne's face he saw her smile to the side, a slow secret smile, and Ghyl did not know what to think.

Ghyl danced no better than he had promised, but Shanne seemed not to notice and indeed did very little better, apparently not attending the rhythm of the music; once again Ghyl was assured that she was a young lady.

Of course! She would not row with him on the river for fear of kidnap; obviously she could not bring a Garrion into the skiff! Ghyl chuckled. Instantly Shanne's head bobbed up. "Why do you laugh?"

"Exhilaration," said Ghyl gravely. "Shanne the girl vagabond is the loveliest creature I have ever known."

"Tonight at least I am Shanne the girl vagabond," she said, somewhat wistfully.

"Tomorrow?"

"Shh." She put her hand cross his lips. "Never say the word!" With a quick look to right and left she led Ghyl through the crowd and back to their bench.

The revelry was approaching abandon. Dancers swayed, kicked, pranced, eyes glittering through their dominoes. Some made extravagant pirouettes; others paused to embrace, feverishly, oblivious to all else.

Intoxicated by color and sound and beauty as much as by the wine, Ghyl put his arm around Shanne's waist; she laid her head on his shoulder, looked up into his face. "Did you know that I can read minds?" she said in a husky whisper. "I like yours. You are strong and good and intelligent—but you are far, far, far too severe. What do you fear?" As she spoke her face was close to his. Ghyl, feeling as if he walked in a dream, bent close, close, closer; their faces met, he kissed her. Ghyl's whole inner being exploded. Never would he be the same, never again! How craven, how dull had been the Ghyl Tarvoke of old! Now nothing exceeded his competence; his previous goals—how abject they seemed! . . . He kissed

Shanne again; she sighed. "I am shameless. I have known you only an hour."

Ghyl reached to her domino, lifted it, gazed into her face. "Much longer." He raised his own domino. "Do you recognize me?"

"Yes. No. I don't know."

"Think back . . . eight years? Perhaps nine. You were on your space-yacht: a black and gold Deme. Two ragamuffins skulked aboard. Now do you remember?"

"Of course. You were the defiant one. You rascal, but you deserved your beating."

"Very likely. I thought you so heartless, so cruel . . . so remote."

Shanne giggled. "I don't seem so remote now?"

"You seem—I can't find the word. But that wasn't the first time we met."

"No? When before?"

"When I was small my father took me to see Holkerwoyd's puppets. You sat in the front row."

"Yes. I remember. How strange that you should notice me!"

"How could I avoid it? I must have foreseen this moment."

"Ghyl . . ." She sighed, sipped her wine. "I do so love the ground! Here are the strong things, the passions! Oh you are lucky!"

Ghyl laughed. "You can't really mean that. You wouldn't trade your life . . . for, say, hers." He pointed to Sonjaly. The music had just stopped; Nion and Sonjaly were walking from the floor. Nion spied Ghyl; his stride slowed, he turned his head, stared, continued.

"No," said Shanne. "I would not. Do you know her?"

"Yes. Also the young man."

"The swaggerer. I watched him. He wasn't what . . ." Her voice dwindled away. Ghyl wondered what she had started to say.

For a period they sat quietly. The music started again; Sonjaly danced past with the lord in black and brown. In a kind of dreamy curiosity Ghyl looked for Floriel and Nion, but neither was visible.

"There goes your friend," whispered Shanne, "with someone I know. And shortly they will be gone." She squeezed his arm. "I have no more wine."

"Oh! I'm sorry. Just a moment."

"I'll come with you."

They went to a booth. "Buy a whole flask," whispered Shanne. "The green."

"Yes, of course," said Ghyl. "And then?"

She said nothing. A meaningful silence. Ghyl secured the wine, took her arm. They walked outside, along the river-bank. A hundred yards along Ghyl halted, kissed Shanne. She responded fervently. They wandered on, and presently found a stretch of grassy bank. Damar, at the quarter, laid a quiver-ing trail of tarnished copper on the water.

Shanne removed her domino, Ghyl did the same; they drank wine. Ghyl stared at the river, then up to the moon. Shanne said, "You are quiet; are you sad?"

"In a way. Do you know why?"

She put her hand across his mouth. "Never speak of it. What must be, will be. What can never be . . . can never be."

Ghyl turned to look at her, trying to divine every last scin-tilla of her meaning.

"But," she added in a soft voice, "what can be . . . can be."

Ghyl drank from the wine bottle, set it down, turned to her, held out his arms. She held out hers, the two were one, and what ensued was as far beyond Ghyl's fantasies and musings as a magical reappearance of Emphyrio himself.

There was a pause, while the two sat pressed together, and they drank wine. Ghyl's head whirled. He started to speak, but once again Shanne halted him and, rising on her knees, hugged his head to her bosom, and once again for Ghyl the skies reeled and Damar blurred in and out of focus.

At last there was calm. Ghyl held the flask up against the moonlight. "Enough for you and for me."

"My head whirls," said Shanne.

"Mine as well." He took her hand. "After tonight, what?"

"Tomorrow I fly back to my tower."

"But when will I see you?"

"I don't know."

"I must see you! I love you!"

Shanne, sitting forward, clasped her knees with her arms, smiled up toward Damar. "In one week from today I travel. I travel, I travel, I travel! To distant worlds, beyond the stars!"

Ghyl cried out, "If you go, I'll never see you again!"

Shanne shook her head, her smile wistful. "Very likely that is so."

A harsh cold effluvium seethed up through Ghyl's veins and there turned to ice. He felt stiff, vaguely terrified: aghast at the prospect of the future. He recovered control of his voice. "You provoke me to all sorts of outrageous conduct."

"No, no," said Shanne in her sweet whisper. "Don't ever consider it! You might be rehabilitated, or whatever dreadful thing they do to you."

Ghyl gave a slow, fateful nod. "There is that chance." He turned to Shanne once more; he took her in his arms, kissed her face, her eyes, her mouth. She sighed, melted against him. Ghyl's mood was now less tender; he felt as old as Damar, wise in the lore of all the worlds.

At last they rose to their feet. Ghyl asked, "Where will you go now?"

"To the pavilion. I must find my father; he will be wondering where I am."

"Won't he be worried?"

"I don't think so."

Ghyl put his hands on the girl's shoulder. "Shanne! Can we go off together, away from Ambroy? To South Continent! Or the Mang Islands! And there live our lives together?"

Shanne once more touched his mouth with her hands. "It would never be feasible."

"And I will never see you more?"

"Never more."

There was a sound behind them, a quiet footstep. Ghyl turned to look, to see a black hulk standing patiently beside the moonlit river.

"Just my Garrion," said Shanne. "Come, let us return to the pavilion."

Ghyl turned away. They walked back along the riverbank. Behind, at a discreet distance, came the Garrion.

CHAPTER 13

At the pavilion Shanne kissed Ghyl on the cheek, then, donning her domino, slipped off through the colored shadows to a group of lords and ladies.

Ghyl watched a moment, then turned away. How different seemed the universe! How strange seemed his life of a week ago! There was Floriel. Ghyl went to him. "Well then, here I am. Where is Sonjaly? Where is Nion?"

Floriel gave a mirthless laugh. "You missed all the fun."

"Oh?"

"Yes. A lord in armor—perhaps you noticed him—took interest in Sonjaly. Nion resented his attentions. When the two went outside to walk along the riverbank Nion ran after them, though really it was no affair of his. Mine, if anyone's. Well, I went behind to watch. Nion challenged the lord; the Garrion seized him, beat him, and threw him in the river. The lord went off with Sonjaly. Nion floated off downstream, splashing and cursing. Splendid! I've seen no more of him."

Ghyl laughed: a caw of such harsh mirth that Floriel looked at him in wonder. "And how did you fare? I saw you earlier with a girl in white."

"Are you ready to leave?"

"Why not? A miserable evening. I'll not come to the County Ball again. It's all froth and frivolity, with not an ounce of true entertainment. Well, let us go."

They walked through the night to the dock, and Floriel sculled the skiff across the river. Damar had set; an ash-colored light welled up into the eastern sky. A lamp flickered in the main room of the cottage. Here sat Nion, huddled under a blanket, drinking tea. He looked up as Floriel and Ghyl entered, and gave a grunt of mingled greeting and disapproval. "So you've finally returned. What kept you so long? Do you know that the Garrion beat me and threw me in the river?"

"It serves you right," said Floriel. He poured tea, handed a cup to Ghyl. The three sat in brooding silence. Ghyl at last made a sound, halfway between a sigh and a groan. "Life at Ambroy is futile. It is life wasted."

"Are you just now becoming aware of that?" asked Nion bitterly.

"Life is probably futile anywhere," remarked Floriel with a sniff.

"That's all that's keeping me at Ambroy," declared Nion. "That, and the fact that I can make a decent living here."

Ghyl clenched his hands around the cup. "If I had any courage—if any of us had courage—we'd go forth to find . . . something."

"What do you mean . . . 'something'?" asked Nion in a cantankerous voice.

"I'm not sure. Something meaningful, something grand. The chance to work a remarkable good, to right a terrible wrong, to do high deeds, to inspire men for all time! Like Emphyrio!"

Nion laughed. "Emphyrio again? We worked him once for what he was worth, which wasn't much."

Ghyl paid no heed. "Somewhere the truth regarding Emphyrio exists. I want to learn the truth. Don't you?"

Floriel, more perceptive than Nion, surveyed Ghyl curiously. "Why does this mean so much to you?"

"Emphyrio has haunted me all my life. My father died on the same account; he thought of himself as Emphyrio. He wanted to bring truth to Ambroy. Why else did he dare so much?"

Nion shrugged. "You'll never grease your pan with 'truth.'" He glanced at Ghyl appraisingly. "The girl you were sitting with—wasn't she a lady?"

"Yes. Shanne." Ghyl uttered the name softly.

"She seemed attractive, judging from her figure. Are you seeing her again?"

"She's going traveling. I'll be left behind."

Nion looked at him with raised eyebrows. He gave a sour little bark of a laugh. "I do believe," he told Floriel, "that the lad's smitten!"

Floriel, still smarting over Sonjaly's faithlessness, was not particularly interested. "I suppose it happens."

Nion addressed Ghyl in an earnest, if condescending, voice. "My dear fellow, you should never take these people seriously! Why do you think they come to the County Ball? No other reason but to have a little fling. They purge themselves of tension and emotion; after all, they live unnatural lives up on those eyries. They detest each other's vanity and arrogance and chill. Hence they come down to the County Ball and warm themselves at the fire of honest passion!"

"Nonsense," muttered Ghyl. "The situation was not at all like this."

"Ha! Did she say she loved you?"

"No."

"Did she show any shyness or reluctance?"

"No."

"Did she agree to see you again?"

"No. But she'll be traveling in a short time. She explained it all to me."

"Oh?" Nion pulled thoughtfully at his chin. "She told you when she was departing?"

"Yes."

"And when will it be?"

Ghyl looked sharply at Nion Bohart, whose voice had suddenly become far too casual. "Why do you ask?"

"I have my reasons. . . . Peculiar that she should be so confiding. They're usually the most secretive of folk. You must have plucked at her heartstrings."

Ghyl gave a hollow laugh. "I doubt if she has a heart."

Nion considered a moment, then looked at Floriel. "Would you be ready?"

Floriel grimaced. "As ready as I'll ever be. But we don't know when they debark, or from where."

"Presumably at the Godero space-port."

"Presumably. But we don't know the boat," Floriel looked at Ghyl. "Did she mention what kind of space-yacht she would travel in?"

"I know the space-yacht."

Nion jumped to his feet. "Do you then? Wonderful! Our problems are solved. What about it? Would you care to join us in a venture?"

"You mean, to steal the space-yacht?"

"Yes. It is an unusual opportunity. We know, or rather you know, the departure date: when the yacht will be fueled and victualed and crewed and ready for space. All we need do is step aboard and take charge."

Ghyl nodded. "What then?"

Nion hesitated a barely perceptible instant. "Well, we'll try to ransom our captives; that's only reasonable."

"They won't ransom themselves any more, they've compacted together."

"So I'm told. Well, if they won't pay, they won't pay. We can drop them off on Morgan or some such spot, and then fly off in search of wealth and adventure."

Ghyl sipped his tea, and looked out at the flowing river. What was left for him in Ambroy? A lifetime of wood-carving and Schute Cobol's admonitions? Shanne? Had she, after all, thought of him as no more than a maudlin brute? If she thought of him at all.

Ghyl winced. He said slowly, "I'd like to take the space-yacht, if only to find the Historian, who knows the entire history of the human race."

Floriel gave an indulgent laugh. "He wants to scrutinize the life of Emphyrio."

"Why not?" asked Nion easily. "This is his privilege. Once we've taken the space-yacht and earned a few vouchers, there's nothing in the way."

Floriel shrugged. "I suppose there's no reason why not."

Ghyl looked from one to the other. "Before I listen to another word, an absolutely fundamental matter: we must agree: no killing, no looting, no kidnaping, no piracy."

Nion laughed in exasperation. "We're pirates the minute we take the space-yacht! Why mince matters?"

"True."

"The lords will be carrying a large sum of money for their expenses," Floriel pointed out. "There is no reason why we should leave that to them."

"I agree there also. Lords' property is fair game. If we steal their space-yacht it is foolishness to boggle at dipping into their pouches. But thereafter we prey on no one, perform no harmful acts; agreed?"

"Yes, yes," said Nion impatiently. "Now then, when does the space-yacht depart?"

"Floriel, what of you?"

"I agree, certainly. All we want is the yacht."

"Very well; a solemn compact. No killing—"

"Unless in self-defense," inserted Nion.

"—no kidnaping, or plunder, or harm."

"Done," said Floriel.

"Done," said Nion.

"The space-yacht leaves in less than a week—a week from yesterday. Floriel knows the craft very well. It is a black and gold Deme, from which long ago we were ejected."

"Well, well, well," marveled Floriel.

"One other point," Ghyl went on. "Assuming that we

succeed in seizing the yacht, who can navigate? Who can operate the engines?"

"No problem there," said Nion. "The lords don't navigate either; they use a crew of Lusch technicians, who will serve us obediently, as long as their salaries are paid."

"So there," said Floriel, "all is decided. The space-yacht is as good as ours!"

"How can we fail?" demanded Nion. "We'll need two or three others, of course: Mael and Shulk, and Waldo Hidle; Waldo will find us our weapons. Wonderful! To a new life for all of us!" He held up his mug; the conspirators toasted their desperate venture in tea.

CHAPTER 14

Ghyl returned to Undle Square with the feeling of revisiting a place he had known long ago. A high overcast shrouded the sky, allowing an umber light to seep into the square. An unnatural silence hung in the air, the stillness before a thunderstorm. Few recipients were aboard, and these hurried to their destinations, cloaks drawn up around their heads, like insects fleeing the light. Ghyl let himself into the shop, closed the door. The familiar odor of shavings and polishing oil came to his nostrils; bots buzzed against the windowpane. As always, Ghyl turned a glance toward Amiante's bench, as if he half-expected someday to find there the dear familiar hulk. He went to his own bench, and for several minutes stood contemplating the screen which now he would never complete.

He had no regrets. Already his old life seemed remote. How dull and constricted seemed that old life! . . . What of the future? It was formless, vacant: a great windy space. He could not begin to imagine the direction of his existence—presuming, of course, that the forthcoming act of piracy turned out successfully. He looked around the shop. His tools and belongings, Amiante's accumulation of oddments—all must be abandoned. Except Amiante's old portfolio, which Ghyl could never give up. He took it from the cabinet, stood holding it irresolutely. It was too large to carry in its present condition. He made a parcel of the most valuable contents, those which Amiante had prized most dearly. As for the rest—he would simply walk away and never return. It was heart-wrenching. There were many memories to this room with the amber-paned windows, the shavings on the floor.

The next morning Nion, Floriel, Mael, and Waldo Hidle came to the shop and the group formulated plans. Nion proposed a scheme which was simple and bold, with all the virtues of directness. He had noticed that Garrion were never halted at the wicket controlling access to the south area of the space-port, but passed back and forth unchallenged. The group would disguise themselves as Garrion and thereby gain access to the avenue along which the space-yachts were parked. They would conceal themselves near the black and gold Deme. When the Lusch crew came aboard, probably with a Garrion or two, the group, with due discretion and minimum violence—this at Ghyl's insistence—would over-power the Garrion, intimidate the crew, and take control of the yacht. Nion and Floriel wanted to wait for the lords, to let them board the ship, to take them as hostages and hold them for ransom. Ghyl argued against this proposal. "In the first place, the longer we wait the greater our chances of fail-ure and rehabilitation. Secondly, the lords won't pay ransom; this is their compact, to protect themselves from kidnaping."

"Bah," said Nion. "They'll pay, don't worry about that. Do you think they'd be all that self-sacrificing? Not much."

Waldo Hidle, a tall, sharp-featured young man, with rust-orange hair and pale yellow eyes, took Ghyl's side. "I'm for taking the ship and leaving fast. Once we make our move we're vulnerable. Suppose a message arrives and we don't make the correct response, or suppose we neglect some tri-fling formality? The patrol would be on us at once."

"That's all very well," said Nion. "Let's assume we escape with the ship. What are we going to use for money? We must be practical. Kidnaping is a means to earning the money."

Floriel added, "If they refuse to pay ransom, as Ghyl sug-gests, then we're no worse off. We'll simply set them down somewhere."

"Also," said Nion, "they'll undoubtedly have sums of money on their persons, which we can use very nicely."

Ghyl could summon no convincing counter-argument, and after a good deal of further discussion, Nion's plan was adopted.

Every day the conspirators met in the shop, to practice the Garrion stance and mode of walking. Waldo Hidle and Nion secured Garrion masks and costumes; thereafter the re-hearsals were done in costume, with each criticizing inac-curacies or falsities in the other's deportment.

On three occasions they paid discreet visits to the space-port and planned their precise mode of action.

The night before the critical day all gathered at the wood-carving shop and tried to sleep, with little success; all were tense.

Before dawn they were awake, to tone their skins the purple-brown of the Garrion, and strap themselves into the now-familiar Garrion harness. Then, muffling themselves in cloaks, they departed.

Ghyl was last to leave. For a moment he stood in the doorway looking back across the familiar old benches and tool racks, tears making his eyes heavy. He shut the door, turned, followed his comrades.

Now they were committed. They were abroad in Garrion costume, which was irregulationary. If they were apprehended they would face a very searching inquiry at the very least.

Overtrend took them to the space-port, each touching his Garrion shoulder to the registry plate. At some time in the future each would be billed for the ride, but none would be on hand to pay: or so they hoped. Coming up into the depot they crossed the echoing old chamber, using their much-practiced Garrion stride. No one glanced twice at them.

At the control wicket came the first test. The guard glanced across the counter with a blank expression, pressed the unlock button. The door slid ajar; the conspirators stalked out upon the south sector of the field.

They marched down the access avenue, past space-yacht after space-yacht, and took up stations behind the nose-block and rear structure of the ship next to the Deme, that same black and gold space-yacht from which Ghyl and Floriel so long ago had been ejected.

Time passed. The sun rose into the sky; a small red and black freighter sank down upon the north sector, to be met by landing authorities.

Nion spoke in a husky voice: "Here they come." He indicated a group coming along the avenue: six Lusch crewmen, two Garrion.

The plan now devolved upon who entered the ship first: the crew or Garrion. The crew would not be armed, but if they witnessed a struggle they would surely raise an alarm. In the optimum situation the crew would board the ship while the Garrion paused outside an extra few seconds to release the nose-chock or some other such small duty.

The optimum situation did not occur. The Garrion mounted the ramp, unlocked the port, turned and stood facing the avenue, as if alert for just such an assault as the conspirators had planned. The crew scrambled up the ramp and entered the ship. The Garrion followed. The port swung closed.

The marauders watched silently, taut with frustration. There had been no opportunity to act. The instant they had showed themselves, the Garrion would have brought weapons to bear.

"Well, then," hissed Nion, "we wait for the lords. Then—we must *act!*"

An hour passed, two hours, the conspirators fidgeting with nervousness. Then along the avenue came a little dray, loaded with gay cases and parcels: personal baggage. The dray halted under the Deme; an after hatch opened, a cargo flat descended, the cases and parcels were transferred and hoisted into the belly of the Deme. The dray returned the way it had come.

The air became heavy with imminence. Ghyl's stomach began to pull and jerk; it seemed that all his life had been spent crouched under a space-yacht's nose-block.

"Here come the lords," muttered Floriel at last. "Everybody back."

Three lords and three ladies came along the avenue. Ghyl recognized Shanne. Behind marched two Garrion. Nion muttered to Floriel on one side of him, to Mael on the other.

The party turned off the avenue, ascended the Deme's boarding ramp. The entry port opened.

"Now!" said Nion. He stepped forth, stalked up the ramp, the others behind him. The Garrion instantly seized their weapons, but Nion and Mael were ready. Energy struck from their guns; the Garrion toppled, rolled to the ground.

"Quick!" snapped Nion to the lords. "Into the ship! Co-operate as you value your lives!"

The lords and ladies, aghast, retreated into the ship; behind came Nion, Mael, and Floriel, then Ghyl and Waldo.

They burst into the saloon. The two Garrion who had come aboard with the crew stood glowering and indecisive; then they rushed forward, clicking their mandibles. Nion, Mael, and Floriel fired their weapons and the Garrion became steaming wads of dark flesh. The ladies began to wail in horror; the lords made hoarse sounds.

From the depot came the wail of a siren, hoarse and wild by turns; it appeared that someone in the tower had glimpsed the attack. Nion Bohart ran to the engine room, waved his weapon at the Luschein crew. "Take the ship aloft! We have taken control; if we are threatened you will die first!"

"Fool!" cried one of the lords. "You will kill us all! The tower has orders to shoot down any seized ships, no matter who is aboard; did you not know that?"

"Quick!" bellowed Nion. "Up with the ship! Or we're all dead!"

"The coils are barely warm; the trans-gain system has not been checked!" wailed the Luschein engineer.

"Take us up—or I'll burn off your legs!"

Up went the ship, weaving and tottering on its unbalanced propulsors, and so perhaps was saved from destruction when the energy guns directed from the tower were brought to bear. Before this, the ship had gained velocity and vanished into space-drive.

CHAPTER 15

Nion Bohart had assumed command of the ship, a fact tacitly accepted by his fellows and enforced upon the lords. He wore his authority with a swashbuckling swagger; but there was no doubting his earnestness, his dedication, and his pure pleasure in the success of the exploit.

He held his weapons upon the lords while Floriel searched them. He found no weapons, nor the large sums of money which had been expected.

"Well then," said Nion in a dire voice. "Where are your funds? Do you carry vouchers or valuta or whatever?"

The lord who owned the ship, a thin-faced saturnine individual in a suit of silver foil and pink velvet, with a gallant hat of silver mesh, turned a sneer of disgust upon Nion. "The money is in our luggage; where else?"

Nion, not at all disturbed by the lord's contempt, shoved his weapons back in his belt. "Names please?"

"I am Fanton the Overtrend. This is my consort, the Lady Radance; this is my daughter, the Lady Shanne."

"Very well. You, sir?"

"I am Ilseth the Spay; my consort, the Lady Jacinth. "

"You, sir?"

"I am Xane the Spay."

"Good. You may all sit, if you are so inclined."

The lords and ladies remained standing a moment; then Fanton muttered something, and the group went to settees along the bulkhead.

Nion looked around the saloon. He gestured to the Garrion corpses. "You, Ghyl, you, Waldo: eject this rubbish."

Ghyl stood stiffly, burning with resentment. Certainly, in any group such as this, there was need for a leader; nonetheless, in Ghyl's opinion, Nion had arrogated this privilege to himself somewhat high-handedly. If now he obeyed the order without complaint, he thereby conceded Nion's authority. If he did not obey, he initiated contention. And he would gain Nion's instant and abiding hatred. So—submit or fight.

He decided to fight.

134

"The emergency is over, Nion. We began this venture as a group of equals; let's keep it that way."

"What's this?" barked Nion. "Do you object to unpleasant work?"

"No. I object to your giving orders in regard to the unpleasant work."

For a tense moment the two faced each other, Nion smiling but obviously discomfited. He snarled, "We can't bicker over every little detail; somebody has to give orders."

"In that case, let's rotate the leadership. Floriel can start, I'll take it next, or Mael, or you or Waldo—it makes no great difference. But let's keep our group an association of equals, rather than a captain and his followers." Ghyl, sensing that now was the appropriate time to seek support, looked around to the others. "Do you fellows agree?"

Waldo spoke first, hesitantly. "Yes, I agree. There is no need for anyone to give orders, as long as we are not faced with emergency."

"I don't like orders," Mael agreed. "As Ghyl says, we're a group. Let's make the decisions together, then act."

Nion looked at Floriel. "What of you?"

Floriel licked his lips. "Well, I'll go along with whatever everyone else thinks."

Nion gave in gracefully. "Good enough. We're a group, we'll act as a group. Still, we've got to have rules and direction, otherwise we fall to pieces."

"No argument there," said Ghyl. "I suggest then that we confine our guests, passengers, prisoners—whatever they are—in staterooms, and hold a conference."

"Very good," said Nion, and then with heavy sarcasm: "Perhaps, Mael, you and Floriel will so confine our guests. I and Waldo, and Ghyl, if he so decides, will eject the corpses."

"A moment before you hold your conference," spoke Lord Fanton. "What are your designs in regard to us?"

"Ransom," said Nion. "As simple as that."

"In that case, you must revise your plans. We will request none. If we did, none would be paid. This is our law. Your piracy is in vain."

"Not altogether," said Nion, "even if what you say is true. We have possession of the ship, which represents wealth. If you pay no ransom we will take you to the man-markets in Wale. The women will go to brothels, the men will work in the mines or gather silicon flowers on the desert. If of course you prefer this to ransom."

" 'Preference' is not involved," said Ilseth the Spay, who seemed less absolute than Fanton. "This is the law, imposed upon us."

Ghyl spoke, to forestall Nion. "We'll discuss the situation at our conference. We intend no harm upon you, if you give us no trouble."

Nion said, "To the staterooms then, if you please."

The ship floated quietly in space, propulsors at rest, while the five young pirates sat at conference.

The question of leadership was first discussed. Nion Bohart was all sweet reason. "In a situation of this sort someone has to act as the coordinator. It is a matter of responsibility, of competence, of confidence and mutual trust. Does anyone want the job of leader? I don't. But I'm willing to tackle it because I feel responsible to the group."

"I don't want to be leader," said Floriel virtuously, with a rather malicious glance toward Ghyl. "I am quite content to let anyone competent take over the job."

Mael grinned uncomfortably. "I don't want the job, but on the other hand I don't want to do the dirty work, to run here and there while somebody plays king."

"Nor I," echoed Waldo. "Perhaps we do not really need a leader. It is easy enough to discuss and reconcile differences and arrive at a consensus."

"It means a constant argument," grumbled Floriel. "Much easier to give the job to a man we know to be competent."

"There won't be arguments if we establish a set of rules and abide by them," said Ghyl. "After all, we are not pirates; we intend no pillage or desperate work."

"Oh?" inquired Nion. "How do you expect to exist? If we don't get ransom money, we have a space-yacht but no means to maintain it."

"Our original compact was explicit," said Ghyl. "We agreed not to kill. Four Garrion are dead, unavoidably I suppose. We agreed to try for ransom; and why not, after all? The lords are parasites and fair game. But most importantly we agreed to use the space-yacht not for pillage or plunder but for travel! To the far worlds all of us have longed to visit!"

"All very well," said Floriel, with a glance at Nion, "but

what do we eat when the provisions run out? How do we pay port fees?"

"We can let the ship for charter, we can convey folk here and there, perform explorations or special ventures. Surely there must be honest profit to be gained from a space-yacht!"

Nion shook his head with a quiet smile. "Ghyl, my friend, this is a cruel universe. Honesty is a noble word, but meaningless. We can't afford to be sentimental. We have committed ourselves; we can't back down now."

"This is not our original agreement!" said Ghyl. "We pledged: no killing; no plunder."

Nion shrugged. "What do the others think?"

Floriel said easily, "We have to live. I have no qualms."

Mael shook his head uncomfortably. "I don't object to theft, especially from the rich. But I don't care to kill, or enslave, or kidnap."

"I feel about the same," said Waldo. "Theft in one way or another is a law of nature; every living thing steals from another, in the process of survival."

A slow, quiet smile was forming on Nion's face. Ghyl cried passionately, "This is not our compact! We agreed to live as honest men, after taking the yacht. To break the compact would be intolerable! How could we trust each other? Did we not embark upon this venture to search for truth?"

" 'Truth'?" barked Nion. "Only a fool would use such a word! What does it mean? I don't know."

"One aspect of truth," said Ghyl, "is the keeping of promises. That is what concerns us most at the moment."

Nion began, "Are you suggesting—" but Mael, jumping to his feet, held up his hands. "Let's not quarrel! It's insanity! We've got to work together."

"Exactly," said Floriel, with a scornful glance toward Ghyl. "We've got to think of the common good, and profit for everyone."

Waldo said, "But let's be honest with each other. No denying that we did make the compact, exactly as Ghyl states."

"Perhaps so," agreed Floriel, "but if four of us wish to make certain changes, must we all be thwarted because of Ghyl's idealism? Remember, the search for 'truth'—"

"Whatever that is," interjected Nion.

"—won't put food in our stomachs!"

"Forget my 'idealism' for a moment," said Ghyl. "I insist only that we keep to the terms of our compact. Who knows? We might do better as honest men than as thieves. And isn't it better not to have to worry about apprehension and punishment?"

"Ghyl's got a sound point there," admitted Waldo. "At least we should give it a try."

"I've never heard of anyone making a good living with only a space-yacht," grumbled Nion. "And be sensible: who's to trouble us if we indulge in a few quiet confiscations?"

"Our compact was clear and definite," Ghyl reminded him. "No theft, no piracy. We've succeeded in our main enterprise: we now own a space-yacht. If five men such as we can't make a good honest living for ourselves, we deserve to starve!"

There was a silence. Nion made a mulish grimace of disgust. Floriel fidgeted and looked up and down, every which way but at Ghyl.

Mael said heavily, "Very well then. Let's give it a trial. If we don't make a go of it, we'll have to try something else—or perhaps split up."

"In that case," demanded Nion, "what of the space-yacht?"

"We could sell it and divide the money. Or cast lots."

"Bah. What a sorry state of affairs."

"How can you say that?" cried Ghyl. "We've succeeded! We've got our space-yacht! What more could we ask?"

Nion turned his back, went to look out the forward port. Floriel said, "We can still try for ransom. I say, tax the lords one at a time; winkle the truth out of them. I can't believe that they won't pay to save themselves from Wale."

"Let's talk to them, by all means," agreed Waldo, anxious to restore the bonds of cooperation and good fellowship.

Lord Fanton was the first brought back to the saloon. Eyes snapping with rage, he looked from one face to the other. "I know what you want: ransom! You will have none."

Nion spoke in a suave voice, "Surely you want to save yourself and your family from the man-markets?"

"Naturally. But I can pay no ransom, nor can my friends. So do your worst. You will get no more wealth from us."

"Only the value of your persons," said Nion. "Very well, return to your stateroom."

Xane the Spay was brought forth, Nion swaggered forward, hands on hips, but Ghyl spoke first. "Lord Xane, we wish to cause no one undue hardship, but we were hoping to collect ransom for your safe return."

Lord Xane held out his hands helplessly. "Hopes are cheap. I also have hopes. Will mine be realized? I doubt it."

"Is it literally true that you can command no ransom?"

Xane the Spay gave an embarrassed laugh. "In the first place, we control very little ready cash."

"What?" demanded Mael. "With 1.18 percent of all the income to Ambroy?"

"Such is the case. Grand Lord Dugald the Boimarc is a strict accountant. After he deducts for expenses, taxes, overhead, and other costs, there is little residue, believe me or not."

"I for one do not believe you," spat Floriel. " 'Expenses,' 'taxes'—do you take us for fools?"

Nion asked in a silky voice, "Where does all the money go? It is a sizable sum."

"You must put your question to Grand Lord Dugald. And remember, our law forbids the payment of as much as a twisted sequin in ransom."

Lord Ilseth the Spay made a similar statement. Like Fanton and Xane, he declared that not a sequin of ransom could be paid.

"Then," said Nion grimly, "we will sell you on Wale."

Ilseth made a despairing gesture. "Isn't this carrying vindictiveness too far? After all, you have Lord Fanton's space-yacht and our funds."

"We want an additional two hundred thousand vouchers."

"Impossible. Do your worst." Ilseth departed the saloon. Nion called after him, "Don't worry; we will!"

Mael said gloomily, "They certainly are an obdurate group."

"Curious that they should plead poverty," mused Ghyl. "What in the world becomes of all their money?"

"I consider the statement an insolent lie," sniffed Floriel. "I feel that we should show them no mercy."

"It certainly seems strange," agreed Waldo.

"They'll bring a thousand vouchers apiece on Wale," said Nion briskly. "Five thousand or better for the girl."

"Mmph," said Floriel. "Nine thousand is a far cry from two hundred thousand, but it's better than nothing."

"So then: to Wale," said Nion. "I'll give orders to the crew."

Ghyl declared, "No, no, no! We agreed to put the lords off on Morgan! These are the terms of our compact!"

Floriel gave a wordless cry of outrage. Nion turned a smiling, sinister face toward Ghyl. "Ghyl, this is the third time you have obstructed the common will."

"The third time, rather, that I have reminded you of your promises," retorted Ghyl.

Nion stood negligently, with folded arms. "You have brought dissension to the group, which is absolutely intolerable." He unfolded his arms and it could be seen that he held a hand-weapon. "An unpleasant necessity but . . ." He aimed the weapon at Ghyl.

Waldo cried, "Have you gone mad?" He struggled to his feet, grabbed for Nion's arm. The weapon discharged, directly into Waldo's open mouth, and he fell forward. Mael, clawing at his own weapon, jumped to his feet; he pointed the gun at Nion, but could not bring himself to shoot. Floriel dodged behind Nion, fired, and Mael spun to the deck. Ghyl leapt back into the engine room, drew his own weapon, aimed at Nion, but held his fire for fear of missing and sending a bolt through the hull. Floriel, against a settee, was more vulnerable; but again Ghyl could not bring himself to fire; this was Floriel, his childhood friend!

Nion and Floriel retreated to the forward part of the saloon. Ghyl could hear them muttering. Behind him the Luschein crew watched with terrified eyes.

Ghyl called out, "You two can't win. I can starve you. I control the engines, the food, the water. You must do as I say."

Nion and Floriel muttered at length together. Then Nion called out, "What are your terms?"

"Stand, with your backs toward me, hands in the air."

"Then what?"

"I'll lock you in a stateroom, put you down on a civilized planet."

Nion laughed harshly. "You fool."

"Starve then," said Ghyl. "Go thirsty."

"What of the lords? The ladies? Do they starve and go thirsty as well?"

Ghyl considered. "They can come aft one at a time to eat, when necessary."

Again came Nion's jeering laughter. "Now I'll tell you our terms. Surrender, and I'll put *you* down on a civilized planet."

"Surrender? What for? You don't have any bargaining power."

"But we do." There was the sound of motion, a scuffle, low voices. Into the saloon walked Lord Xane the Spay, stiffly.

"Halt," said Nion. "Right there." And he raised his voice

to Ghyl. "We have no great bargaining power, perhaps—but we have enough. You dislike killing, so perhaps you'll try to prevent the death of our guests."

"How do you mean?"

"We will kill them, one at a time, unless you agree to our terms."

"You would do no such heartless deed!"

The gun cracked; Lord Xane the Spay collapsed, with his head burned black. "Do you now believe?" called Nion. "Next: the Lady Radance!"

Ghyl wondered: could he run forward and kill the two of them before he himself was killed? No chance whatever.

Nion spoke, "Do you agree? Yes or no?"

"Do I agree to what?"

"Surrender."

"No."

"Very well; we will kill the lords and ladies one by one, then blow a hole in the side of the ship, and all of us will die. You cannot win."

"We will proceed to a civilized planet," said Ghyl. "You may go ashore. These are my terms."

There was more noise, footsteps, a whimper of fear. The Lady Radance staggered into the saloon.

"Wait!" cried Ghyl.

"Will you surrender?"

"I'll agree to this. We will proceed to some civilized planet. The lords, the ladies, and I will go ashore. The ship will be yours."

Nion and Floriel muttered a moment. "Agreed."

The space-yacht descended upon the world Maastricht, fifth planet of the star Capella: a destination chosen after careful and emotion-charged discussion between Lord Fanton, Ghyl, and Nion Bohart.

Air composition and pressure had been justified; those who were to disembark had dosed themselves with toners, ameliorators, and antigens specific against the biochemical complexes of Maastricht.

The saloon port opened, to admit a flood of light. Fanton, Ilseth, Radance, Jacinth, and Shanne went into the entry chamber, alighted, to stand blinking and dazzled.

Ghyl did not dare to cross the saloon. Nion Bohart was vindictive and wicked; Floriel, now completely under his control, was no better. Ghyl retired into the engine room, opened the heavy-goods port. He dropped out parcels of food and water, then the lords' luggage, from which he had previously abstracted all the money: a large sum. Tucking his own bundle of belongings into his jacket, he dropped to the ground, and dodged behind the bole of a nearby tree, prepared for anything.

But Nion and Floriel seemed content to leave well enough alone. The ports closed; the propulsors hummed; the yacht raised into the air, gathered speed, and disappeared.

CHAPTER 16

The gold and black Deme was gone. Solitude was complete. The group stood on a vast savannah, confined somewhat to east and west by low sugar-loaf humps of bald granite or limestone. The sky was a rich soft blue, completely unlike the dusty mauve sky of Halma. An ankle-deep carpet of coarse yellow stalks tipped with scarlet berries spread as far as the eye could reach, the color muting to mustard-ocher in the distance. Here and there stood clumps of dark shrubs, an occasional heavy black tree, all shags and tatters. It soon became apparent that the time was morning. The sun, Capella, hung halfway up the sky, surrounded by a zone of white glimmer: something like the light over an ocean, and the landscape to the east was shrouded in a bright haze.

Well, then, thought Ghyl: here was the far world he had yearned to visit all of his life. He gave a sardonic chuckle. Never in his wildest imaginings had he anticipated being marooned with two lords and three ladies. He appraised them, where they stood in the shade of a sponge bush, the lords still wearing their splendid garments and proud, wide-brimmed hats. Again Ghyl was impelled to a snort of amusement. If he felt discomfited it was clearly nothing compared to the incongruous, almost farcical, spectacle presented by the lords. They spoke quickly among themselves, making nervous gesticulations, looking this way and that, but seeming to bend their most serious attention toward the hills. Now they took note of Ghyl, inspecting him with glares of detestation.

Ghyl went to join them; they moved fastidiously back. Ghyl asked, "Does anyone know where we are?"

"This is Rakanga Steppe, on the planet Maastricht," said Fanton tersely and turned away, as if to exclude Ghyl from the conversation.

Ghyl asked politely, "Are there cities or towns nearby?"

"Somewhere; we do not know where," said Fanton over his shoulder.

Ilseth, a trifle less brusque than Fanton, said, "Your friends did their best to make our lot difficult. This is the wildest section of Maastricht."

"I suggest," said Ghyl, "that we let bygones be bygones. True, I was part of the group which confiscated your ship, but I meant none of you harm. Remember, I saved your lives."

"We are sensible of the fact," said Fanton coldly.

Ghyl pointed off across the far savannah. "I see a watercourse in the distance; at least a line of trees. If we go to this, and if it is a stream, it should eventually lead us to a settlement."

Fanton appeared not to hear and engaged Ilseth in an earnest discussion, both staring toward the hills with an expression almost of longing. The older women muttered together. Shanne looked at Ghyl with an unfathomable expression. Ilseth turned to the ladies. "Best that we verge to the hills, to escape these hellish open plains. With luck we can find a grotto or covered shelter of some kind."

"Aye," said Fanton. "We would not be exposed to the sky during the whole of a strange night."

"Ah no!" whispered Lady Jacinth in a voice of hushed horror.

"Well then, let us be off." Fanton bowed to the ladies, extended his arm in a brave flourish. The ladies, casting apprehensive eyes at the sky, scurried off across the savannah, followed by Lords Fanton and Ilseth.

Ghyl, nonplussed, looked after them. He called out, "Wait! The food and water!"

Fanton spoke over his shoulder: "Bring it."

Ghyl stared in mingled rage and amusement. "What! You want me to carry all of it?"

Fanton paused, inspected the parcels. "Yes, all. Even so, I doubt if there will be sufficient."

Ghyl laughed incredulously. "Carry your own food and water."

Fanton and Ilseth looked around, eyebrows lofted in irritation.

"Another matter." Ghyl pointed toward the hills, where a large, hump-backed black beast stood watching. As they looked, it lifted up on its hindquarters to gaze more intently. "That is a wild beast," said Ghyl. "It is quite possibly ferocious. You have no weapons. If you value your lives, do not march off by yourselves, without food or water."

Ilseth grumbled. "There is something in what he says. We have not much choice."

Fanton grudgingly returned. "Give me the weapon then, and you may carry the provisions."

"No," said Ghyl. "You must carry your own provisions. I am walking north, toward the river, which undoubtedly will lead to a human settlement. If you go to those hills you will suffer hunger and thirst, and will probably be killed by the wild beasts."

The lords frowned up toward the sky, looked north across the open savannah without enthusiasm.

Ghyl said politely, "I discharged your luggage from the yacht. If you have garments more durable, I suggest you change into them."

The lords and ladies paid him no heed. Ghyl divided the provisions into three lots; with vast distaste the lords slung their share of the parcels over their shoulders, and so they set out.

As they trudged across the savannah, Ghyl thought, Twice now I have saved these lords from death. Beyond all doubt, on the instant that I deliver them to civilization, they will denounce me for a pirate. I will be expelled, or whatever the local penalty. So then, what shall I do?

Had Ghyl been less concerned for the future he might have enjoyed the journey across the savannah. The lords were a constant source of wonder. By turns they patronized and insulted Ghyl, then refused to acknowledge his existence. He was continually surprised by their superficiality and petulance, by their almost total inability to come to rational terms with their environment. They were in awe of open spaces and ran to reach the shelter of a tree. Their heritage, so Ghyl decided, was responsible for their conduct. For centuries they had lived like pampered children, required to make no decisions, to meet no emergencies. They were concerned, therefore, with little beyond the immediate moment. Their emotions, though dramatic, were never profound. After the first few hours Ghyl accepted their foibles with equanimity. But how to deliver them safely to civilization and at the same time escape with a whole skin? The prospect of becoming a fugitive on a strange planet caused Ghyl foreboding.

The lords immediately made it clear that they preferred night to day as a time for travel. With disarming candor they informed Ghyl that the spaces seemed not so vast, and the glare of brilliant Capella would thereby be avoided. But a number of sinister beasts roamed the savannah. Ghyl feared one in particular: a sinuous creature twenty feet long with a thin, flat body and eight long legs. This he thought of as "the slinker," from its mode of movement. In the dark it could slide up to them unobserved and seize them in its claws. There were other creatures almost as horrid; short, bounding beasts like metal barrels studded with spikes; giant serpents gliding on a hundred minuscule legs; packs of hairless red wolves, which twice forced the group to climb into trees. So despite the inclination of the lords, Ghyl refused to travel after dark. Fanton threatened to go forward without him, but after hearing a set of ominous calls and hoots decided to remain near the protection of the weapon. Ghyl built a roaring fire under a big sponge tree and the group ate a portion of the food.

Now Ghyl broached the subject which was at the top of his mind. "I am in a peculiar position," he told Fanton and Ilseth. "As you know, I was a member of the group which thrust these inconveniences upon you."

"The fact is seldom out of my mind," said Fanton curtly.

"This then is my dilemma. I meant no harm for you or the ladies. I wanted only your yacht. Now I feel it my duty to help you to civilization."

Fanton, looking into the fire, responded only with a grim and ominous nod.

"If I left you alone," Ghyl went on, "I doubt if you would survive. But I also must think of my own interests. I want your word of honor that if I help you to security you will not denounce me to the authorities."

Lady Jacinth sputtered in outrage. "You dare make conditions? Look at us, our indignities, discomfort, and yet—"

"Lady Jacinth, you misunderstand!" exclaimed Ghyl.

Ilseth made an indifferent gesture. "Very well, I agree. After all, the man has done his best for us."

"What?" demanded Fanton in a passionate voice. "This is the spiteful lout who robbed me of my yacht! I promise only that he'll be well punished!"

"In that case," said Ghyl, "we shall separate, and go different ways."

"As long as you leave the weapon with us."

"Ha! I'll do nothing of the sort."

Ilseth said, "Come, Fanton, be reasonable. This is an unusual situation. We must be large-hearted!" He turned to Ghyl. "As far as I am concerned, the piracy is forgotten."

"And you, Lord Fanton?"

Fanton gave a sour grunt. "Oh, very well."

"And the ladies?"

"They will remain discreet, or so I suppose."

A soft breeze came out of the dark, wafting a vile scent which caused Ghyl a prickling uneasiness. The lords and ladies seemed not to notice.

Ghyl rose to his feet and peered out into the darkness. He turned back to find the lords and ladies already composing themselves for rest.

"No, no!" he said urgently. "For safety we should climb the tree, as high as possible."

The lords gazed stonily at him, making no movement.

"As you wish," said Ghyl. "Your lives are your own." He stoked the fire with the limbs of a dead tree, evoking a peevish complaint from Fanton. "Must you make such a furious blaze? Fire is detestable."

"There are beasts out yonder," said Ghyl. "The fire will at least allow us to see them. And I urge that everyone climb the tree."

"Ridiculous, perched in the branches," declared Lady Radance. "How could we rest? Is there no consideration for our fatigue?"

"You are very vulnerable on the ground," said Ghyl politely. "In the tree you will not rest as well but you will be more secure." He scrambled up into the branches and wedged himself into a high crotch.

On the ground the lords and ladies muttered uneasily. At last Shanne jumped to her feet and climbed the tree. Fanton assisted Lady Radance; together they scrambled to a branch near Ghyl. Lady Jacinth, complaining bitterly, refused to climb higher than a heavy limb ten feet from the ground. Ilseth shook his head in exasperation and perched himself on another branch somewhat higher.

The fire burnt low. From the darkness came a set of thudding sounds, a far wail. Everyone sat quietly.

Time passed. Ghyl dozed fretfully. Halfway through the night he became aware of a vile stench. The fire was almost dead.

There came a sound of heavy slow footsteps. A huge dark creature came padding across the turf. It paused beneath the tree, with one foot in the embers. Then it reached up, plucked Lady Jacinth from the low branch, and carried her off screaming horribly. Ghyl could not see to aim the weapon. All climbed higher and slept no more.

The night was long indeed. Fanton and Ilseth crouched in silence near the top of the tree. Lady Radance made an intermittent fluting sound, like the warbling of a petulant bird; from Shanne came an occasional forlorn wail. The air became cold and clammy with settling dew; Lady Radance and Shanne became still and stiff.

Finally a ribbon of green light formed across the eastern sky, expanding upward to become the rim of a pink suffusion: then a spark of intense white light, then a dazzling cusp, then a disk, as Capella cleared the horizon.

Down from the tree came the haggard group. Ghyl made a fire, which he alone seemed to find cheerful.

After a glum breakfast, the five once more set off toward the north. To Ghyl's perplexity Lord Ilseth displayed neither grief nor shock at the loss of Lady Jacinth, nor did any of the others seem overly concerned. What strange folk! marveled Ghyl. Do they have feelings or do they just play at life? And he listened as the lords and ladies, recovering something of their aplomb, began to converse among themselves, ignoring Ghyl as if he did not exist. Fanton and Ilseth once more gestured toward the hills and began to veer west, until Ghyl called them back to the original course.

About midmorning black clouds boiled up from the south. There were whistling gusts of wind; then a hailstorm surpassing any of Ghyl's experience pelted the travelers with pebbles of ice. Ghyl stood with his arms over his head; the lords and ladies ran back and forth, beating at the hailstones as if they were insects, while Ghyl watched in amazement.

The storm passed as suddenly as it had come; in an hour the sky was clear again; Capella blazed down upon the glistening savannah. But the lords and ladies had become dismal, forlorn, black-hearted. Their wonderful broad-brimmed hats drooped, their slippers were torn, their filigreed garments were stained. Only Shanne, perhaps because of her youth, failed to become venomously cantankerous, and she began to trail back with Ghyl. For the first time since the pirates had taken the ship they spoke together. To Ghyl's utter amazement, he found that she had not recognized him as the young man of the County Ball; indeed she seemed to have forgotten the episode. When Ghyl recalled it to her memory she looked at him in perplexity. "But—what a coincidence! You at the County Ball—and you here now!"

"A strange coincidence," agreed Ghyl sadly.

"Why are you so evil? A pirate, a kidnaper! You seemed so trusting and innocent, if I remember rightly."

"Yes, you remember rightly. I could explain the change, but you would not understand."

"It makes no difference, one way or another. My father will denounce you as soon as we reach civilization. Do you realize that?"

"Last night he and Ilseth agreed not to do so!" cried Ghyl.

Shanne gave him a blank look, and for a space said no more.

At noon they reached the line of trees, which indeed bordered a dank trickle of water. Late in the afternoon they came to the place where the trickle joined a shallow river, with a faint trail along the bank, and not long after the travelers came upon an abandoned village, consisting of a dozen huts of bleached gray timber leaning every which way. In the soundest of these Ghyl proposed to spend the night, and for once the lords agreed without controversy. The inner walls of the shack were sealed with a pasting of old newspapers, printed in characters illegible to Ghyl. He could not restrain a pang of illogical awe at the sight of so much duplication. Here and there were faded pictures: men and women in peculiar costumes, space-ships, structures of a sort unfamiliar to Ghyl, a map of Maastricht, which Ghyl studied half an hour without enlightenment.

Capella sank in a glorious coruscation of gold, yellow, scarlet, vermilion, totally unlike the sad mauves and alebrown sunsets of Halma. Ghyl built a fire on the old stone hearth, which irritated the lords.

"Need it be so warm, so bright, with all those little whips and welts of flame?" complained Lady Radance.

"I suppose he wants to see to eat," said Ilseth.

"But why must the fool toast himself like a salamander?" demanded Fanton crossly.

"If we had maintained a fire last night," Ghyl returned, "and if the Lady Jacinth had used my advice to climb high in the tree, she might be alive now."

At this the lords and ladies fell silent, and their eyes flickered nervously up and down. Then they retreated into the darkest corners of the shack and pressed themselves to the walls: a form of conduct which Ghyl found startling.

During the night something tried the rickety door of the cabin, which Ghyl had barred shut. Ghyl sat up, groped for his gun. From the embers in the fireplace came a faint glow. The door shook again; then outside Ghyl heard steps, and they seemed like the steps of a man. Ghyl followed the sound around the walls to a window. Silhouetted against the starlit sky he thought he saw the shape of a human or near-human head. Ghyl threw a chunk of wood at the head. There was a thud, an exclamation. Then silence. Somewhat later Ghyl heard sounds at the front door: heavy breathing, scratching and scraping, a small squeak. Then once again silence.

In the morning Ghyl went cautiously to the door, opened it with the utmost care. The ground outside seemed undisturbed. There was no booby trap over the lintel, no tripstring no barbs or hooks. What then had been the meaning of last night's activity? Ghyl stood in the doorway, searching the ground for signs of a deadfall.

Lord Ilseth came up behind him. "Stand aside, if you will."

"A moment. Best make sure it's safe."

" 'Safe'? Why should it not be safe?" Ilseth pushed Ghyl aside and strode forth. The ground gave way under his foot. He snatched up his leg, and fixed to his ankle was a plump, purple-cheeked creature like a fat fish or an enormous elongated toad. Ilseth ran wailing through the village, kicking and clawing at the thing on his ankle. Then he gave a sudden great caw of agony and bounded off across the landscape in great wild hops. He disappeared behind a row of feathery black bushes and was seen no more.

Ghyl drew a deep breath. He prodded with a stick and discovered four additional traps. Fanton, watching over his shoulder, said nothing.

Lady Radance and Shanne, moaning in perplexity and terror, at last were prevailed upon to come forth from the hut. The group cautiously departed the dreadful village and set forth along to bank of the little river. For hours they walked in the shade of tremendous trees with fleshy russet trunks and succulent green foliage. Hundreds of small open-work creatures, like monkey skeletons, hung in the branches, rasping and chittering, occasionally dropping twigs; in and out of the sunlight shimmered air-snakes. Behind, from time to time, Ghyl thought he noticed someone or something following. On other occasions a ripple, a turblence in the water, seemed almost to keep pace with thme. At noon these indications disappeared, and an hour later they came to cultivated country. Fields were planted with vines and bushes yielding green pods, bulbs of black pulp, gourds. Soon they entered a small town: huts and cottages of unpainted timber in a long untidy straggle along the river, which at this point connected with a canal. The townspeople were small and brown-skinned, with round heads, black eyes, harsh heavy features. They wore coarse brown and gray cloaks with conical hoods, long-toed leathern slippers; each displayed cabalic signs tattooed on his cheeks. They were not an affable people, and eyed the travelers with surly incuriosity. Fanton spoke to them sharply, and was answered in a language which Ghyl was surprised to find that he could understand, though the accent was thick.

"What town is this?"

"Attegase."

"How far is the nearest large city?"

"That would be Daillie—a matter of two hundred miles."

"How does one reach Daillie in the swiftest manner?"

"There is no swift manner. We have no reason for haste. Five days from now comes the water bus. You can ride to Reso and take the air-float to Daillie. "

"Well then, I must communicate with the authorities. Where is the Spay system?"

"Spay? What is that?"

"The communication device. The telephone, the long-distance radio."

"We don't have any. This is Attegase, not Hyagansis. If you want all those trinkets and gimcracks, you better go there."

"Well then, where is this 'Hyagansis'?" demanded Fanton, at which the man and all the bystanders set up an uproar of laughter. "Isn't any Hyagansis! That's why!"

Fanton sucked in his cheeks, turned away. Ghyl asked, "Where can we stay for five days?"

"Bit of a tavern over by the canal, used by the tipplers and canal-tenders. Maybe old Voma will take care of you. Maybe not, if she's been eating reebers. She gets too bloated to do much more than take care of herself."

The travelers limped to the tavern beside the canal: a strange place built of stained wood, with an enormous high-peaked roof, grotesquely high, from which crooked dormers thrust out in all manner of unexpected angles. One corner was cut away to provide a porch, and diagonally in the corner of this porch, under a tremendous beam, was the entrance.

The tavern was more picturesque from without than within. The innkeeper, a slatternly woman in a black apron, agreed to house the group. She held out her hand, rubbing thumb to forefinger. "Let's see your money. I can't spare good food for those who will not pay, and I've never seen a more clownish set of loons, excuse my saying so. What happened to you? You jump from an air-dock?"

"Something of the sort," said Ghyl. With a side-look toward Fanton, he brought forth the money he had taken from Fanton's luggage. "How much do you require?"

Voma inspected the coins. "What are these?"

"Interplanetary valuta," barked Fanton. "Have you never had off-world visitors?"

"I'm lucky to get some from off the canal and then they want me to write 'em a tab. But don't take me for a dolt, sir, because I'm inclined to outrages of the spirit, and I've been known to pull noses."

"Show us our rooms then. You will be paid, never fear."

The rooms were reasonably clean, but the food—boiled black tubers with a rancid odor—was beyond the noble-folks' eating. Ghyl asked, "These are 'reebers,' no doubt?"

"Reebers they are and right. Tingled with pap and bugspice. I can't touch them myself, or I pay for it."

"Bring us fresh fruit," suggested Fanton. "Or some plain broth."

"Sorry, sir. I can get you a pot of swabow wine, now."

"Very good, bring the wine, and perhaps a crust of bread."

So passed the day. During the course of the evening, Ghyl, sitting in the pot-room, mentioned that they had walked down from the south, after leaving a wrecked air-boat. Conversation halted. "Down from the south? Across the Rakanga?"

"I guess that's what it's called. Something attacked us in the deserted village. Who or what would that be?"

"The Bouns, most likely. Some say they are men. It's why the village is deserted. Bouns got them all. Crafty cruel things."

The following day Ghyl came upon Shanne, strolling alone beside the canal. She made no protest to his joining her, and presently they sat on the bank, shaded from Capella by a tinkling silver and black disk-tree.

For a space they watched the canal boats ease past, powered by billowing square sails, in some cases by electric-field engines. Ghyl reached to put his arms around her, but she primly evaded him.

"Come now," said Ghyl. "When we sat by another river you were not so hoity-toity."

"That was the County Ball: a different case. And you were not then a vagabond and a pirate."

"I thought that the piracy had been put by the boards."

"No indeed. My father plans to denounce you the instant we reach Daillie."

Ghyl raised on his elbow. "But he promised, he gave me his word!"

Shanne looked at him in smiling surprise. "You can't believe that he would hold to an agreement with an underling? A contract is struck between equals. He always intended that you should be punished, and severely."

Ghyl nodded slowly. "I see. . . . Why did you warn me?"

Shanne shrugged, pursed her lips. "I suppose I am perverse. Or coarse. Or bored. There is no one to talk with but you. And I know that you are not innately vicious, like the others."

"Thank you." Ghyl rose to his feet. "I believe I will be returning to the inn."

"I will come along too. . . . In so much light and air I easily become nervous."

"You are a bizarre people."

"No. You are . . . unperceptive. You are not aware of texture and shadows."

Ghyl took her hands and for a moment they stood face to face on the riverbank. "Why not forget you are a lady and come with me? It would mean sharing the life of a vagabond; you would be giving up all that you are accustomed to—"

"No," said Shanne, with a cool smile for the opposite bank of the river. "You must not misunderstand me—as you most obviously do."

Ghyl bowed as formally as he knew how. "I am sorry if I have caused you embarrassment."

He walked back to the inn and sought out Voma. "I am departing. Here"—he gave her coins—"this should cover what I owe."

She gazed slack-mouthed down at the coins. "What of the others? That sour Lord Fanton, he told me that you would pay for all."

Ghyl laughed scornfully. "What kind of a fool do you take me for? See that he pays his score."

"Just as you say, sir." Voma dropped the coins into her pouch. Ghyl went to his room, took his parcel, ran down to the canal, arriving just in time to leap aboard a passing barge. It was piled high with hides and tubs of pickled ree-bers and reeked with an offensive odor; nevertheless it was transportation. Ghyl came to an arrangement with the boat-man and took himself and his parcel to the windward section of the foredeck. He settled himself to watch the passing coun-tryside and considered his circumstances. Travel, adventure, financial independence: this was the life he had yearned for, and this was the life he had achieved. All but the financial in-dependence. He counted his money: two hundred and twelve interplanetary exchange units: the so-called valuta. Enough for three or four months' living expenses, perhaps more if he were careful. Financial independence of a sort. Ghyl leaned back against a bale of hides and, looking up at the slowly passing treetops, mused of the past, the malodorous present, and wondered what the future would bring.

CHAPTER 17

A week later the barge verged alongside a concrete dock on the outskirts of Daillie. Ghyl jumped ashore, half-expecting to be greeted by welfare agents, or whatever the nature of the local police. But the dock was vacant except for a pair of roustabouts handling lines for the barge, and they paid him no heed.

Ghyl found his way to the street. To either side were warehouses and manufacturing plants built of white concrete, panels of blue-green ripple glass, soft convex roofs of white solidified foam: all glaring and flashing in the light of Capella. Ghyl set off to the northeast, toward the center of the city. A fresh wind blew briskly down the street, fluttering Ghyl's ragged clothes and, he hoped, blowing away the reek of hides and reebers.

Today seemed to be a holiday, the sreets were uncannily empty; the clean crisp structures were silent; there was no sound except for the rush of the wind.

For an hour Ghyl walked along the bright street, seeing not a single person. The street lifted over the brow of a low hill; beyond spread the immense city, dominated by a hundred glass prisms of various dimension, some as tall or taller than the skeletal structures of Vashmont Precinct, all glittering and winking in the blaze of Capella-light.

Ghyl set off down the sun-swept street, into a district of cubical white dwellings. Now there were people to be seen: brown-skinned folk of no great stature, with heavy features, black eyes, black hair, not a great deal different from the inhabitants of Attegase. They paused in their occupations to watch as Ghyl passed; he became ever more conscious of the reek of hides, his stained off-world garments, his growth of beard, his untidy hair. Down a side street he spied a market: an enormous nine-sided structure under nine translucent roof panels, each a different color. An aged man, leaning on a cane, gave him counsel and directed him to a money changer's booth. Ghyl gave over five of his coins and received a handful of metal wafers in return. He bought local garments

155

and boots, went to a public rest room, cleaned himself as well as possible, changed clothes. A barber shaved and trimmed him to the local mode; cleaner and less conspicuous. Ghyl continued toward the center of Daillie, riding most of the way on a public slideway.

He took a room at an inexpensive hostelry overlooking the river and immediately bathed in a tall octagonal room paneled with strips of aromatic wood. Three children, shaved bald and of indeterminate sex, attended him. They sprayed him with unctuous foam, beat him with whisks of soft feathers, turned gushes of effervescent water over him, the first warm, the second cold.

Much refreshed, Ghyl resumed his new clothes and sauntered out into the late afternoon. He ate in a riverside restaurant with windows shaded by screens much like those carved at Ambroy. Ghyl's interest, momentarily aroused, waned when he saw the material to be a homogeneous synthetic substance. It occurred to him that he had seen little natural material in Daillie. There were vast masses of foamed concrete, glass, synthetic stuff of one sort or another, but little wood or stone or fired clay, and the lack invested Daillie with a curious sterility, a clean sun- and wind-swept emptiness.

Capella sank behind the glass towers. Dusk fell over the city; the interior of the restaurant grew dim. To each table was brought a glass bulb containing a dozen luminous insects, glowing various pale colors. Ghyl leaned back in his seat and, sipping pungent tea, divided his attention between the luminous insects and the vivacious folk of Daillie at nearby tables. Rakanga Steppe, the Bouns of the deserted village, Attegase, and Voma's Inn were remote. The events aboard the space-yacht were a half-forgotten nightmare. The woodworking shop on Undle Square? Ghyl's mouth moved in a wistful half-smile. He thought of Shanne. How pleasant it would be to have her across the table, chin on knuckles, eyes reflecting the insect lights. What sport they could have exploring the city together! Then traveling on to other strange planets!

Ghyl gave his head a wry shake. Impossible dream. He would be sufficiently fortunate if Lord Fanton, through impatience or press of circumstances, failed to lodge a complaint against him. Had he remained with the group, always within eye-range, a continual reminder of outrages and offenses, nothing could have deterred Lord Fanton from charging him with piracy. But out of sight, out of mind: Lord Fanton might well conceive it beneath his dignity to exert himself against an underling. . . . Ghyl returned to the inn and went to sleep, certain that he had seen the last of Lord Fanton, Lady Radance, and Shanne.

Daillie was a city vast in area and population, with a character peculiarly its own yet peculiarly fugitive and hard to put a name to. The components were readily identifiable: the great expanses of sun-dazzled streets constantly swept by wind; the clean buildings essentially homogeneous in architecture, cleverly built of synthetic substances: a population of mercurial folk who nevertheless gave the impression of self-restraint, conventionality, absorption in their own affairs. The space-port was close to the center of the city; ships from across the human universe came to Daillie but seemed to arouse little interest. There were no enclaves of off-world folk, few restaurants devoted to off-world cuisines; the newspapers and journals concerned themselves largely with local affairs: sports, business events and transactions, the activities of the Fourteen Families and their connections. Crime either was nonexistent or purposely ignored. Indeed, Ghyl saw no law enforcement apparatus: no police, militia, or uniformed functionaries.

On the third day of his stay, Ghyl moved to a less expensive hostelry near the space-port; on the fourth day he learned of the Civic Bureau of Information, to which he immediately took himself.

The clerk noted his requirements, worked a few moments at an encoding desk, then punched buttons on a sloping keyboard. Lights blinked and flashed, a strip of paper was ejected into a tray. "Not much here," the clerk reported. "Enverios, a pathologist of Gangalaya, died last century. H.I. . . . No? Here's an Emphyrio, early despot of Alme, wherever that is. H.I. Is that you man? There's also an Enfero, a Third Era musician."

"What of Emphyrio, despot of Alme? Is there further information?"

"Only what you have heard. And the H.I. reference, of course."

"What is 'H.I.'?"

"The Historical Institute of Earth, which provided the item."

"The Institute could provide more information?"

"So I would suppose. It has detailed records of every important event in human history."

"How can I get this information?"

"No problem whatever. We'll put through a research requisition. The charge is thirty-five bice. There is, of course, a wait of three months, the schedule of the Earth packet."

"That's a long time."

The clerk agreed. "But I can't suggest anything quicker— unless you go to Earth yourself."

Ghyl departed the Bureau of Information and rode by surface car to the space-port. The terminal was a gigantic half-bubble of glass surrounded by green lawn, white concrete runways, parking plats. Magnificent! thought Ghyl, recalling the dingy space-port of Ambroy. Nonetheless, he felt a lack. What could it be? Mystery? Romance? And he wondered if the lads of Daillie, visiting their space-port, could feel the awe and wonder that had been his when he had skulked the Ambroy space-port with Floriel . . . Perfidious Floriel. The train of thought thus stimulated set Ghyl to wondering about Lord Fanton. He had barely set foot into the terminal when his speculations were resolved. Hardly fifty feet away stood Shanne. She wore a fresh white gown, silver sandals; her hair was glossy and clean; nevertheless, she herself seemed haggard and worn, and her complexion showed an unhealthy pink flush.

Making himself inconspicuous behind a stanchion, Ghyl sought around the terminal. At a counter stood Lord Fanton and Lady Radance, both harsh and gaunt, as if even now the hardships they had undergone preyed on them. They completed their transaction; Shanne joined them; the three moved off across the terminal, conspicuous even here, where travelers from half a hundred worlds mingled, for their aloofness and withdrawal: for the Difference!

Ghyl now felt assured that Lord Fanton had not denounced him to the authorities: in fact, Fanton probably believed that Ghyl had departed the planet.

Keeping a wary lookout, Ghyl conducted his own business. He learned that any of five different shipping lines would convey him to Earth, in whatever degree of luxury and style he chose. Minimum fare was twelve hundred bice: far more than the sum in Ghyl's possession.

Ghyl departed the space-port and returned to the center of Daillie. If he wished to visit Earth he must earn a large sum of money, though by what means he had not the slightest idea. Perhaps he would simply request the Bureau of Information to secure the information he sought. . . . Thus musing, Ghyl strolled along the Granvia, a street of luxury shops dealing in all variety of goods, and here he chanced upon an object which diverted him completely from his previous concerns.

The object, a carved screen of noble proportions, occupied a prominent position in the display window of Jodel Heurisx, Mercantile Factor. Ghyl stopped short, approached the window. The screen had been carved to represent a lattice festooned with vines. Hundreds of small faces looked earnestly forth. REMEMBER ME, read the plaque. Near the lower right-hand corner Ghyl found his own childhood face. Close at hand, the face of his father, Amiante, peered forth.

Ghyl's gaze seemed to blur; he looked away. When once more he could see, he returned to study the screen. The price was marked at four hundred and fifty bice. Ghyl converted the sum into valuta, then into welfare vouchers. He performed the calculation again. A mistake, surely: only four hundred and fifty bice? Amiante had been paid the equivalent of five hundred bice: little enough, certainly, considering the pride and love and dedication which Amiante gave his screens. Curious, thought Ghyl; curious indeed. In fact—astonishing.

He entered the shop; a clerk in a black and white robe of a mercantile functionary approached him. "Your will, sir?"

"The screen in the window—the price is four hundred and fifty bice?"

"Correct, sir. Somewhat costly, but an excellent piece of work."

Ghyl grimaced in puzzlement. Going to the cabinet, he inspected the screen carefully, to learn if it might have been damaged or misused. It seemed in perfect condition. Ghyl peered close, then all his blood turned cold and seemed to drain to his feet. He turned slowly to the clerk. "This screen is a reproduction."

"Of course, sir. What did you expect? The original is priceless. It hangs in the Museum of Glory."

Jodel Heurisx was an energetic, pleasant-faced man of early middle age, stocky, strong, and decisive in his manner. His office was a large room flooded with sunlight. There was little furniture: a cabinet, a table, a sideboard, two chairs, and a stool. Heurisx half-leaned, half-sat on the stool; Ghyl perched on the edge of a chair.

"Well then, young man, and who are you?" asked Heurisx.

Ghyl had difficulty framing a coherent statement. He blurted, "The screen in your window, it is a reproduction."

"Yes, a good reproduction: in pressed wood rather than plastic. Nothing as rich as the original, of course. What of it?"

"Do you know who carved the screen?"

Heurisx, watching Ghyl with a speculative frown, nodded. "The screen is signed 'Amiante.' He is a member of the Thurible Cooperative, no doubt a person of prestige and wealth. None of the Thurible goods come cheap, but they are all of superlative quality."

"May I ask from whom you obtained the screen?"

"You may ask, I will answer: from the Thurible Cooperative."

"It is a monopoly?"

"For such screens, yes."

Ghyl sat a half-minute, chin resting on his chest. Then: "Suppose that someone were able to break the monopoly?"

Heurisx laughed and shrugged. "It is not a question of breaking a monopoly, but destroying what appears to be a strong cooperative organism. Why, for instance, should Amiante care to deal with a newcomer when he already has a good thing going for himself?"

"Amiante was my father."

"Indeed? 'Was,' did you say?"

"Yes. He is dead."

"My condolences." And Jodel Heurisx inspected Ghyl with cautious curiosity.

"For carving that screen," said Ghyl, "he received about five hundred bice."

Jodel Heurisx leaned back in shock. "What? Five hundred bice? No more?"

Ghyl gave a snort of sad disgust. "I have carved screens for which I earned seventy-five vouchers. About two hundred bice."

"Astounding," murmured Jodel Heurisx. "Where is your home?"

"The city Ambroy on Halma, far from here, beyond Mirabilis."

"Hmm." Heurisx plainly knew nothing of Halma, or perhaps of the great Mirabilis Cluster. "The craftsmen of Ambroy sell, then, to Thurible?"

"No. Boimarc is our trade organization. Boimarc must deal with Thurible."

"Perhaps they are one and the same," suggested Heurisx. "Perhaps you are being cheated by your own folk."

"Impossible," muttered Ghyl. "Boimarc sales are verified by the Guild-masters, and the lords take their percentage from this sum. If there were peculation, the lords would be cheated no less than the underlings."

"Someone enjoys vast profits," mused Heurisx. "So much is clear. Someone at the top end of the monopoly."

"Suppose then, as I asked before, you were able to break the monopoly?"

Heurisx tapped his chin with his finger. "How would this be accomplished?"

"We would visit Ambroy in one of your ships and buy from Boimarc."

Heurisx held up his hands in protest. "Do you take me for a mogul? I am small beer compared with the Fourteen. I own no space-ships."

"Well then, can a space-ship be chartered?"

"At considerable expense. Of course the profit likewise would be large—if the Boimarc group would sell to us."

"Why should they not? If we offer double or triple the previous rate? Everyone gains: the craftsmen, the guilds, the welfare agents, the lords. No one loses but Thurible, who has enjoyed the monopoly long enough."

"It sounds reasonable." Heurisx leaned back against the table. "How do you envisage your own position? As of now you have nothing further to contribute to the enterprise."

Ghyl stared incredulously. "Nothing but my life. If I were caught I'd be rehabilitated."

"You are a criminal?"

"In a certain sense."

"You might do best to disengage yourself at this moment."

Ghyl could feel the warmth of anger on the skin of his face; but he carefully controlled his voice. "Naturally I would like financial independence. But no matter about that. My father was exploited; he was robbed of his life. I want to destroy Thurible. I would be happy to achieve no more than this."

Heurisx gave a short bark of a laugh. "Well, you can be assured I do not care to cheat you or anyone else. Suppose, after due reflection, that I agree to provide the ship and assume all financial risks—then I believe that I should receive two-thirds of the net profit, and you one-third."

"That is more than fair."

Come back tomorrow and I'll communicate my decision."

Four days later Jodel Heurisx and Ghyl met at a riverside café where the factors of Diallie consummated much of their business. With Heurisx was a young man, ten years or so older than Ghyl, who had little to say.

Heurisx said, "I have obtained the use of a ship: the *Grada*. It is larger than I had intended; on the other hand it costs no charter fee, and in fact belongs to my brother, Bonar Heurisx." He indicated his companion. "We will participate jointly in the venture; he will convey a cargo of specialty instruments to Luschein, on Halma, where, according to Rolver's Directory, there is a ready market for such articles. There wil be no great profit, but enough to defer costs. Then, you and he will take the *Grada* to Ambroy, to buy craft-goods in the manner you describe. The financial risk is reduced to a minimum."

"My personal risk unfortunately remains."

Heurisx tossed a strip of enamel upon the table. "This, when impressed with your photograph, will identify you as Tal Gans, resident of Daillie. We will dye your skin, depilate your scalp, and fit you with fashionable clothing. No one will recognize you, unless it be an intimate friend, whom you will no doubt take pains to avoid."

"I have no intimate friends."

"I consign you then to the care of my brother. He is somewhat more wayward then myself, somewhat less cautious: in short, just the man for such a venture." Jodel Heurisx rose to his feet. "I will leave the two of you together, and I wish you both good luck."

CHAPTER 18

Strange to return to Ambroy! How familiar and dear, how remote and dim and hostile was the ramshackle half-ruined city!

They had found no difficulties at Luschein, though the instruments sold for considerably less than Bonar Heurisx had anticipated, causing him despondency. Then up and around the planet, over the Deep Ocean, north beside the Baro Peninsula and Salula, out over the Bight, with the low coast of Fortinone ahead. For the last time Ghyl rehearsed the various aspects of his new identity. Ambroy spread below. The *Grada* accepted a landing program from the control tower and descended upon the familiar space-port.

The landing formalities at Ambroy were notoriously tedious; two hours passed before Ghyl and Bonar Heurisx walked through the wan midmorning sunlight to the depot. Calling the Boimarc offices by Spay, Ghyl learned that, while Grand Lord Dugald was on the premises, he was extremely busy, and could not be seen without prior appointment.

"Explain to Lord Dugald," said Ghyl, "that we are here from the planet Maastricht to discuss the Thurible marketing organization; that it will be to his advantage to see us immediately."

There was a wait of three minutes, after which the clerk somewhat sourly announced that Lord Dugald would be able to give them a very few minutes if they would come immediately to the Boimarc offices.

"We will be there at once," said Ghyl.

By Overtrend they rode out to the far verge of East Town, a district of abandoned streets, flat areas strewn with rubble and broken glass, a few buildings yet occupied: a forlorn region not without a certain dismal beauty.

In a thirty-acre compound were two structures, the Boimarc administrative center and the Associated Guilds warehouse. Ghyl and Bonar Heurisx, passing through a portal in the barbed fence, proceeded to the Boimarc offices.

From a cheerless foyer they were admitted to a large room

where twenty clerks worked at desks, calculators, filing devices. Lord Dugald sat in an alcove with glass walls, slightly elevated from the main floor, and, like the other Boimarc functionaries, appeared to be extremely busy.

Ghyl and Bonar Heurisx were taken to a small open area directly before Lord Dugald's alcove, under his gaze to a somewhat uncomfortable degree. Here they waited, on cushioned benches. Lord Dugald, after a swift glance through the glass, paid them no heed. Ghyl examined him with vast curiosity. He was short and heavy and sat slumped in his chair like a half-filled sack. His black eyes were close together; tufts of dark gray hair rose above his ears; there was an unnatural purplish overtone to his complexion. He was, almost comically, the realization of a caricature Ghyl had somewhere seen . . . of course! Lord Bodbozzle, of Holkerwoyd's Puppets! And Ghyl worked hard to restrain a grin.

Ghyl watched while Lord Dugald examined, one after another, yellow sheets of parchment, apparently invoices or requisitions, and stamped each with a handsome instrument topped with a great globe of polished red carnelian. The invoices, so Ghyl noted, were prepared by a clerk sitting before an illuminated inventory board, of a sort he had seen at Daillie; the stiff sheets so prepared were then presented to Lord Dugald for the validation of his personal stamp.

Lord Dugald approved the last of the requisitions and hung the stamp by its carnelian globe under his desk. Only then did he make a curt signal to indicate that Bonar Heurisx and Ghyl were to come forward.

The two stepped up into the glass-enclosed alcove; Lord Dugald signaled them to seats. "What is this of Thurible Cooperative? Who are you? Traders, you say?"

Bonar Heurisx spoke carefully. "Yes, this is correct. We have only just arrived from Daillie, on Maastricht, in the *Grada.*"

"Yes, yes. Speak then."

"Our research," Bonar Heurisx went on more briskly, "leads us to believe that Thurible Cooperative is performing inefficiently. To be brief, we can do a better job with considerably greater return for Boimarc. Or if you prefer, we will buy directly from you, at a schedule also yielding greatly augmented profits."

Lord Dugald sat immobile except for his eyes, which flicked back and forth, from one to the other. Curtly he responded, "The suggestion is not feasible. We enjoy excellent relations with our various trading organizations. In any case, we are bound by long-term contracts."

"But the system is not to your best advantage!" Bonar protested. "I will offer new contracts at double payment."

Lord Dugald rose to his feet. "I am sorry. The subject is not open to discussion."

Bonar Heurisx and Ghyl, crestfallen, looked at him. "Why not give us a try, at least?" argued Ghyl.

"Absolutely not. Now, if you will please excuse me . . ."

Outside, walking west along Huss Boulevard, Bonar said despondently, "So much for that. Thurible holds a long-term contract." After a moment's reflection he grumbled, "Obvious, of course. We're beaten."

"No," said Ghyl. "Not yet. Boimarc has contracted with Thurible, but not the guilds. We shall go to the source of the merchandise, and bypass Boimarc."

Bonar Heurisx gave a skeptical snort. "To what avail? Lord Dugald spoke with clear authority."

"Yes, but he has no authority over the recipients. The guilds are not bound to sell to Boimarc, craftsmen need not produce for the guilds. Anyone can go noncup as he wishes, if he cares to lose his welfare benefits."

Bonar Heurisx shrugged. "I suppose that it does no harm to try."

"Exactly my feeling. Well then, first to the Scriveners' Guild, to inquire about hand-crafted books."

They walked south through the old Merchants' Quarter into Bard Square, upon which most of the guild-houses fronted. Bonar Heurisx, who had been glancing over his shoulder, presently muttered, "We're being followed. Those two men in black capes are watching our every move."

"Special Agents," said Ghyl with a glum smile. "Hardly a surprise. . . . Well, we're doing nothing irregulationary, as far as I know. But I'd better not appear too well acquainted with the city."

So saying he halted, looked around Bard Square with an expression of perplexity, and asked directions of a passerby who pointed out the Scriveners' Hall, a tall structure of black and brown brick with four looming gables of ancient timber. Evincing uncertainty and hesitation for the benefit of the Special Agents, Ghyl and Bonar Heurisx considered the building, then chose one of the three portals and entered.

Ghyl had never before visited the Scriveners' Hall and was

taken aback by the almost indecorous volume of chatter and badinage, deriving from apprentice classes in rooms to either side of the foyer. Climbing a staircase hung with samples of calligraphy, the two found their way to the Guild-master's office. In the anteroom sat a score of fidgeting, impatient scriveners, each cluthing a case containing his work-in-progress.

In dismay Bonar Heurisx looked at the crowd. "Must we wait?"

"Perhaps not," said Ghyl. He crossed the room, knocked on a door which swung open to reveal an elderly woman's peevish countenance. "Why do you pound?"

Ghyl spoke in his best Daillie accent. "Please announce us to his excellency, the Guild-master. We are traders from a far world; we wish to arrange new business with the scriveners of Ambroy."

The woman turned away, spoke over her shoulder, then looked back to Ghyl. "Enter, if you please."

The Scriveners' Guild-master, a waspish old man with a wild ruff of white hair, sat behind a vast table littered with books, posters, calligraphic manuals. Bonar Heurisx stated his proposal, to the Guild-master's startlement. "Sell you our manuscripts? What an idea! How could we be sure of our money?"

"Cash is cash," declared Bonar.

"But—how absurd! We use a long-established method; this is how we have derived our livelihood for time out of mind."

"All the more reason then to consider a change."

The Guild-master shook his head. "The current system works well; everyone is satisfied. Why should we change?"

Ghyl spoke. "We will pay double the Boimarc rate, or triple. Then everyone would be even more satisfied."

"Not so! How would we calculate the welfare deduction, the special assessments? These are handled now with no effort on our part!"

"With all charges met you would still receive twice your previous income."

"What then? The craftsmen would become avaricious. They would work two times less carefully and two times as fast, hoping for financial independence or some such nonsense. They know now that they must use scrupulous care to secure an Acme or a First. If they were teased by prosperity and set up a great clamor, what of our standards? What of our quality? What of our future markets? Should we throw away security for a few paltry vouchers?"

"Well then, sell us your Seconds. We will take them across the galaxy and dispose of them there. The craftsmen will double their income and your present markets are safe."

"And thereafter produce only Seconds, since they sell as well as Firsts? The same considerations apply! Our basic stock-in-trade is high quality; if we abandon this principle we debase our merchandise and become mere triflers."

In desperation Ghyl exclaimed, "We'll then, let us be the agent for your sales. We will pay the going rate, we will pay twice this sum into a fund for the benefit of the city. We can clear ruined areas, finance institutes and entertainments."

The Guild-master glared in outrage. "Are you attempting to deceive me? How can you do so much on the output of the scriveners?"

"Not just the scriveners alone! On the output of all the guilds!"

"The proposal is far-fetched. The old way is tried and true. No one becomes financially independent, no one becomes pompous and self-willed; everyone works meticulously and there is no contention or complaint. Once we introduce innovation, we destroy equilibrium. Impossible!"

The Guild-master waved them away; the two left the Guild Hall in discouragement. The Special Agents standing nearby, discreet rather than surreptitious, watched with open curiosity.

"Now what?" asked Bonar Heurisx.

"We can try the other important guilds. If we fail, at least we will have tried our hardest."

Bonar Heurisx agreed to this; they continued to the Jewelers' Syndicate, but when finally they gained the ear of the Guild-master and made their proposal, the response was as before.

The Glassblowers' Guild-master refused to speak to them; at the Lute-makers' they were referred to the Guild-masters Conclave, eight months hence.

The Enamel, Faience, and Porcelain-workers' Guild-master put his head into an anteroom long enough to hear their proposition, said "No" and backed out.

"The Wood-carvers' Guild remains," said Ghyl. "It is probably the most influential; if we receive a negative response there, we might as well return to Maastricht."

They crossed Bard Square to the long low building with

the familiar façade. Ghyl decided that he dared not go in. The Guild-master, while no intimate acquaintance, was a man with a keen eye and a sharp memory. While Ghyl waited in the street Bonar went into the office alone. The Welfare Specials who had been following approached Ghyl. "May we ask why you are visiting the Guild-masters? It seems a curious occupation for persons new to the planet."

"We are inquiring after trading possibilities," said Ghyl shortly. "The Boimarc Lord would not listen to us; we thought to try the guilds."

"Mmf. The Welfare Agency would disapprove such an arrangement in any case."

"It does no harm to try."

"No, of course not. Where is your native planet? Your speech is almost that of Ambroy."

"Maastricht."

"Maastricht, indeed."

The after-work movement to the Overtrend kiosk had begun; people were pushing past. A lank, well-remembered female figure loped by, then stopped short, turned to stare. Ghyl looked away. The young woman craned her neck, peered into Ghyl's face. "Why, it's Ghyl Tarvoke!" cawed Gedée Anstrut. "What in the world are you doing in that outlandish costume?"

The Welfare Specials leaned forward. One cried, "Ghyl Tarvoke? Have I not heard that name?"

"You have made a mistake," Ghyl told Gedée.

Gedée drew back, her mouth open. "I forgot. Ghyl Tarvoke went off with Nion and Floriel . . . oh my!" She put her hand to her mouth, backed away.

"Just a moment, please," said the Welfare Special. "Who is Ghyl Tarvoke? Is that your name, sir?"

"No, no, of course not."

"Yes it is too!" shrieked Gedée. "You're a filthy pirate, a murderer. You are the terrible Ghyl Tarvoke!"

At the Welfare Agency, Ghyl was thrust before the Social Problems Clinic. The members, sitting in a long box behind desks of iron, examined him with expressionless faces.

"You are Ghyl Tarvoke."

"You have seen my identification."

"You have been recognized by Gedée Anstrut, by Welfare Agent Schute Cobol, and by others as well."

"As you like then. I am Ghyl Tarvoke."

The door opened; into the room came Lord Fanton the Spay. He approached, stared into Ghyl's face. "This is one of them."

"Do you admit to piracy and murder?" the chairman of the Social Clinic asked Ghyl.

"I admit to confiscating the ship of Lord Fanton."

" 'Confiscate'? A pretentious word."

"My ambitions were not ignoble. I intended to learn the truth of the Emphyrio legend. Emphyrio is a great hero; the truth would inspire the people of Ambroy, who are sorely in need of truth."

"This is beside the point. You are accused of piracy and murder."

"I committed no murder. Ask Lord Fanton."

Lord Fanton spoke in a pitiless voice: "Four Garrion were killed, I know not by which of the pirates. Tarvoke stole my money. We made a terrible march during which the Lady Jacinth was devoured by a beast and Lord Ilseth was poisoned. Tarvoke cannot avoid responsibility for their deaths. Finally he left us stranded in a squalid village without a check. We were forced to make the most unpleasant compromises before we reached civilization."

"Is this true?" the chairman asked Ghyl.

"I saved the lords and ladies from slavery and from death, several times."

"But you originally put them into the predicament?"

"Yes."

"No more need be said. Rehabilitation is denied. You are sentenced to perpetual expulsion from Ambroy, via Bauredel. Expulsion will occur at once."

Ghyl was taken to a cell. An hour passed. The door opened; an agent motioned to him. "Come. The lords want to question you."

Two Garrion took Ghyl into custody. He was thrust into a sky-flitter, conveyed up through the sky toward Vashmont. Down to an eyrie the flitter descended, landing upon a blue-tiled terrace. Ghyl was taken within.

His clothes were removed; he was led stark naked into a high room at the top of a tower. Three lords came into the room: Fanton the Spay, Fray the Underline, and Grand Lord Dugald the Boimarc.

"You have been a busy young man," said Dugald. "Exactly what did you have in mind?"

"Breaking the trade monopoly which strangles the folk of Ambroy."

"I see. What is this hysterical yammer in regard to 'Emphyrio'?"

"I am interested in the legend. It holds a special meaning for me."

"Come, come!" demanded Dugald with surprising sharpness. "This cannot be truth! We demand that you be frank!"

"How do I help myself telling other than the truth?" asked Ghyl. "Or anything but untruth, for that matter."

"You are quick as mercury!" stormed Dugald. "You shall not evade us, I warn you! Tell us all, or we will be forced to process you, so that you cannot help yourself."

"I have told the truth. Why do you not believe me?"

"You know why we do not believe you!" And Dugald motioned to the Garrion. They seized Ghyl, propelled him, sick and trembling, through a narrow trapezoidal portal into a long narrow room. They seated him in a heavy chair, clamped him so that he could not move.

Dugald said, "Now we shall proceed."

The inquiry was over. Dugald sat spraddled-legged, looking at the floor. Fray and Fanton stood across the room studiously avoiding each other's eyes. Dugald suddenly turned to stare at them. "Whatever you heard, whatever you presumed, whatever you even conjectured must be forgotten. Emphyrio is a myth; this young would-be Emphyrio will shortly be less than a myth." He signaled the Garrion. "Return him to the Welfare Agency. Recommend that expulsion occur at once."

A black air-wagon waited at the rear of the Welfare Agency. Wearing only a white smock, Ghyl was brought forth, thrust into the air-car. The port clanged shut; the air-car throbbed, lifted, and swept off to the north. The time was late afternoon; the sun wallowed in a bank of yeast-colored clouds; a wan and weary light bathed the landscape.

The air-car bumped to a landing beside a concrete wall which marked the Bauredel frontier. A brick road between two subsidiary walls led up to an aperture in the boundary wall. A two-inch stripe of white paint marked the exact Fortinone-Bauredel boundary. Immediately behind the stripe the aperture was stopped by a plug of concrete stained and spotted a horrid dull brown.

Ghyl was seized and turned out upon the brick road, between the walls which led to the frontier. A Welfare Special clapped on the traditional broad-brimmed black hat and in a portentous voice read the banishment decree: "Depart from our cherished land, oh evil man who have been proved guilty of great harm! Glorious Finuka has proscribed killing throughout the cosmic realm; thank Finuka then for the mercy to be bestowed upon you, more than you showed your own victim! You are then to be banished perpetually, and for all time, from the territory of Fortinone, and into the land of Bauredel. Do you care to leap a final rite?"

"No," said Ghyl in a husky voice.

"Go then as best you may, go with Finuka's aid into the land of Bauredel!"

A great concrete piston, entirely filling the alley, moved forward, thrusting Ghyl toward that single inch of Bauredel territory available for his occupancy.

Ghyl backed up against the piston, planted his feet against the crumbling brick. The piston thrust forward. Sixty feet to the border. A film of sunlight, pale as lymph, slanted into the avenue, outlining uneven edges of the brick, framing the concrete plug of the portal with a black shadow.

Ghyl stared at the bricks. He ran forward, tugged at a brick, then another, then another, until his fingernails broke and his fingertips were bloody. By the time he found a loose brick, the piston had denied him all but forty feet of avenue. But after the first brick came up, others pulled up without difficulty. He rushed to carry the bricks to the wall, stacked them into a pile, ran back for more.

Bricks, bricks, bricks: Ghyl's head pounded, he gasped and wheezed. Thirty feet of avenue, twenty feet, ten feet. Ghyl scrambled up the pile of bricks; they collapsed below him; frantically he stacked them again, with the piston looming over his shoulder. Up once more, and as the pile gave way he scrambled to the top of the wall. The piston thrust upon the bricks. A crunch, a crush: the bricks compressed into a friable red cake.

Ghyl lay flat on top of the wall, concealed by the walls of the avenue and by the piston, ready to drop over into Bauredel territory should the welfare agents see fit to investigate.

Ghyl lay flat as a limpet. The sun fell behind clouds; sunset was a somber display of dark yellow, watery browns. A cold breeze blew in across the waste.

Ghyl could hear no sound. The machinery of the piston

was silent. The Welfare Specials had departed. Ghyl rose cautiously to his knees, peered in all directions. Bauredel to the north was dark: a waste swept by a sighing wind. To the south a few far lights glimmered.

Ghyl rose to his feet, stood swaying. The air-car had departed; the shack which housed the piston machinery was dark, but Ghyl was only half-convinced that he was alone. The area was pervaded with terror. The thin wailing of the wretches expelled in the past still seemed to hang in the air.

Ghyl looked south toward Ambroy, forty miles distant, where the *Grada* represented security.

Security? Ghyl gave a hoarse laugh. He wanted more than security. He wanted vengeance: retribution for years upon years of fraud, dreary malice, the sadness of wasted lives. He dropped to the ground and started south across the barrens, toward the lights of the village. His legs, at first limp, regained their strength.

He came to a fenced pasture, where biloa stalked sedately back and forth. In the dark, when aroused, biloa had been known to attack men. Ghyl veered around the pasture and presently came to an unpaved road, which he followed to the village.

He halted at the edge of town. The white smock rendered him conspicuous: if seen he would be recognized for what he was, and the local welfare agent would be summoned. . . . Ghyl moved stealthily through the shadows, down a side lane and to the rear of the town's beer garden, where he conducted a careful reconnaissance. Dropping to his hands and knees, he crawled around the periphery to where a portly gentleman had draped his beige and black cloak over the railing. While the gentleman engaged the barmaid in conversation, Ghyl took the cloak, and, retreating under the trees, threw it over his shoulders and, drew the hood over his head, to hide his Daillie haircut. Across the square he noted an Overtrend station with a concrete rail receding to the south.

Hoping that the portly gentleman would not immediately notice the loss of his cloak, Ghyl walked briskly to the station.

Three minutes later a car arrived; with a last look over his shoulder toward the beer garden, Ghyl stepped aboard and was whisked south. Mile after mile after mile: into Walz and Batra, then Elsen and Godero. The car halted; Ghyl stepped out upon the slideway, was carried to the escalator, raised and discharged into the space terminal. He swung back the hood of the stolen cloak, advanced with a forthright tread to the north gate. The control officer stepped forward. "Identification, sir?"

"I have lost it," said Ghyl, striving for a Daillie accent. "I am from the *Grada*—that ship yonder." He leaned over the book. "Here is my signature: Tal Gans. This official here"—Ghyl indicated a clerk, who stood nearby—"passed me through the gates."

The guard turned to the clerk indicated. "Correct?"

"Correct."

"Please be more careful with your papers, sir. They might be misused by some unscrupulous person."

Ghyl gave a lofty nod, and strode out upon the field. Five minutes later he was aboard the *Grada*.

Bonar Heurisx regarded him with astonishment. "I have been intensely concerned! I thought never to see you again!"

"I have had a fearful day. Only by chance am I alive." He told Heurisx of his adventures; and Heurisx, looking at him, marveled at the changes done in a single day. Ghyl's cheeks were hollow, his eyes burned; he had put the trust and hope of his youth forever behind him.

"Well then," said Bonar Heurisx, "so much for our plans, which were chancy at best."

"Not so fast," said Ghyl. "We came here to trade; trade we will."

"Surely you're not serious?" demanded Heurisx.

"Something may still be possible," said Ghyl. He went to his locker, threw off the white smock, donned dark Daillie trousers, a tight dark shirt.

Bonar Heurisx watched in puzzlement. "We're not going forth again tonight?"

"I, not you. I hope to make some sort of arrangement."

"But why not wait till tomorrow?" complained Bonar Heurisx.

"Tomorrow will be too late," said Ghyl. "Tomorrow I'll be calm, I'll be reasonable, I won't be desperate with anger."

Bonar Heurisx made no response. Ghyl finished his preparations. Because of the officials at the control gate, he dared not carry the articles he might have wished, and so contented himself with a roll of adhesive tape, a dark beret over his shaved head. "I'll be gone possibly two hours. If I do not return by morning, you had best depart."

"All very well, but what do you plan?"

"Trade. Of one sort or another."

Ghyl departed the ship. He returned to the control gate, submitted to a lackadaisical search for contraband, and was issued a new landing permit. "Be more careful of this than the last, if you please. And mind the tavern girls. They'll importune, and you'll wake in the morning with a sour taste and never a coin in your pocket."

"I'll take care."

Ghyl once more rode Overtrend to East Town: by night the most forlorn and dismal of regions. Once again he approached the thirty-acre compound surrounding the Associated Guilds warehouse and the Boimarc offices. Furtive as an animal, he approached the fence. The warehouse was dark save for a light in the guards' office. The Boimarc offices showed a set of illuminated windows. A pair of floodlights, to either side, shone across the compound, where during the day lift-trucks worked loading and unloading air-vans and drays.

Standing in the shadow of a broken signal stanchion, Ghyl examined the entire vicinity. The night was dark and damp. To the east were gutted ruins of ancient row houses. Far south the Vashmont eyries showed a few high, yellow lights; much closer he saw the red and green glimmer of a local tavern. In the compound, mist blowing in from the ocean swirled around the floodlights.

Ghyl approached the gate, which was closed and barred, and undoubtedly equipped with sensor alarms. It offered no hope of access. He started around the edge of the compound and presently came to a spot where wet earth had collapsed into a ditch, leaving a narrow gap. Ghyl dropped to his knees, enlarged the gap, and presently was able to roll under the fence.

Crouching, sliding through the dark, he approached the Boimarc offices from the north. He peered through a window, into the empty rooms. There was ample illumination, but no sound, no sense of occupancy.

Ghyl looked right and left, backed away, circled the building, cautiously testing doors and windows, but as he expected all were locked. At the east end a small annex was under construction. Ghyl clambered up the new masonry to a setback in the main structure and thence to the roof. He listened. No sound.

Ghyl stole across the roof and presently found an insecure ventilator which he detached and so was able to drop down into an upper storage chamber.

Quietly he made his way to the ground floor, his senses

sharp and questing, and at last peered into the main offices. Light exuded calmly, evenly, from glow-panels. He heard the ticking of an automatic instrument. The room, as before, was empty.

Ghyl made a quick investigation, taking note of the various doors, should he need to make a hurried exit. Then more confidently he turned back toward Lord Dugald's alcove. He peered behind the desk; there in its socket, hung the stamp. On the desk were new requisitions, as yet unvalidated. Ghyl took three of these, and, going to the inventory mechanism, set himself to puzzle out the form and coding and the method by which the requisitions were printed. Then he studied the read-outs on the automatic inventory calculator.

Time passed. Ghyl essayed a few sale requisitions; then referring constantly to the sample forms and the operator's schedule, he prepared a requisition. He checked it with care. So far as he could see—perfect.

He removed the evidences of his work and replaced the sample requisitions. Then, taking Lord Dugald's stamp from its socket, he validated the requisition.

And now: what to do with the requisition? Ghyl studied a notice taped to the console of the computer: a schedule of lead times and deadlines, and verified his supposition: the requisition must be conveyed to the dispatcher in the warehouse.

Ghyl departed the offices the way he had come, not daring to use the doors for fear of exciting an alarm.

Standing in the shadows he looked across at the warehouse, which was dark except for lights in the watchman's cabin.

Ghyl approached the warehouse from the rear, climbed up a ramp to the loading dock, went in a stealthy half-run to a corner of the building. He peered around and saw nearby the booth in which sat two guards. One knit a garment, the other rocked back and forth with his feet on a shelf.

Ghyl backed away, walked along the dock, testing doors. All were securely locked. Ghyl heaved a sad sigh. He found a length of half-rotten wood, took up a position and waited. Fifteen minutes passed. The guard who knitted glanced at a timepiece, arose, flicked on a lantern, spoke a word to his comrade. Then he went forth to make his rounds. He came past Ghyl whistling tunelessly between his teeth. Ghyl shrank back in the shadows. The watchman stopped by a door, fumbled with his keys, inserted one in the lock.

Ghyl crept up behind, struck down with the length of

wood. The guard dropped in his tracks. Ghyl took his
weapon, his lantern, bound and gagged the man with adhesive tape.

With a final glance to right and left he eased open the
door, entered the dark warehouse. He flashed the light here
and there: up and down bales of merchandise, crates and
boxes, in bays marked *Acme, First, Second*. The dispatcher's
office was immediately to the left. Ghyl entered, turned his
light along the counters, the desks. Somewhere he should see
a sheaf of stiff yellow sheets. . . . There, in a cubicle to the
side. Ghyl stepped forward, inspected the requisitions. The
top sheet was the earliest, carrying the lowest number. Ghyl
removed this sheet, wrote its number on his own requisition,
added it to the pile.

He ran back to the door. The watchman lay groaning, still
unconscious. Ghyl dragged him into the warehouse, near a
pile of crates. He lifted two crates to the floor, beside the
watchman's head, disarranged the remaining crates. He replaced the lantern, the weapon, the keys on the watchman's
person, removed the adhesive bonds, and departed hastily.

Three-quarters of an hour later Ghyl was back and aboard
the *Grada*, to find Bonar Heurisx taut with anxiety. "You've
been gone so long! What have you accomplished?"

"A great deal! Almost everything! Or so I hope. We'll
know in the morning." In exultation Ghyl explained the circumstances. ". . . and all Acmes and Acme Reserved I ordered out the choicest goods in the warehouse! The best of
the best! Oh what a trick to play on Lord Dugald!"

Heurisx heard him aghast. "The risk! Suppose the substitu-
tion is detected?"

Ghyl gave a reckless fling of the arms. "Unthinkable! But
still—we want to be ready to leave, and leave at once. I agree
as to that."

"Never have I stolen a copper!" cried Bonar Heurisx in
distress. "I will not steal now!"

"We do not steal! We take—and pay!"

"But when? And to whom?"

"In due course. To whomever will accept the money."

Bonar sunk into a chair, rubbed his forehead wearily.
"Something will go wrong. You will see. Impossible to
steal—"

"Excuse me: to 'trade.' "

"—to steal, trade, swindle, whatever you care to call it, with such facility."

"We shall see! If all goes well, the drays will arrive soon after sunrise."

"And if all goes ill?"

"As I said before—be ready to leave!"

The night passed; dawn came at last. On tenterhooks, Ghyl and Bonar Heurisx waited, either for loaded drays or the black five-wheeled cars of the Special Agents.

An hour after dawn a port official mounted the loading ladder. "Ahoy, aboard the *Grada*."

"Yes, yes?" called Bonar Heurisx. "What is it?"

"Are you expecting cargo?"

"Certainly."

"Well, then, open your hatches, prepare to stow. We like to do things efficiently here at Ambroy."

"Just as you say."

Ten minutes later the first of the drays pulled up beside the *Grada*.

"You must rate highly," said the driver. "All Acmes and Acme Reserves."

Bonar Heurisx made only a noncommittal sound.

Six drays in all rolled up to the *Grada*. The driver of the sixth dray said, "You're cleaning us out of Acmes. I've never seen such a cargo. Everyone at the warehouse is wondering about it."

"Just another cargo," said Ghyl. "We're full to our chocks; don't bring any more."

"Precious little more to bring," grumbled the driver. "Well then, sign the receipt."

Ghyl took the invoice and, prompted by a sudden whimsy, scrawled 'Emphyrio' across the paper.

Bonar Heurisx called to the crew, "Close the hatches, we're taking off!"

"Only just soon enough," said Ghyl. He pointed. "There come the Special Agents."

Up into the air lifted the *Grada;* on the field below a dozen Special Agents jumped from their black cars to stand looking after them.

Ambroy dwindled below; Halma became a sphere. Damar, lowering and purple-brown, fell back to the side. The propulsors whined more hoarsely, the *Grada* went into space-drive.

Jodel Heurisx was stupefied by the quality and quantity of the cargo. "This is not merchandise; this is treasure!"

"It represents the hoard of centuries," said Ghyl. "All goods of Acme grade. Notice this screen, the Winged Being—the last screen my father carved. I polished and waxed it after his death."

"Put it aside," said Jodel Heurisx. "Keep it for your own."

Ghyl shook his head glumly. "Sell it with the rest. It brings me melancholy thoughts."

But Jodel Heurisx would not allow Ghyl his sentimentality. "Someday you will have a son. Would not the screen be a fine present to make to him?"

"If such an unlikely event ever comes to pass."

"The screen then is yours, and it will be kept in my home until you need it."

"Oh, very well. Who knows what the future holds?"

"The rest of the cargo we will convey to Earth. Why trifle the provincial markets? On Earth are the great fortunes, the ancient palaces; we will attract the money of connoisseurs. A sum shall be reserved for the Ambroy guilds. We shall deduct the expenses of the voyage. The remainder will be divided into three parts. There will be wealth for all of us. You shall be financially independent, Ghyl Tarvoke!"

CHAPTER 19

All his life Ghyl had heard speculation as to the provenance of man. Some declared Earth to be the source of the human migration; another group inclined toward Triptolemus; others pointed to Amenaro, the lone planet of Deneb Kaitos; a few argued spontaneous generation from a universal float of spores.

Jodel Heurisx resolved Ghyl's uncertainty. "You may be sure: Earth is the human source! All of us are Earthmen, no matter where we were born!"

In many ways the reality of Earth was at odds with Ghyl's preconceptions. He had thought to find a dismal world, the horizon spiked with rotting ruins, the sun a flaming red eye, the seas oily and stagnant from the seepage of ages.

But the sun was warm and yellow-white, much like the sun of Maastricht; and the sea seemed considerably more fresh than Deep Ocean to the west of Fortinone.

The people of Earth were another surprise. Ghyl had been ready for weary cynicism, a jaded autumnal lassitude, inversions, eccentricities, subtle sophistications; and in this expectation he was not completely wide of the mark. Certain of the people he met displayed these qualities, but others were as easy and uncomplicated as children. Still others perplexed Ghyl by their fervor, the intensity of their conduct, as if the day were too short for the transaction of all their business. Sitting with Jodel Heurisx at an outdoor café of old Cologne, Ghyl remarked upon the variety of people who walked past their table.

"True enough," said Jodel Heurisx. "Other cities on other planets are cosmopolitan enough, but Earth is a universe in itself."

"I expected the people to seem old—sedate—wise. Some do, of course. But others—well, look at that man in the green suede. His eyes glitter; he looks right and left as if he were seeing everything for the first time. Of course, he might be an outworlder, like us."

"No, he's an Earthman," said Jodel Heurisx. "Don't ask

me how I know; I couldn't tell you. A matter of style: small
signs that betray a man's background. As for his air of restlessness, sociologists declare that material well-being and psy-
chic stability vary in counter-proportion. Barbarians have no
time either for idealism or its observe, phychosis. The people
of Earth, however, concern themselves with 'justification' and
'fulfillment,' and a few, such as, perhaps, that man in green,
become over-intense. But there are enormous variations.
Some devote their energies to visionary schemes. Other turn
inward to become sybarites, voluptuaries, connoisseurs, col-
lectors, aesthetes; or they concentrate upon the study of some
arcane specialty. To be sure, there are numerous ordinary
folk, but somehow they are never noticed, and only serve to
heighten the contrast. But then, if you remain on Earth for a
period, you will discover much of this for yourself."

The *Grada*'s cargo was sold, and profitably. At Tripoli,
Ghyl took leave of Jodel and Bonar Heurisx. He promised
someday to return to Daillie. Jodel Heurisx told him, "On
that day my home will be your home. And never forget that I
hold for you your wonderful screen: the 'Winged Being.'"

"I won't forget. For now—good-bye."

"Good-bye, Ghyl Tarvoke."

Feeling somewhat melancholy, Ghyl watched the *Grada*
lift into the windy blue African sky. But when the ship at last
dwindled and disappeared, his spirits rapidly rose: far worse
fates than to be on Earth for the first time, with the equivalent of a million vouchers in his pouch! Ghyl thought of his
childhood: a time unreal behind a golden haze. How often he
and Floriel had lain in the yellow grass on Dunkum's
Heights, talking of travel and financial independence! Both,
in separate ways, had achieved their ambition. And Ghyl
wondered what region of space Floriel now wandered;
whether he were alive or dead. . . . Poor Floriel! thought
Ghyl, to be so lost.

For a month Ghyl roamed Earth, exploring the cloud-tow-
ers of America, the equally marvelous submarine cities of the
Great Barrier Reef, the vast wilderness parks over which air-
cars were not permitted to fly. He visited the restored dawn-
cities of Athens, Babylon, Memphis, medieval Bruges,
Venice, Regensburg. Everywhere, often light but sometimes
so heavy as to be oppressive, lay the weight of history. Each
trifling area of soil exhaled a plasm: the recollection of a million tragedies, a million triumphs; of births and deaths; kisses

exchanged; blood spilled; the char of fire and energy; songs, glees, incantations, war-chants, frenzies. The soil reeked of events; history lay in strata, in crusts; in eras, continuities, discontinuities. At night ghosts were common, so Ghyl was told: in the precincts of old palaces, in the mountains of the Caucusus, on the heaths and moors of the north.

Ghyl began to believe that Earth-folk were preoccupied with the past, a theory reinforced by the numerous historical pageants, the survival of anachronistic traditions, the existence of the Historical Institute, which recorded, digested, cross-filed, and analyzed every shred of fact pertinent to human origin and development. . . . The Historical Institute! Presently he would visit the Institute's headquarters in London, although—for some reason he did not care to analyze—he was in no great hurry to do so.

At St. Petersburg he met a slim blond Norwegian girl named Flora Eilander, who occasionally reminded him of Shanne. For a period they traveled together, and she pointed out aspects of Earth he had not before noticed. In particular she scoffed at his theory that Earth-folk were preoccupied with the past. "No, no, no!" she told him with a delightful lilting emphasis. "You miss the whole point! We are concerned with the soul of events, the intrinsic essences!"

Ghyl could not be sure that he had comprehended her exposition, but this was no longer a novelty. He found the people of Earth bewildering. In every conversation he felt a thousand subtleties and indirections, a frame of mind which found as much meaning in the unstated as the stated. There were, he finally decided, niceties of communication which forever would be denied him: allusions through twitches of mannerism, distinctions of a hundredth of a second between a pair of contradictory significances, nameless moods which must instantly be countered or augmented in kind.

Ghyl became angry with himself and quarreled with Flora, who compounded the situation by condescension. "You must remember that we have known everything, tried every pang and exhilaration. Therefore it is only natural—"

Ghyl gave a harsh laugh. "Nonsense! Have you ever known grief or fear? Have you ever stolen a space-yacht and killed Garrion? Have you known a County Ball at Grigglesby Corners with the lords and ladies coming forth like magicians in their wonderful costumes? Or stumbled through a rite at Finuka's Temple? Or looked down dreaming from the Meagher Mounts across old Fortinone?"

"No, of course; I have done none of these." And Flora, giving him a long slow inspection, said no more.

For another month they wandered from place to place: Abyssinia, where the sunlight evoked aloes, bitumen, old dust; Sardinia when its olive trees and asphodel; the haze and murk of the Gothic north.

One day in Dublin, Ghyl came upon a placard which froze him in his tracks:

FRAMTREE'S ORIGINAL PERIPATEZIC ENTERCATIONERS

The Wonderful Trans-Galactic Extravaganza!

Hear the blood-curdling screams of the Maupte Bacchanids!
Goggle at the antics of Holkerwoyd's puppets!
Smell the authentic fetors of two dozen far planets!
Much more! Much More!

At Casteyn Park, seven days only

Flora was uninterested but Ghyl insisted that they instantly take themselves to Casteyn Park, and for once Flora was the one to be perplexed. Ghyl told her nothing other than that he had known the show in his childhood; there was nothing more he could tell her.

Beside a stand of giant oaks Ghyl found the same gaudy panels, the same placards, the same sounds and outcries he had known as a child. He sought out Holkerwoyd's Puppet Show and sat through a mildly amusing revue. The puppets squeaked and capered, trilled topical songs, caricatured local personalities, then a group dressed as punchinellos performed a series of farces.

After the show, leaving the bored but indulgent Flora in her seat, Ghyl approached the curtain at the side of the stage: it might have been the identical curtain that once before he had pushed through, and he fought the impulse to look over his shoulder to where his father must surely be sitting. Slowly he pulled aside the curtain, and there, as if he had not moved during all the years, sat Holkerwoyd, mending a bit of stage property.

Holkerwoyd had aged; his skin was waxen, his lips had drawn back; his teeth seemed yellow and prominent; but his eyes were as keen as ever. Seeing Ghyl, he paused in his work, cocked his head. "Yes, sir?"

"We have met before."

"I know this." Holkerwoyd looked away, rubbed his nose with a gnarled knuckle. "So many folk I've seen; so many places I've been; a task to set all out in order. . . . Let me see. We met long years ago, on a far planet, in the ditch at the edge of the universe. Halma. It hangs below the green moon Damar, where I buy my puppets."

"How could you remember? I was a small boy."

Holkerwoyd smiled, wagged his head. "You were a serious fellow, puzzled at the way the world went. You were with your father. What of him?"

"Dead."

Holkerwoyd nodded without surprise. "And how goes your life? You are far from Ambroy."

"My life goes well enough. But there is a question which troubles me to this day. You performed the legend of Emphyrio. And the puppet was executed."

Holkerwoyd shrugged and returned to his mending. "The puppets are not useful forever. They become aware of the world, they begin to feel real. Then they are spoiled and must be destroyed before they infect the troupe."

Ghyl grimaced. "Puppets presumably are cheap."

"Cheap enough. But just barely. The Damarans are sly dealers, cold as steel. How they love the chink of valuta! To good effect! They live in palaces while I sleep on a cot, starting up at odd noises." Holkerwoyd became agitated and waved his mending in the air. "Let them lower prices, and lavish less splendor on themselves! They are deaf to all my remonstrances. Would you like to see Emphyrio once more? I have a puppet who is becoming perverse. I have warned and scolded but I continually find him looking across the footlights at the audience."

"No," said Ghyl. He backed toward the curtain. "Well then, for the second time I bid you good-bye."

Holkerwoyd gave a casual wave. "We may yet meet again, though I suspect not. The years come fast. Some morning they'll find me lying stark, with the puppets climbing over me, peering in my mouth, tweaking my ears . . ."

Back at the Black Swan Hotel, Ghyl and Flora sat in the saloon bar, with Ghyl staring glumly into a glass of wine. Flora hade several attempts to speak but Ghyl's mind had wandered far away, beyond Mirabalis, and he gave back monosyllabic answers. Looking into the wine, he saw the narrow-fronted house on Undle Square. He heard Amiante's quiet voice, the thin scrape of chisels on wood. He felt the wan Ambroy sunlight, the drifting across the mud flats at the mouth of the Insse; he recalled the smells of the docks of Nobile and Foelgher, the gaunt Vashmont towers, the moldering ruins below.

Ghyl was homesick, even though Ambroy could no longer be considered home. Meditating on Amiante's humiliation and futile death, Ghyl became so bitter that he turned the whole glass of wine down his throat. The decanter was empty. A waiter in a white apron, sensing Ghyl's mood, hastened to bring a new decanter.

Flora rose to her feet, looked down at Ghyl a second or two, then sauntered from the room.

Ghyl thought of his expulsion, of the looming piston, the crushed bricks, the hour he lay huddled on the wall while the sad twilight gathered around him. Perhaps he had deserved the punishment; undeniably he had stolen a space-yacht. Still, was not the crime justifiable? Did not the lords use Boimarc, or Thurible Cooperative, whatever the case, to swindle and cheat and victimize the recipients? Ghyl brooded and sipped wine, wondering how best to disseminate his knowledge to the recipients. Useless to work either through the guilds or the Welfare Agency; both were conservative to the point of obsession.

The problem required reflection. Ghyl turned the last of the wine down his throat and went up to his suite. Flora was nowhere in evidence. Ghyl shrugged. He would never see her again: this he knew. Perhaps it was just as well.

On the following day he crossed the Irish Channel to ancient London. Now, at last, he would visit the Historical Institute.

But the Historical Institute was not to be approached so easily. Ghyl's questions to Telescreen Information met, first bland evasiveness, then a recommendation to a guided tour of Oxford and Cambridge universities. When Ghyl persisted, he was referred to the Bureau of Weights and Measures, which passed him on to Dundee House. This proved to be the headquarters of some sort of intelligence agency, the function of which Ghyl never fully understood. A clerk politely inquired the reason for his interest in the Historical Institute, whereupon Ghyl, controlling his impatience, mentioned the legend of Emphyrio.

The clerk, a golden-haired young man with crisp mustache, turned away and spoke a few quiet words, apparently to the empty air, then listened, apparently to the air itself. He turned back to Ghyl. "If you will remain at your hotel, an agent of the Institute will shortly make contact with you."

Half-amused, half-irritated, Ghyl set himself to wait. An hour later he was met by an ugly little man in a black suit and a gray cloak: Arwin Rolus, sub-director of Mythological Studies at the Institute. "I understand that you are interested in the legend of Emphyrio."

"Yes," said Ghyl. "But first: explain to me the reason for so much stealth and secrecy?"

Rolus chuckled, and Ghyl saw that he was not really ugly after all. "The situation may seem extravagant. But the Historical Institute, by the very nature of its being, accumulates a great deal of secret intelligence. This is not the Institute's function, you understand: we are scholars. Still, from time to time we are able to resolve difficulties for more active folk." He looked Ghyl up and down with an appraising eye. "When an outworlder comes inquiring about the Institute, the authorities ensure that he doesn't intend to bomb the place."

"No danger of that," said Ghyl. "I want information, no more."

"Precisely what information?"

Ghyl handed him the fragment from Amiante's portfolio. Without apparent difficulty Rolus read the crabbed old characters. "Well, well, indeed. Interesting. And now you want to find what happened? How the story ended, so to speak?"

"Yes."

"May I ask why?"

The Earthers were a suspicious lot! thought Ghyl. In a measured voice he stated, "I have known half the legend since my childhood. I promised myself that if I ever were able to learn the rest, I would do so."

"And this is the only reason?"

"Not altogether."

Rolus did not pursue the question. "Your home planet is . . ." He raised his bushy gray eyegrows.

"Halma. It is a world back of the Mirabilis Cluster."

"Halma. A remote world. . . . Well, perhaps I can gratify your curiosity." He turned to the wall-screen, tapped with his fingertips to project a coded signal. The screen responded with a run of references, one of which Rolus selected. "Here," he said, "is the entire chronicle, indited by an unknown writer of the world Aume, or, as some say, Home, about two thousand years ago."

The screen displayed a message, printed in Archaic. The first few paragraphs were those of Ghyl's fragment; then:

In the Catademnon sat those without ears to hear, who owned no souls and knew neither ease nor fellowship. Emphyrio brought forth his tablet and called for peace. They gave alarms and waved green pennants. Emphyrio urged fellowship; without ears to hear and eyes averted, none would understand, and they waved blue pennants. Emphyrio pled for the kindness which differentiated man from monster, or lacking that, mercy. They broke the tablet of truth underfoot and waved red pennants. Then they lifted Emphyrio in their hands aloft, they held him high to a wall, and through his skull they drove a great nail so that he hung on the wall of the Catademnon. When all had looked to see how fared the man who would have spoken truth, they took him down and under the beam where they nailed him, there in the crypt they immured him forever!

But what was their profit?

Who was the victim?

On the world Aume, or Home, the brutes of Sigil no longer wasted the land. They looked eye to eye and asked: "Is it true, as Emphyrio avers, that we are creatures for whom there is dawn and dusk, pain and pain's ease? Why then do we waste the land? Let us make our lives good; for we have none other." And they threw down their arms and retired to those places which were the most pleasant to them, and at once became the easiest of folk, so that all men wondered at their first ferocity.

Emphyrio died imploring the dark ones to the ways of man, and that they should curb their begotten monsters. They refuted him; they hung him to the wall on a nail. But the monsters, at first insensate, were now, through truth, of all folk the easiest. If there be here lesson or moral, it lies beyond the competence of him who inscribes this record.

CHAPTER 20

A sheet printed with the message issued from the wall; Rolus handed it to Ghyl, who read it a second time, then placed it with Amiante's fragment.

"The world Aume—is it Halma? Is Sigil the moon Damar?"

Rolus brought further information to the screen, in a script unfamiliar to Ghyl. "Aume is Halma," he said. "A world with a complicated history: do you know it?"

"I suspect not," said Ghyl. "We learn very little at Ambroy." He could not keep the bitterness from his voice. "Very little indeed."

Without comment Rolus read from the screen, occasionally expanding or interpolating. Two or three thousand years before Emphyrio, and long before men appeared, the Damarans had established colonies on Halma, using space-ships provided by a race of star-wanderers. But war came; the Damarans were expelled and forced back to Damar, where they contrived a means to destroy the star-wanderers. Through the facility of their procreative systems, the Damarans were able to duplicate whatever genetic material might be presented to their glands. They decided to produce an army of irresistible warriors, ruthless and ferocious, who would tear the star-wanderers into shreds. First they prepared a prototype, then built artificial glands to produce the creatures in quantity. When the army was assembled they sent it down from Sigil, or Damar, but isolated in their caves they had lapsed half a thousand years behind the times. The star-wanderers were gone, no one knows where, and men had arrived to take possession of the plant. The army from Damar seemed an act of wanton aggression. The Wirwan—to name the monsters—seemed like fiends from hell. In certain details they were similar to their progenitors. They lacked an accurate sense of hearing, and communicated by means of radio waves. Emphyrio apparently devised a mechanism which translated human words into Wirwan radiation. He was the

187

first man to communicate with the invaders. They were singu-
larly innocent, he discovered, having been trained to one purpose. He made them aware of themselves; he corrupted their
innocence, so to speak. Almost magically they became hesi-
tant and retiring, and retreated into the mountains. Encouraged by his success, Emphyrio traveled across the gap to
Sigil, hoping to pacify those who had dispatched the army.

"Emphyrio's ultimate fate is uncertain," said Rolus. "The
account you just read states that the Damarans drove a nail
through his head and killed him. Another source declares that
Emphyrio negotiated a truce and returned to Aume, where he
became the first lord. There are other reports to the effect
that the folk of Sigil held Emphyrio a prisoner in perpetuity,
preserving him in a state of suspended life. The facts are uncertain. All is changed now. The Damarans produce puppets
and manikins in their artificial glands. The Wirwans, a forlorn race, survive on the slopes of Mount Meagher. The men
are as you know."

Ghyl heaved a sigh. So then: the tale was told. Fortinone,
scene of the early campaigns, was now placid. On Damar the
puppet-makers catered to the tourists and bred puppets. And
Emphyrio? His fate was uncertain. Ghyl recalled his childhood visit to the Meagher Mounts when he had traced imag-
inary campaigns upon the topography. He had been more
accurate than he ever could have dreamed.

Arwin Rolus was preparing to take his departure. "Is there
anything more you wish to know?"

"Does the Institute collect information from Halma now?
From Fortinone?"

"Yes, of course."

"You have a correspondent at Ambroy?"

"Several."

"Their identity is secret?"

"Of course. If they were known, they might be com-
promised. We are required to stay aloof from events. Not all
are able to do this. Your father, for instance."

Ghyl turned to stare at Rolus. "My father? Amiante Tarvoke? Was he a correspondent?"

"Yes. For many years."

Ghyl took himself to a cosmetic surgeon. His nose was
narrowed, bridged, and peaked; his eyebrows set in a new
slant. The tattoo on his shoulder was expunged; the prints

of his tongue, fingers, palms, and soles were altered. His skin was toned dull olive-bronze, his hair was dyed black, and finally only the contents of his brain remained to identify him as Ghyl Tarvoke.

At Ball and Sons, Haberdashers, Ghyl fitted himself out with Earth-style garments and was astounded by the hologram. Who would associate this debonair young gallant with poor, harried Ghyl Tarvoke of old?

Fictitious identification papers were hard to come by. Finally Ghyl called Dundee House and presently was connected with Arwin Rolus.

Rolus recognized Ghyl at once, which caused Ghyl exasperation and uneasiness. Ghyl stated his requirements but Rolus was reluctant to offer assistance. "Please understand the Institute's position. We profess didactic dispassion and nonpartisanship in all circumstances. We record, analyze, interpret—but we do not interfere or promulgate. If I, as an officer of the Historical Institite, were to assist your intrigue, I would be intruding the Institute upon a flow of history."

Ghyl thought that Rolus had unnecessarily emphasized one of his phrases. Ghyl said quickly, "I did not mean this to be an official call. I thought only to turn to you, as my single acquaintance on Earth, for some quiet advice."

"I see," said Rolus. "Well, in that case . . ." He thought a moment. "Of course I know nothing of these matters. But"—a slip of paper issued from the wall-slot in Ghyl's room—"if you call this code, someone at least will listen to you without wincing."

"I also have a question for you in your official capacity."

"Well then. What is the question?"

"Where is the Catademnon, where on Damar?"

Rolus gave a brisk nod, as if Ghyl's question came as no surprise. "I will put the question into process; the information will reach you shortly and the service charge will be added to your hotel addition."

Ten minutes later a sheet of paper issued from the wall-slot. The message read:

> The Catademnon, hall of the war lords of ancient
> Sigil, now known as Damar, is a ruin in the mountains ten miles southwest of the present Old City.

During the evening Ghyl made contact with the man

whose code Arwin Rolus had supplied. The next day he picked up his new documents, and assumed the identity of Sir Hartwig Thorn, Grandee. He immediately booked passage for Damar, and the same evening departed Earth.

CHAPTER 21

Damar was an eerie little world, half the diameter of Halma, but with one-sixth Halma's mass and two-thirds its surface gravity. There were great expanses of bog across the polar regions, mountains and crags of astonishing dimension in the middle latitudes, an arid zone where grew Damar's unique equatorial thicket: a tangle of barbs and tendrils ten miles wide and occasionally a half-mile high. What with bogs, crags, gorges, and the thicket, there were few areas convenient for habitation. Garwan, the tourist center, and Damar Old City were at opposite ends of the Great Central Plain, this apparently a scar inflicted by the glancing blow of a meteor.

At Garwan were hotels, restaurants, baths, sporting areas; luxury in bizarre surroundings. Puppet theaters provided spectacle and diversion: farce, historical pageants, macabre drama, erotic display. The puppet performers were a special breed: handsome little creatures four or five feet tall, vastly different from the half-simian imps supplied to such as Holkerwoyd.

The Damarans themselves seldom ventured from their residences under the hills, upon which they spent prodigious fortunes. The typical residence was a complex system of chambers swathed in soft fabrics, illuminated with meticulous nicety. Silver light shone on gray and nacreous curtains; red, carmine, and magenta were used against blues and pale pink. Globes giving off deep purple of plangent sea-green hung behind films and layers of gauze. The residences were never complete, always in the process of alteration and extension. On rare occasions a man whom the Damaran wished to please, or one who paid a sufficiently large fee, might be invited into a residence: a visit preceded by an extraordinary ritual. Twittering puppets bathed the visitor, sprayed him with mist, muffled him head to foot in a white robe, fitted him with sandals of white felt. Thus sanitized, deodorized, and padded, he would be conducted along interminable vistas of hangings and draperies, into grottoes hung with waving webs and gauzes, through blue lights and gray-green lights, finally to emerge awed and bewildered, if by nothing else other than the vast expenditures of wealth. The average excursionist, however, saw the Damarans only as silent shapes at the back of an office or shop.

Arriving at Garwan, Ghyl established himself at one of the "Old Damar" hotels: a pyramidal heap of white domes and hemispheres, with a few small windows placed seemingly at random. Ghyl was lodged in two domed rooms on different levels, draped with panels of pale green, and floors cushioned by a heavy black carpet.

Leaving the hotel, Ghyl entered a tour and travel agency. On a shadowed balcony stood a Damaran, each eye-bulb glinting with a luminous star: a creature smaller, softer, more flexible than a Garrion, but otherwise much the same. On the counter a screen responding to a radio-frequency projection showed luminous characters: "You wish?"

"I want to hire an air-car." The words became tremulous shapes on the screen, which the Damaran read at a glance.

The response came: "This is possible, though expensive. A tour by sight-seeing tube costs no more and is preferable, in safety and deluxe comfort."

"No doubt," said Ghyl. "But I am a scholar at a university of Earth. I wish to look for fossils. I want to visit the puppet factories and look through the old ruins."

"It is possible. There is a depletion fee upon the export of fossils. It is not advisable to visit the puppet factories, due to the delicacy of procedures. A visitor would not be amused. There are not ruins of interest. The sight-seeing tube will offer greater value, and will cost less."

"I prefer to hire an air-car."

"You must post a bond for the value of the car. When do you want it?"

"Early tomorrow morning."

"Your name?"

"Hartwig Thorn."

"Tomorrow morning the car will be at the back of the hotel. You may now pay three thousand one hundred standard valuta units. Three thousand is the deposit. It will be returned to you. The air-car charge is one hundred units a day."

Ghyl walked about the city for an hour or two. With the coming of evening, he seated himself in an open-air café, to drink ale imported from Fortinone. Halma swam up into the sky, an enormous amber half-disk, vaguely marked with familiar outlines.

A man walked into the café, followed by a woman; each in turn was silhouetted against Halma. Ghyl altered the focus of his vision, watched the couple settle themselves at a nearby table. The man was Schute Cobol; the woman no doubt was his wife; they had come to Damar to spend their hoarded vouchers like any other recipients. Schute Cobol glanced at Ghyl, studied his Earth-style garments, muttered something to his wife, who likewise inspected Ghyl. Then they gave their attention to the menu. Ghyl, with a wry grin, looked up through the air toward Halma.

CHAPTER 22

The days and nights of Damar were short. After dining and musing long into the night over a map of Damar, Ghyl had hardly retired to his suite before the sky began to lighten.

He arose with a sense of fatefulness. Long ago Holkerwoyd had pronounced him "fey": laboring under a burden of doom. He dressed slowly, aware of the weight. It seemed that his whole life had been directed toward this day.

The air-car was waiting on a stage behind the hotel. Ghyl examined the controls, decided that they were standard. He climbed in, latched the dome, hitched the control wheel up to a convenient position and locked it. He checked the energy level: the cells were charged; he touched the ON button, pulled up on the wheel. The car lifted into the air. Ghyl slid the wheel forward, tilted it back: the car slid up at a slant.

So far, so good. Ghyl sent the car higher, up over the mountains. Far to the south was the equatorial thicket, a formless gray-brown smudge. Ghyl steered to the north.

The miles slipped past; the thin upper air hissed past the dome. Ahead glinted a single rime-crusted peak: a landmark. Ghyl steered to the north of the peak and saw ahead Damar Old City: an unlovely jumble of long sheds and warehouses. Instinctively preferring that his presence not be noted, Ghyl dropped the air-car low, to within a hundred feet of the surface, and veered to the southeast of Old City.

He searched an hour before he found the ruins: a tumble of stone lost among the rocky debris of the mountainside.

He landed the air-car on a little flat of drifted gravel fifty yards from a low wall, and now Ghyl wondered how he had searched so long, for the structure was of monumental scope and walls were yet standing. He alighted and stood by the car, listening, to hear only the sigh of wind across the harsh surface of the scree. The Old City, ten miles distant, was a formless jumble of gray and white tablets. He could see no moving object, no sign of life.

He took his lamp and hand-gun, approached the broken wall, which was half-drifted over with soil. Beyond was a depression, then a heavier wall of lichen-stained concrete: cracked, sagging, but still upright. Ghyl moved closer, trying to control his awe. This was a hall of giants; Ghyl felt dwarfed and trivial. Still . . . Emphyrio had been a man like himself, with a man's courage and a man's fear. He had come to the Catademnon—and then?

Ghyl crossed the fosse between the two walks and came to a portal, choked with rubble. He scrambled up and peered within, but the sunlight, slanting across the sky, avoided the gap and he saw only black shadows.

Ghyl switched on his lamp, slid down over the debris, into a dank corridor cluttered with the drift of centuries. On the wall hung tatters of fabric spun, perhaps, from fibers of melted obsidian, stained with metal oxides. The patterns were crusted with grime, but nonetheless heroic. They reminded Ghyl of hangings he had seen elsewhere, in circumstances he could not recall. . . . The corridor opened into an oval hall, the roof of which had collapsed. The floor was open to the sky.

Ghyl halted. He stood in the Catademnon. Here Emphyrio had confronted the tyrants of Sigil. There was no sound, not even the rasp of the wind, but the pressure of the past was almost tangible.

At the far end of the hall was a gap with tatters of ancient regalia to either side. Here Ehphyrio might have been lifted and nailed to a beam—if this had indeed been his fate.

Ghyl crossed the floor. He halted, looked up at the stone beam over the gap. There was certainly a scar, an eroded hole, a socket. If Emphyrio had been suspended here, his feet would have dangled to the level of Ghyl's shoulders, his blood would have stained the stone by Ghyl's feet. . . . The stone was crusted with a gray efflorescence.

Ghyl walked under the beam, turned his flash down into the opening. Dust, debris, bits of dry vegetation clogged the first part of a wide set of stairs. Ghyl clambered through, flashing the light to all sides. "Under the beam where they had nailed him, there in their crypt did they immure him forever." The steps gave upon an oval chamber, with three passages leading off into the darkness. The chamber was floored with a dull stone on which lay an undisturbed layer of dust. The crypt? Ghyl turned the light around the chamber, and walked in the direction where the crypt must lie. He looked into a long room, cold and still. On the floor, helter-skelter, were half a dozen cases molded of glass, coated heavily with

dust. Each contained organic remains: chitinous plates; strips
of withered black leather. . . . In one of the cases was a human skeleton, the joints wasted apart, the bones collapsed.
The vacant eyeholes looked up a Ghyl. In the center of the
forehead was a round hole.

Ghyl took the air-car back to Garwan, set it down on the
pad behind the hotel, collected his deposit. Then he went to
his suite, where he bathed and changed into fresh garments.
He went to sit on the terrace overlooking the plaza. He felt
flat, deflated. He had not expected to find what he had found.
The skeleton had been anticlimactic.

He had hoped for more. What of the sense of portent with
which he had started the day? His instinct had played him
false. Everything had gone with footling ease, with such small
difficulty and so little incident that the whole affair seemed
shameful. Ghyl felt uneasy, disatisfied. He had found the remains of Emphyrio: as to this there was no doubt. But
drama? There was none. He knew no more than before. Emphyrio had died uselessly, his glorious life ending in failure
and futility. But there was no surprise: so much had been set
forth in the legend.

The sun fell behind the western hills. Garwan's shape—receding domes, superimposed one on the other, pile on pile—
was black against the ash-brown sky. From an alley beside
the hotel came a dark figure: a Damaran. It sidled along the
jetta hedge that bordered the terrace, halted to look across
the plaza. Then it turned to examine the terrace, as if calcu-
lating the worth of the night's business. Avaricious, hyper-lux-
urious beasts, thought Ghyl, with every sequin, every
voucher, every bice poured into their already extravagant
residences. He wondered if in the old heroic days, during the
time of Emphyrio, the Damarans had been equally sybaritic.
. . . The Catademnon had suggested no great refinement.
Perhaps in those days they had lacked the financial means to
gratify their tastes. . . . Sensing Ghyl's attention, the
Damaran turned its queer, tufted head, stared for several seconds, the yellow-green star in the dull eyes expanding and
contracting. Ghyl stared back, exploring a sudden startling
speculation.

The Damaran abruptly turned, disappeared behind the
hedge. Ghyl leaned back in his seat. He sat for a long while
in a half-mesmerized state of detachment, while excursionists

came, dined, departed. And the twilight faded to a luminous umber and disappeared.

The situation had a queer ambivalence. Ghyl swung between nervous amusement for his own whimsies and a dreadful bleakness of spirit.

As an exercise in abstract logic the problem resolved into a starkly simple solution.

When the arguments were transposed into human terms, the force of the logic remained, but the solution implied such heartbreaking tragedy that it transcended belief.

Still: facts were facts. So many curious little trifles which he had observed with wonder now became firm segments of an intricate whole. Ghyl gave a giddy wild laugh which drew glances of censure from a nearby group of Ambroy excursionists. Ghyl choked back his mirth. They would consider him a maniac. If he went to their table, told them his thoughts, how he would shock them! Their trip, for which they had saved all their lives, would be ruined. Would they welcome such knowledge?

Here was a new predicament: What should he do, what steps should he take?

There was no one to give him counsel; he was alone.

What, given the circumstances, would have been Emphyrio's course of action?

Truth.

Very well, thought Ghyl: it shall be Truth, and let the consequences fall where they may.

Another incidental thought occurred to him, nearly occasioning another outburst of lunatic mirth. What of his premonitions of destiny now? They had been fulfilled, ten times over.

Ghyl signaled for a menu and ordered his dinner. In the morning he would depart for Ambroy.

CHAPTER 23

Ghyl arrived at the familiar old Godero space-port late in the afternoon, Ambroy time. He waited until the excursionists had pushed off the ship, then strolled down the ramp in a manner of languid condescension, hoping to camouflage his inner trepidation.

The control official was a man of bitter disposition. He scowled at Ghyl's Earth-style garments, studied his documents with discouraging skepticism. "Earth, is it? What do you do here in Ambroy?"

"I travel."

"Hmf. Sir Hartwig Thorn. A grandee. We have them here as well. It's all the same. The grandees do the traveling; the underlings work. Duration of stay?"

"Perhaps a week."

"There's nothing here to see. A day is sufficient."

Ghyl shrugged. "It well may be."

"Nothing but drabness and drudgery. You'll find no splendor here, save up on the eyries. Do you know they just raised our percentage? It's 1.46 percent now, when for so long it was 1.18. Do you charge a percentage on Earth?"

"A different system is in force."

"I take it that you are importing no duplicated, machine-manufactured, or plagiarized articles for distribution either gratis or for profit?"

"None."

"Very well, Sir Hartwig. Pass on, if you will."

Ghyl walked out into the well-remembered hall. At a Spay booth he placed a call to Grand Lord Dugald the Boimarc, at his eyrie in Vashmont Precinct.

The screen displayed a white disk on a dark blue ground. A courteous voice spoke: "Grand Lord Dugald is away from his eyrie. He will be pleased for you to leave a memorandum of your business."

"I am a grandee of Earth, just now arrived. Where may I find Lord Dugald?"

"He attends a fête, at the eyrie of Lord Parnasse the Underline."

"I will call there."

A lordling, thin of face, with varnished black hair dressed in a fanciful sweep over his forehead, responded to the second call. He listened with exquisite hauteur, turned away without a word. A moment later Lord Parnasse appeared.

Ghyl put on a style of amused condescension. "I am Sir Hartwig Thorn, touring from Earth. I called to pay my respects to Grand Lord Dugald, and was referred to your eyrie."

Parnasse, thin and keen like the lordling, with a darkly florid complexion, examined Ghyl up and down. "I am honored to make your acquaintance. Lord Dugald is at my eyrie, enjoying an entertainment." He hesitated a barely perceptible instant. "I would be glad to welcome you to my eyrie, especially if your business with Lord Dugald is urgent."

Ghyl laughed. "It has waited many years, and could well wait a day or so longer; but I would be pleased to settle it as soon as possible."

"Very good, sir. You are where?"

"At the Godero space-port."

"If you will go to Bureau C and mention my name, a conveyance will be put at your disposal."

"I will arrive shortly."

It was the common assumption among ordinary recipients that the lords lived in splendor, surrounded by exquisite objects, breathing delightful odors, attended by beautiful youths and maidens. Their beds, by repute, were air-fluff and wildflower down; each meal was said to be a banquet of delicious confections and the choicest Gade wines. Even under the load of his preoccupations, Ghyl felt something of the old thrill and wonder as the air-car rose toward the eyrie. He was discharged upon a terrace enclosed by a white balustrade, with all the expanse of Ambroy below. Two wide steps led to an upper terrace, with the palace of Lord Parnasse beyond.

Ghyl instructed the air-car to wait. He mounted the steps, approached the portal, beside which stood a pair of Garrion in dull red livery. Through tall windows swagged with golden-satin drapes a splendid assembly of lords and ladies was visible.

Ghyl entered the palace without challenge from the Garrion and halted to watch the lords and ladies at their entertainment. There was little noise. All spoke in fluttering, arch whispers, and laughed, when they did so, almost soundlessly, as if each were vying to produce the most animation, the most entrancing visual display, with the least sound.

Ghyl looked around the room: elegance, certainly, and a subtle suffusion of light which disguised and dissembled rather than illuminated. The floor was a checker of moth-wing brown and mustard yellow, with a black rug from the Mang Islands. For furniture there were couches upholstered in bottle-green plush—to Ghyl's eyes of an eccentric and over-refined design, certainly not the work of the Ambroy furniture-makers. The walls were hung with tapestries, apparently imported from Damar. Splendor and luxury indeed, thought Ghyl, but there was also a curious intimation of shabbiness: the make-shift insubstantiality of a stage set. The air, despite the soft lights and sumptuous drapes, lacked ease and richness; the activity lacked spontaneity. It was, thought Ghyl, like watching puppets play at festivity, rather than watching festivity itself. Small wonder, he thought, that lords and ladies attended such functions as the County Ball, where they could participate in the passions of the underlings. . . . As he thought of the County Ball, he saw Shanne, wearing a wonderful gown of muted lemon yellow, with ribbons and flounces of ivory. Ghyl watched her in fascination as she stood talking in hushed half-whispers to a gallant young lord. With what charming eagerness did she perform her wiles: smiles, pouts, roguish tilts of the head, pretty little outrages, sham startlements, mock provocations, grimaces of delight, dismay, bewilderment, consternation.

A tall thin lord approached: Lord Parnasse. He halted, bowed. "Sir Hartwig Thorn?"

Ghyl bowed in return. "I am he."

"I trust you find my eyrie to your liking?" Lord Parnasse's voice was light, dry, with the faintest possible overtone of condescension.

"It is delightful."

"If your business with Lord Dugald is urgent, I will take you to him. When you have finished, you may enjoy yourself without restraint."

"I would not wish to presume upon your hospitality," said Ghyl. "As you see, I have ordered the air-car to wait. My business probably will require no great time."

"As you wish. Be good enough, then, to follow me."

Shanne had noticed Ghyl; she stared at him in fascination.

Ghyl gave her a smile and a nod; it made no great difference if she recognized him. Puzzled and thoughtful, she turned to watch as Ghyl followed Lord Parnasse to a small side-room hung with blue satin. At a little marquetry table sat Grand Lord Dugald the Boimarc.

"Here is Sir Hartwig Thorn of Earth, who has a matter to discuss with you," said Parnasse. He gave a stiff bow, departed.

Grand Lord Dugald, portly, middle-aged, with a plum-colored complexion, stared at Ghyl. "Do I know you? You have aspects I find familiar. What was your name once more?"

"My name is irrelevant," said Ghyl. "You may think of me as Prince Emphyrio of Ambroy."

Dugald stared at him coldly. "This seems an overextravagant joke."

"Dugald, Grand Lord as you are called, your entire life is an extravagant joke."

"Eh? What's this?" Dugald heaved himself to his feet. "What is all this about? You are no man of Earth! You have the voice of an underman. What farce is this?" Dugald turned to summon the Garrion who stood at the end of the hall.

"Wait," said Ghyl. "Listen to me, then decide what to do. If you call the Garrion now, you lose all of your options."

Dugald stared, his face an apoplectic purple, his mouth opening and closing. "I know you, I have seen you. I remember your way of speaking. . . . Can it be? You are Ghyl Tarvoke, who was expelled! Ghyl Tarvoke, the pirate! The great thief!"

"I am Ghyl Tarvoke."

"I should have known, when you said 'Emphyrio.' What an outrage to find you here! What do you want of me? Revenge? You deserved your punishment!" Lord Dugald looked at Ghyl in new wrath. "How did you escape? You were expelled!"

"True," said Ghyl. "Now I am back once more. You destroyed my father, you set about to destroy me. I feel no great pity for you."

Lord Dugald once more turned toward the Garrion; once again Ghyl held up his hand. "I carry a weapon; I can kill you and the Garrion as well. You would do best to hear me out; it will take no great time; then you can decide upon your course of action."

"Speak then!" bugled Lord Dugald. "Say what you must and go!"

"I spoke the name Emphyrio. He lived two thousand years ago, and thwarted the puppet-masters of Damar. He awoke the Wirwan to their own sentience; he persuaded them to peace. Then he went to Damar, and spoke in the Catademnon. Do you know of the Catademnon?"

"No," said Lord Dugald contemptuously. "Speak on."

"The puppet-makers drove a spike through Emphyrio's head, then they contrived a new campaign. What they had not gained by violence, they hoped to take by craft. After the Empire Wars they repaired the city; they installed Overtrend and Underline, they established Boimarc. They also organized Thurible Cooperative, and thereafter Boimarc sold to Thurible, and perhaps bought from Thurible as well. Puppet-makers indeed! What need had the Damarans of puppets? They used the folk of Fortinone for their puppets, and robbed us of our wealth."

Dugald rubbed his nose with his two forefingers. "How do you know all this?"

"How could it be otherwise? You called me a thief, a pirate. But you are the thief and pirate! More accurately, you are a puppet controlled by thieves."

Lord Dugald seemed to swell in his chair. "So now. So now you insult me as well?"

"No insult: the literal truth. You are a puppet of a type created long ago in the Damaran glands."

Lord Dugald stared hard at Ghyl. "You are certain of this?"

"Of course. Lords? Ladies?" Ghyl gave a harsh laugh. "What a joke! You are excellent replicas of man—but you are puppets."

"Who infected you with such fantastic views?" demanded Lord Dugald in a stifled voice.

"No one. At Garwan I watched a Damaran walk; it walked with soft feet, as if its feet hurt. On Maastricht I remembered the lords and ladies walking just so. I remembered how they dreaded the light, the open sky; how they wished to run to the mountains to hide: like Wirwans, like Damarans. I remembered the color of their skin: the tone of pink that sometimes tends toward Damaran purple. On Maastricht I wondered how human-seeming folk could act so strangely. How was I so innocent? And so many generations of men and women: how could they have been so stupid, so unperceptive? Simple enough. A fraud so large cannot be comprehended: the idea is rejected."

As Ghyl spoke, Dugald's face began to quiver and work in a most peculiar fashion, his mouth pulling in and out, his eyes bulging, the side of his head quivering and pulsing, so that Ghyl wondered whether he might be undergoing a seizure. Finally Dugald blurted, "Foolishness . . . trash . . . wicked nonsense . . ."

Ghyl shook his head. "No. Once the idea takes hold, everything is clear. Look!" He pointed to the hangings. "You stifle yourself in cloth like the Damarans; you have no music; you cannot breed children with true men; you even have a strange odor."

Dugald sank slowly into his chair, and for a moment was silent. Then he glanced craftily sidewise at Ghyl. "How far have you communicated these wild suppositions?"

"Widely enough," said Ghyl. "I would not care to come here otherwise."

"Hah! Who have you informed?"

"First, I sent a memorandum to the Historical Institute."

Dugald gave a sick groan. Then, with a pitiful attempt at bravado, he declared. "They will never heed such a farrago! Who else?"

"It would avail you nothing to kill me," said Ghyl politely. "I realize that you would like to do so. I assure you it would be useless. Worse than useless. My friends would spread the news, not only throughout Fortinone, but across the human universe: how the lords are but puppets, how their pride is play-acting, how they have cheated the folk who trusted them."

Dugald hunched down into his chair. "The pride is not counterfeit: it is true pride. Shall I tell you something? Only I, Grand Lord Dugald the Boimarc, of all the lords, have no pride. I am humble, I am purple wtih care—because only I know the truth. All the others—they are blameless. They realize their difference; they assume this to be the measure of their superiority. Only I am not proud; only I know who I am." He gave a piteous groan. "Well, I must pay your demands. What do you want? Wealth? A space-yacht? A townhouse? All these?"

"I want only truth. Truth must be known."

Dugald gave a croak of protest. "What can I do! Would you have me destroy my people? Honor is all we have: what else? I alone am without honor, and look at me! See how I fare! I am different from all the rest. I am a puppet!"

"You alone know?"

"I alone. Before I die I will instruct another and doom him as I long ago was doomed."

Into the alcove came Lord Parnasse. He looked with inquisitive eyes from Ghyl to Lord Dugald. "You are still at your business? We are almost ready to dine." He addressed Ghyl: "You will join us?"

Ghyl gave a strained laugh. Lord Parnasse lifted his eyebrows. "Certainly," said Ghyl. "I will be pleased to do so."

Lord Parnasse bowed curtly, departed the alcove.

Lord Dugald contrived a face of bluff bonhomie. "Well, then let us consider the matter. You are not a Chaoticist; I'm sure you do not wish to destroy a time-tested socialty; after all—"

Ghyl held up his hand. "Lord Dugald, whatever else, the deception must be ended, and restitution must be made to the people you have cheated. If you and your 'socialty' can survive these steps, well and good. I bear malice only toward you and Damarans, not the lords of Ambroy."

"What you demand is impossible," declared Dugald. "You have come here swaggering and threatening, now my patience is exhausted! I warn you, with great fervor, to spread no falsehoods or incitements."

Ghyl turned toward the door. "The first folk to know shall be Lord Parnasse and his guests."

"No!" cried Dugald in anguish. "Would you destory us all?"

"The deception must be ended; there must be restitution."

Dugald held out his arms in despair and pathos. "You are obdurate?"

" 'Obdurate'? I am passionate. You killed my father. You have robbed and cheated for two thousand years. You expect me to be otherwise?"

"I will mend matters. The rate will return to 1.18 percent. The underlings will receive an appreciably higher return; I will so demand. You cannot imagine how insistent are the Damarans!"

"The truth must be know."

"But what of our honor?"

"Depart Halma. Take your folk to a far planet, where none know your secret."

Dugald gave a cry of wild anguish. "How would I explain so drastic an act?"

"By the truth."

Dugald stared Ghyl eye to eye, and Ghyl, for a strange brief instant, felt himself looking into unfathomable Damaran emptiness.

Dugald must also have found a quality to daunt him. He turned, strode from the alcove, out into the great hall, where he climbed up on a chair. His voice rasped through the murmur, the half-heard whispers. "Listen to me! Listen, everyone! The truth must be told."

The company swung around in polite surprise.

"The truth!" cried Dugald, "the truth must be told. Everyone must know at last."

There was silence in the hall. Dugald looked wildly right and left, struggling to bring forth words. "Two thousand years ago," he declared, "Emphyrio delivered Fortinone from those Damaran monsters known as Wirwan.

"Now another Emphyrio has come, to expel anothe race of Damaran monsters. He has insisted upon truth. Now you will hear truth.

"Almost two thousand years ago, with Ambroy in ruins, a new set of puppets were sent from Damar. We are those puppets. We have served our masters the Damarans, and have paid to them money wrung from the toil of the underfolk. This is the truth; now that it is known, the Damarans no longer can coerce us.

"We are not lords; we are puppets.

"We have no souls, no minds, no identities. We are synthetics.

"We are not men, not even Damarans. Most of all, we are not lords. We are whimsies, fancies, contrivances. Honor? Our honor is as real as a wisp of smoke. Dignity? Pride? Ridiculous even to use the words."

Dugald pointed to Ghyl. "He came here tonight calling himself Emphyrio, impelling me to truth.

"You have heard the truth.

"When the truth is finally told, there is no more to say."

Dugald stepped down from his chair.

The room was silent.

A chime sounded. Lord Parnasse stirred, looked around at his guests. "The banquet awaits us."

Slowly the guests filed from the room. Ghyl stood aside.

Shanne passed near him. She halted. "You are Ghyl. Ghyl Tarvoke."

"Yes."

"Once, long ago, you loved me."

"But you never loved me."

"Perhaps I did. Perhaps I loved you as much as I was able."

"It was long ago."

"Yes. Things are different now." Shanne smiled politely, and gathering her skirts went her way.

Ghyl spoke to Lord Dugald. "Tomorrow you must speak to the undermen. Tell them the turth, as you have told the truth to your own folk. Perhaps they will not tear down your towers. If they are enraged beyond control, you must be prepared to depart."

"Where. To the Meagher Mounts to join the Wirwans?"

Ghyl shrugged. Lord Dugald turned, Lord Parnasse waited. They passed into the banquet hall leaving Ghyl standing alone.

He turned and went out on the terrace, and stood for a moment looking over the ancient city, which spread, with faint lights glowing, to the Insse and beyond. Never had he seen so beautiful a sight.

He went to the air-car. "Take me to the Brown Star Inn."

CHAPTER 24

The folk of Ambroy, so careful, so diligent, so frugal, were dazed for several hours after the announcement came over the Spay public announcement system. Work halted, folk went out into the streets, to look blankly into the sky toward Damar, up to the eyries on the Vashmont towers, then across town toward the Welfare Agency.

People spoke little to each other. Occasionally someone would give a short bark of harsh laughter, then become silent once more. Folk began to drift toward the Welfare Agency, and by midday a great crowd stood in the surrounding plaza, staring at the grim old building.

Within was gathered the Cobol clan, holding an emergency meeting.

The crowd began to move restlessly. There were mutters, which, swelling, became a vast susurrus. Someone, perhaps a Chaoticist, threw a stone, which broke a window. A face appeared in the gap, and an arm made admonitory motions, which seemed to irritate the crowd. Before there had been hesitancy and doubt as to the role of the Agency. But the angry gestures from the window seemed to put the Agency in the camp of those who had victimized the recipients; and, after all, had not the welfare agents enforced the regulations which made the swindle possible?

The crowd stirred; the mutter became an ugly growling sound. More rocks were thrown, more windows broken.

A loudspeaker on the roof suddenly brayed, "Recipients! Return to your work! The Welfare Agency is studying the situation, and in due course will make the proper representations. Everyone! Disperse, depart at once: to your homes or places of work. This is an official instruction."

The crowd paid no heed; more rocks and bricks were thrown; and suddenly the Agency had become a place in a state of siege.

A group of young men surged up to the locked portal, tried to force it open. Gunfire sounded; several were laid low. The crowd pushed forward, entered the Agency through the broken windows. There was more gunfire, but the crowd was within the building and many horrible deeds occurred. The Cobols were torn to bits, the structure put to the torch.

Hysteria continued throughout the night. The eyries remained undamaged mainly because the mob had no feasible mode of attack. On the next day the Guild Council attempted to restore order, with some success, and the Mayor set to work organizing a militia.

Six weeks later a hundred space-craft of every description—passenger packets, cargo vessels, space-yachts—departed Ambroy and crossed to Damar. A few Damaran were killed, a few more captured. The rest took refuge in their residences.

A deputation of the captured Damaran was handed an ultimatum:

> For two thousand years you have plundered us without pity or regret. We demand total retribution. Bring forth all of your wealth: every thread of fabric, every precious artifact, all your treasure, in money, credits, foreign accounts and exchange, and all other property of value. These articles and this wealth will thereupon become ours. We will then destroy the residences with explosives. The Damarans must henceforth live on the surface in conditions as bleak as those you inflicted upon us. Thereafter you must pay to the State of Fortinone an indemnity of ten million vouchers each year, for two hundred Halma years.
>
> If you do not immediately agree to these terms you will be destroyed, and not one Damaran will remain alive.

Four hours later the first precious articles began to be conveyed from the residences.

In Undle Square a shrine was erected to shelter a crystal case containing the skeleton of Emphyrio. On the door of a nearby narrow-fronted house with amber glass windows hung a plaque of polished black obsidian. Silver characters read:

> In this house lived and worked the son of Amiante Tarvoke, Ghyl, who, taking the name of Emphyrio for his own, did the name, his father, and himself great credit.